HALO®

RENEGADES

RENEGADES

KELLY GAY

BASED ON THE BESTSELLING VIDEO GAME FOR XBOX®

GALLERY BOOKS

New York | London | Toronto | Sydney | New Delhi

Gallery Books
An imprint of Simon & Schuster, Inc.
1230 Avenue of the Americas
New York, NY 10020

First Gallery Books trade paperback edition February 2019

GALLERY BOOKS and colophon are registered trademarks of Simon & Schuster, Inc.

For information about special discounts for bulk purchases, please contact Simon & Schuster Special Sales at 1-866-506-1949 or business@simonand-schuster.com.

The Simon & Schuster Speakers Bureau can bring authors to your live event. For more information or to book an event, contact the Simon & Schuster Speakers Bureau at 1-866-248-3049 or visit our website at www.simonspeakers.com.

Manufactured in the United States of America

10 9 8 7 6 5 4 3 2 1

Library of Congress Cataloging-in-Publication Data is available.

ISBN 978-1-5011-9279-1
ISBN 978-1-5011-9280-7 (ebook)

For my family, near and far, and those we lost this year:

Chester, Sam, Warren, Randy, and Lynda

Prologue

What a rudimentary way to transport a body, dragging it by the ankle across the sand. Nothing more than scrap, the sum of its existence reduced to mass and decay and a complete lack of dignity.

Four corpses lie ahead in the sand, facedown, dressed in patches of charred skin and bits of burnt cloth. Together with this fifth and final companion, they are all that is left.

The others—and there were many others—perished in the explosion. Perhaps this was a kinder fate, for had any managed to survive, they would have suffocated quite slowly in this planet's thin atmosphere.

I, of course, am the exception.

Always surviving. One way or another. My purpose unfulfilled.

I wonder how many stories I will get, how many beginnings and endings, and when the cycle will finally end.

Perhaps the great Forerunner Theoretical Humble-Through-Study was correct when she posed the idea that the mind never truly dies; it only evolves, each evolution growing further beyond the grasp of those who came before, until finally it is as if the mind no longer exists at all, for we have lost the ability to know it. It is only with great misunderstanding that we view the end.

I am not at an ending, however.

I have just begun.

And this new beginning is quite extraordinary. I am no longer bound by service and compartments and walls. What remains of my thoughts and memories are finally free to roam. Like apparitions, they appear and disappear. Gone. Then back again. I sift through these endless recollections, learning to nurture them in an effort to save them, giving them time to grow and find their proper place once more in the scheme of my long existence. I believe, given time and freedom, I might recover and properly catalog them all.

Equally as extraordinary, fate took my vessel and my humans, but in return gave me shape and mobility instead. A head. Torso. Arms and legs. Feet. Hands. Fingers. . . . This form draws even older memories through the murk and mire of millennia, the past seeping through, refusing to be forgotten, bringing darker recollections I am not yet ready to acknowledge.

I glance at the fingers curled around the pale, bruised ankle. Alloy fingers now, not flesh and bone and blood, but form nonetheless. Hard blue light shines between my alloy plates, giving these parts anchor and design and power. With every slow step, the long, jagged piece of metal I commandeered from the wreckage and repurposed into a staff stabs into the sand, helping to maintain my balance and account for the damaged leg I have yet to repair.

Now that I have pulled the body to lie with its companions, I raise my staff with both hands and jab it into the ground, using it as a tool to bury the remains. The wind blows over the loosened sand, picking it up and sending tiny grains against my metal parts. These hit with a cascade of sounds. The different pitches like . . .

Rain, my memory tells me.

It sounds like rain. And I remember.

As I listen and dig, my mind drifts from one memory to the next before settling on a familiar topic: the notion of culpability.

Calculations are inconclusive, but my actions managed to play a significant role—roughly 62.35 percent—in the demise of the ship and crew, though there were external factors on their part and on the part of others.

Still, the guilt at this unexpected turn weighs heavily. There is regret and sadness as well. These emotions are remembered and permitted to simulate, to flow and saturate into every part of my essence, simulations that I feel quite keenly.

It is the least I owe them. Isn't it?

To feel something.

It is a human thing to do, after all.

And I am *still* human.

Am I not?

I send this stream of thought and deliberation to another sector to be analyzed while I focus on the task at hand.

Digging a mass grave in the sand is not difficult. There is, in fact, no physical exertion whatsoever. My new form uses hard light and costs me nothing but time.

Time . . .

My greatest enemy. My greatest friend.

I pause and glance at the wreckage.

After several days, it still smokes, burns, and sparks. Beyond this scene, on a low rock-strewn dune, rests the antenna I fashioned from the wreckage. Even now it broadcasts my distress call to the stars.

Patience was not an attribute I was born with, but I have endured it and eventually I learned to accept it.

And so . . . I can wait. I am good at waiting.

Someone will hear. They always do.

Ho-hum.

Back to digging I go. . . .

SATCOM T-2
J-Node// RELAY: 75153
New Tyne, Venezia
March 3, 2557
0210 STANDARD

//FORWARD: UNSC TAUROKADO
//AUTHORIZATION KS-67159-021127
//URGENT//
//TO: W. HAHN

AFTER ACTION REPORT: ACE OF SPADES

Hahn, my cover is blown. I lost access to the field pad, ship, and crew. This is my final report.

Per my last transmission, ACE OF SPADES found the SPIRIT OF FIRE's log buoy on Laconia. During departure, we rescued salvage captain RAM CHALVA from Sangheili commander GEK 'LHAR, and left under fire.

Coordinates from the log buoy were obtained by tech and nav officer NIKO, and CAPTAIN RION FORGE initiated a slipspace jump, following the coordinates into uncharted space. Without my field pad, tracker, and nav records from the ship, there is no way to pinpoint or even guess at a sector locale, much less a star system. Sorry.

I can tell you that, near the coordinates, we found complete planetary destruction, namely a dense ring of debris orbiting a dwarf star. No physical evidence of the UNSC SPIRIT OF FIRE was detected upon initial scans. However, we did identify a small Forerunner facility with an operational, though fragmented, AI.

Also, our scans of the debris field revealed that GEK 'LHAR arrived in the general area and made it to the Forerunner facility ahead of us. The Sangheili recovered what CPT. FORGE referred to as a Forerunner device called a "luminary."

Hahn, it didn't end well. There was an altercation at the facility, and we lost our second-in-command, CADE MCDONOUGH.

After this casualty, we recovered the fragmented AI from the facility. CPT. FORGE allowed it to modify the ACE OF SPADES's internal systems. I don't believe this was the right decision, but losing CADE immensely affected her and the crew, so there may not have been completely rational thought in the moment.

The AI, which the crew dubbed "LITTLE BIT," contains memory portions suggesting the SPIRIT OF FIRE was responsible for the system's planetary destruction. I feel confident there is much more to discover in this debris field, both Forerunner and UNSC. However, extreme caution is advised as GEK 'LHAR is now fully aware of its location. To my knowledge, only these three, 'LHAR, FORGE, and LITTLE BIT, possess the location of the debris field.

My true motives for being a part of the ACE OF SPADES crew were discovered by LITTLE BIT. Upon arriving in New Tyne, I left the ship while CPT. FORGE was occupied with unexpected repairs and seeing to the injuries GEK 'LHAR inflicted on RAM CHALVA while he was in captivity.

I'm requesting immediate evacuation from Venezia. Someone died, Hahn. This isn't the song and dance you sold me back on Sedra. I want out. Now.

//END

CHAPTER 1

Komoya, Sverdlovsk system, May 2557

Despite its reputation as the junkyard of the Via Casilina, Komoya was one of Rion Forge's favorite stops along the interstellar trade route.

The small, murky moon might not have the soft-sand beaches of Emerald Cove or the crystal-capped mountain peaks of Forseti, but what it lacked in geographical marvel it more than made up for in its exotic fusion of misfits and adventurers. Komoya was a true galactic melting pot. It had substance and grit and—

"Gnats!"

Niko slapped his neck, then picked a tiny black carcass from his skin and flicked it away in disgust.

"And this *dirt*. I swear it's *everywhere*. I hate Komoya." He walked awkwardly for a few steps, shaking one leg, then the other, to display just how invasive the fine soil had become. "See what I'm dealing with here?"

"Trying *not* to see, actually," Rion said in a dry tone, checking the time. "Who cares about the dirt when you have a view like that?"

From their slightly elevated position on the road, Komoya was laid out amid a filthy halo of multicolored lights. The city might be warm and damp—and, yes, everything was coated in a fine layer of grit—but the scenery was spectacular. Hundreds of derelict, abandoned, and decommissioned starships sprawled over eleven square kilometers of Komoyan mudflats and low plains, all connected by a web of dirt roads and makeshift bridges.

In the center of this immense collection sat the CAA *Chalybeate*, a decrepit colony vessel that had landed here almost sixty years ago for repairs and never left, becoming the unofficial capital of Komoya. At nearly a kilometer and a half long and with the capacity to hold ten-thousand-plus colonists, it was a city unto itself, its fusion reactor still generating power, and the ship's AI not only continuing its function as superintendent but taking the role of chief administrator among the other working ship AIs. They saw to everything from orbital surveillance and defense to communications satellites and municipal functions.

Chalybeate's hatches and doors and cargo bays had long been exposed to the elements, roads having been built to link directly *through* the ship, over the muck to the next ship, and the next, and the next . . .

Each vessel had transformed into its own small district, complete with apartments, interior marketplaces, public works and services, and exterior bazaars, which lined the makeshift streets and alleys between ships. Overall, it was a rowdy, patchwork kind of place, home to scouts, salvagers, pirates, and opportunists of every stripe, all contending with an ever-growing population of ex-Covenant species.

Despite the influx, most coexisted amid the chaos, each trader needing the others to survive. They'd evolved into a tidy, unpretentious ecosystem existing here in the sludge, and Rion—unlike Niko—liked it just fine.

Insects, drawn by the night lights and the constant spew of carbon dioxide from Komoya's residents, bit and buzzed and played their familiar songs, competing with the sounds of conversation, music, and the general ambient drone of the city.

Rion could have chosen to hide out on any number of moons or planets or asteroids within three star systems, but Komoya had several things going for it. It was close (relatively speaking) to their home base on Venezia; it boasted one of the best shipyards in the Outer Colonies; and Rion just happened to own a warehouse located at the edge of the city.

"I'll be glad to get off this hellhole," Niko muttered, kicking at the dirt beneath his feet as they walked. "I don't know why you had to drag me outside."

"Believe we covered that already."

He rolled his eyes. "Well, just so we're clear: there's no such thing as spending too much time in my lab. *And* there's no fresh air *anywhere* on Komoya." He glanced at the glades and canals along this portion of road and wrinkled his nose in disgust.

"Are you going to complain all the way back too?" Because he'd done the same on the way *to* the shipyard, and despite her fondness for the tall, gangly young man, with his chaotic hair, ridiculous IQ, and amusing personality, Rion had her limits.

And those limits had been sorely tested the last few months.

Niko glanced over his shoulder at the shipyard they'd left a few minutes earlier. Pieced together over the years, it appeared to be a random jumble of scaffolding, cranes, docking stations, repair berths, and large outbuildings. "Drained you dry, huh?"

Ace of Spades—her ship, her workhorse, her home, her passage to the stars—had just passed her flight test. She was back there in berth, ready to fly. Five weeks just to get parts to repair a fried FTL drive, and another four for the techs to install it and make sure *Ace* was spaceworthy.

"Yeah, kid, drained me dry." Three entire bank accounts had been wiped clean. Parts and labor—and the bribes necessary to ensure that *Ace*'s repairs stayed off the books and, more importantly, off local chatter—had erased half of her life's savings.

One more blow like that, and she'd be out of business.

Not to mention the fact that her financials wouldn't stay off the radar for much longer.

"Have no one to blame but me," she said under her breath.

"Don't be too hard on yourself, Cap. Or on Little Bit. He didn't mean to fry the FTL. Our technology couldn't keep up."

"Something he could easily have calculated."

"Sure, had he not been fragmented," Niko reminded her.

Rion let out a soft snort. They'd had this argument too many times to count in the last several weeks. Niko worshipped the AI, and ever since they'd fled Venezia and arrived on Komoya, the kid had holed up in his corner lab with the colloquially named Little Bit, quizzing the thing, learning to make sense of LB's fragmented leaps from clarity to nonsense, working out answers to old questions and forming new ones.

"Less thinks you're becoming obsessed." She checked the time again.

"Less likes her labels." He waved at another insect. "If you could only see what I see. . . . We think we're so advanced, but the Forerunners were a gazillion years ahead of us. Our advances are child's play in comparison. They could build entire planets, Cap. We saw it for ourselves—well, the aftermath, but still. *Planets*.

"And now we have this gateway to the past in our possession. *We* have LB. Not the military, not intelligence, not the science or tech sector. We do." He shoved his hands in his pockets and turned to walk backward so he could face her. "Just imagine what we could learn. All knowledge and tech that's been withheld from us in the name of 'defense.' All the things we can create and understand and share with the little guys, all the places LB can point us to, the things we can uncover about the past."

Rion lifted a brow. "That's a lovely little speech."

He turned around and fell in step beside her. "Okay, fine. I might be a little obsessed, but who wouldn't be?"

Me, she wanted to say.

Rion had taken the ancient, fragmented AI on board her ship, where it immediately began evaluating *Ace*'s systems. But it had been *her* decision to allow it in, to modify and change. . . . She'd sat there on the bridge, watching the pod carrying Cade's body sail into a nearby dwarf star, and permitted the AI to reconfigure *Ace*'s engines without thinking too deeply of the consequences.

LB had created a streamlined slipspace portal that had gotten them from uncharted space back to Venezian orbit in record time.

The jump ended up killing her drive and causing something he casually referred to as "just a minor bobble in space-time reconciliation," whatever the hell that meant.

It was a miracle they'd made it back to Venezia in one piece.

"He's not all bad, you know. The tech we've been working on couldn't be built without him. And he *did* save our asses from Kip. . . ."

LB's discovery of their engineer's treachery had bought them enough time to settle Ram Chalva in the hospital and call in a favor to get a tow out of town and straight to Komoya. It hadn't taken long, though, for Kip's true employer, the Office of Naval Intelligence, to come calling—a week later an Agent Hahn began sending Rion private messages through trade forums and chatter, asking for information on *her* debris field. . . .

All of which she ignored.

Rion had an entire galaxy in which to hide. ONI wouldn't find her until she began accessing her accounts. Today was that day, and Rion intended to be long gone before the spooks could arrive.

She had plans. Plans to avenge Cade's death, plans to recoup their losses, and plans to go back to the debris field to look for her father and his missing ship.

Rion checked the time again.

One more thing to do and then they'd be gone.

"Heads up, guys," Lessa's voice finally buzzed through comms. "Can't believe I'm saying this, but he's here. I got eyes on Gek 'Lhar."

Rion had been expecting the news, but hearing it and knowing the alien bastard who'd murdered one of their crew was nearby stalled her in her tracks. Fresh grief rushed in, causing a sharp stab of pain through her chest. Ten weeks was hardly enough time to mourn the loss of the man she'd known and loved, in one way or another, for a decade. Not nearly enough time . . .

Niko stared at her with wide, emotional eyes, and for a moment she didn't know what to say. His grief was just as legitimate as hers, Cade having been a mentor and a stable father figure where none had ever been before. And while she wanted to comfort him, now was not the time. Instead, she grabbed his shoulders and gave them a good squeeze. "Put it in a box, kid," she said softly. "Remember the plan."

He nodded quickly, attempting to regroup. "Destroy the roach."

"That's right. His honor, his dignity, his standing, his credits, his ship . . . we're taking it all, everything. Until he's left with nothing but those dog tags on his shoulder. And when it's all gone, when we've broken him, we'll take those too, and send him straight to hell where he belongs." She released his shoulders, let out a deep sigh to regroup as well, and ruffled his hair. "You good?"

His wrecked smile nearly did her in. "Yep. I'm good."

He *wasn't* good. None of them were. If that were the case, they'd be organizing their next salvage op instead of putting their lives on the line in the name of vengeance.

"He just landed over in West Glades," Lessa said, clearing her throat and sounding a little emotional too.

As Komoyan airfields went, it was the perfect spot for the Sangheili. Farthest from the city center, on a bit of dry ground and surrounded on three sides by murky mudflats and natural clearings.

"Looks like Nor's intel was right again," Niko said. "Elld's auction was enough to draw him in."

One of the preeminent dealers of salvaged goods and military surplus along the Via Casilina, and a trusted business ally, Venezia-based Nor Fel had contacted Rion a few days prior with news that Gek 'Lhar would be attending a private auction held on Komoya by the Yonhet trader known only as Elld—news that was both troubling and surprising because, unlike Nor, who refused to sell weapons of mass destruction, Elld didn't have such limitations.

And according to Nor, not only was Gek attending, but he'd taken specific steps to procure an invitation, which raised more than a few eyebrows. 'Lhar was a Sangheili commander—he didn't attend auctions. He and his cronies *took* what they wanted. *Killed* for what they wanted. They scoured the galaxy for military surplus to rebuild the Covenant into its former glory.

Playing by Elld's rules put the Sangheili in a rare and vulnerable position, one which Rion would, naturally, use to her advantage. But he had to know the risk he was taking. He'd left the debris field—a veritable goldmine of Forerunner salvage—to come here. What else could he possibly want or need?

"You really think he'll fall in line and play by auction rules?" Lessa asked. "I mean, that's not really his M.O."

"No, but he's outmatched here and he knows it."

"I'd like to see him try something," Niko said. "Komoya has, what, sixty or seventy ships with working cannons?"

And used together, they could create a formidable anti-aircraft barrage, potentially blasting anything out of the sky. Not to mention that, during the auction, house rules severely handicapped anyone in attendance.

"Roger that, little brother," Less agreed. "I'll get a few more images and then meet you guys back at the warehouse."

"We're about fifteen minutes out," Rion said, picking up the pace as they entered the eastern edge of the city.

As they navigated through the narrow dirt streets and canal bridges, through one vast cargo hold after another, Rion barely saw or heard the sights and sounds and people. Gek 'Lhar's image loomed large in her mind. There hadn't been a day in the last ten weeks that she hadn't seen him in her thoughts and dreams, standing over Cade's body, a triumphant leer on his saurian face.

The only bit of solace Rion had was the wound she'd given him with her M6. She'd been trying to kill, not maim. The bullet had sliced across the left side of his face, destroying his eye and leaving a deep jagged mark that could never be hidden. A smear on his precious honor. A wound given to him not in glorious battle against a worthy foe, but by an unclean human female.

While she took immense pleasure from that, she wouldn't be satisfied until the hinge-head was utterly broken.

At the northwestern edge of the city sat the *Loren*, a large transport barge 327 meters in length and 38 meters wide. Its original storage compartments and separate entries made perfect warehouses to rent to the good citizens and patrons of Komoya. A small airfield had been cleared nearby, which made the unloading and transporting of goods and storage a breeze.

As Rion punched in the entry code to her compartment, an old beat-up Mongoose ATV caked in dirt and mud pulled up and parked next to her. Lessa shoved her dirty goggles to the top of her unruly blond curls and tugged a dusty handkerchief from the bottom half of her face. She cut the ignition and hopped off the quad, handing Rion a datapad as the warehouse door slid open. "Gek's still using that atrocious old war freighter."

The datapad contained recon images Lessa had just taken. "Any support vessels?" Rion asked. "How many crew?"

"I counted seven Sangheili plus him. No other ground support I could see. Niko will have to take a peek inside *Chalybeate*'s orbital surveillance to see if he brought any friends."

After they filed inside, Niko entered the code to lock the door behind them and then tossed Lessa a towel from one of the workbenches. "Does Ram know?" he asked.

Lessa wiped the grime from her face. "If he had his comms on . . . I don't know."

Rion set the datapad on the countertop. "I'll go talk to him."

"He was on the roof when I left," Lessa said.

Rion headed for the stairs built into the far-side bulkhead wall. Her boots echoed on the metal rungs as she climbed the two flights and then ducked through the open hatch, stepping out onto the roof of the warehouse.

Ram Chalva sat in his usual spot, both legs dangling over the edge, watching the ships coming and going across the many airfields positioned around Komoya, a bottle of local marsh-cane whiskey at his side. She wondered if he even saw what was before him or if he was wandering around in circles again inside his own head.

Rion had lost two crewmembers, and in their place was Ram Chalva, a damn fine jack-of-all-trades and former captain of his own salvage ship. A wounded, pissed-off Komoyan who had shown up on his homeworld a few days ago asking around about Rion and the *Ace of Spades*.

She'd watched him for a day before approaching him at a bar

on the upper deck of the *Erstwhile*. Rion had pulled up a stool next to a very surprised Ram, ordered a drink, and done a little asking of her own. They ended up talking for hours. . . .

"I was the last of my crew. Gek was done with me. I knew I wasn't leaving Laconia alive. Without you picking me up, I never would have made it." Ram lifted his whiskey glass in salute, and they drank. "I'm sorry about Cade," he said. "He was a stand-up guy."

They toasted Cade and drank again.

"I'm sorry about your crew," she said.

Another toast. Another drink.

They toasted a lot of things that night. And Rion learned way more than she'd ever wanted to know about what it was like to be the prisoner of a hinge-head. The things Gek 'Lhar and his soldiers had done to Ram and his crew were unspeakable, and she was surprised he'd lasted as long as he had.

He was right. If they hadn't rescued him when they did, putting him in a medically cryo-induced state to halt the advance of his injuries until they returned to Venezia, Ram would have died.

"So, what now?" she asked him, assuming he would hang up his salvager hat.

"Well, I'm out a ship, my crew is gone"—they toasted his crew again—*"and I'm back to square one." After a moment of thought, he asked, "What would* you *do, if you had the choice?"*

She didn't want to think about what he'd endured and the loss of his people. A longtime crew was like family, and he'd lost them all. . . .

Would she throw in the towel? Start a new life with boots on the ground, leaving the stars behind?

Out there was a world of hurt. A world of unknowns.

Yet despite her own losses, it still called to her, and she imagined it always would. She could no more leave behind the life she'd chosen than she could the Ace of Spades or her crew. "Well, I suppose I'd find a new ship, start over. . . ."

He smiled. And they toasted again. "To the scrap."

"To the stars."

And they drank.

"Let me crew with you for a while," he said unexpectedly. "I'm still healing, but I'm a good pilot and engineer, I know the job, and I can work any systems you got on that black bird of yours."

"What about being captain of your own ship? I know you've got a stash of credits somewhere. We all do. . . ."

He dipped his head in agreement. "And I could go out and find a decent ship somewhere, hire a new crew, be back up there in a few weeks. . . ."

"But?"

He twirled the clear liquid in his glass for a moment. "Between you and me, I'm not ready to call the shots just yet. I have a lot going on up here at the moment." He pointed to his head. "And to be honest . . . I'm leery."

"Of what?"

"Of too much time on the ground. The longer I'm down here . . . Too much time passes, and . . . Well, I'm not sure I'll have the heart to get back in the game. Not after Laconia." He shrugged. "Crewing with you will keep me in—"

"Without the pressures of being captain," she finished.

He nodded.

Rion couldn't say she was surprised. After what had happened to Cade, she still wasn't sure she was ready herself. It was a hell of a lot of responsibility for one person to bear, even for a pro like Ram

Chalva. She gestured to where he'd pointed at his head. *"And will that be a problem?"*

"No. That's on me. I'll deal with it. I'm good enough to fly, don't worry about that."

What could she say? She'd lost two of her crew, Kip the traitor, and Cade the . . . everything. And there was no replacing him; no one could.

But the extra set of experienced hands, especially if they ran into trouble again, was an opportunity that didn't come around very often.

"Tell you what. We'll give it a go. You can fill in as engineer on our next run, and then we'll see, all right?"

Ram's mouth was tight as he nodded, staring at his glass for a long moment before meeting her gaze. He was a tough man, a long-time rival and good friend, and she hated seeing the suffering behind his grateful look.

He lifted his glass and gave her a dry grin. "Here's to old rivals."

"And friends."

They clinked glasses and drank again. . . .

Ram glanced over his shoulder as Rion approached. He was short and stocky, with a deep olive complexion and eyes so dark they nearly matched his black hair and beard. He wore his shoulder-length hair pulled back in a band and always had a thin hand-rolled cigarette tucked behind his ear or stashed in his front pocket. His hands and arms were covered in faded constellation tattoos.

She joined him, taking a seat on the edge.

He didn't wait for her to spell it out. "I heard," was all he said.

"You gonna be okay?"

"What choice do I have?"

Rion hesitated. "I need to be sure you'll stay frosty and stick to the plan."

He watched a shuttle take off in the distance. "Death is too easy for the things that bastard has done. Don't worry about me. I'm with you. We're going to take everything from him, make him miserable, alone, dishonored." He studied her for a hard second before a slow smile split through the beard to reveal white teeth. "And *then* we'll kill him."

At that point, they might not have to. In a culture based on military prowess and loyalty to master and clan, honor was the foundation upon which the Sangheili carried their very existence. A true Sangheili warrior would choose death over dishonor any day.

"How much time do we have?" Ram asked.

"Less than an hour until the auction."

"You *sure* Elld will let you in, coming in at the last minute?"

"That's the thing about greed," she said, getting up. "Makes folks predictable."

And while Rion didn't prefer showing up uninvited, she really didn't have a choice, thanks to Kip and ONI. Once she sought out an official invite, Elld would run his standard financial check on her accounts—a prerequisite for entry. The credit inquiry, no matter how "secret" it was supposed to be, would light up ONI's advanced surveillance boards like a goddamn laser show. Better to do it all at the last second before entering the auction than to give ONI a head start on her location.

Rion regarded the man as he returned his attention to the night sky and lifted the bottle to his lips for another swallow. "Just be ready," she said.

He finished his drink and then tipped the bottle toward her to show that he heard loud and clear.

CHAPTER 2

HRB *Flintlock*, financial district, Komoya, Sverdlovsk system

The *Flintlock* served as the center of Komoya's west-side financial district. In its former life, it had been part of a fleet of bank-owned securities transit vessels. Now meticulously upgraded with the latest surveillance technology and armed to the teeth, it made the perfect place for Komoya's high-end black market and an even better place for very private, very below-board auctions.

Every vendor, browser, and buyer came armed; to frequent the market without protection was a mistake made only once. Even the credit runners, transporters, and messengers were packing, and Rion always had a sneaking suspicion that the old marsh-cane vendor near the stairs sported a few rifles under her table of sweets.

Rion leaned casually against the second-story railing of the old ship's cargo stairwell, chewing on a stick of sweet marsh cane and watching the crowd. Not that she needed the bird's-eye view. The three Sangheili warriors marching into the market had little care for stealth or for anyone unfortunate enough to be in their path. They stood out not because they were Sangheili—there were enough mercenaries of that ilk around these days—but because of the way they cut through the mob, patrons either scrambling or knocked aside.

Rion tossed her cane stick into the trash and headed down the stairwell. "He's here. Two guards with him."

"Sounds about right," Less said over comms. "I'm counting five hinge-heads left on the ship. They're keeping it warm, Cap. He doesn't plan to be here long."

Rion made it to the cargo bay's main floor and began easing her way into the Sangheili's chaotic wake with unhurried steps. She wasn't worried about losing them—she knew exactly where they were headed.

"Little Bit, is it there?" she asked, ducking beneath an awning and stepping over a spilled basket of salvaged motherboards.

"Is what there, Captain Forge?" came the congenial voice of their adopted Forerunner AI.

Niko's whisper crackled through the comm speaker. "The luminary."

"Of course!" LB said, remembering. "The luminary is indeed on board the war freighter."

Rion rolled her eyes and dodged a few persistent sellers. How many times had they gone over the plan? "*Where* on the freighter?"

"Oh, yes. . . . The bridge, Captain. The luminary is on the bridge."

"Ram?"

"Five is no problem. They'll be out like a light in no time. We've got it covered on this end."

"As soon as you've got the luminary, get to *Ace* and request launch codes. We're all paid up with the yard chief, so there shouldn't be any issues getting the go-ahead to burn. I'll be with you guys shortly."

"Roger that," Ram said. "We'll keep *Ace* running."

After a chorus of good lucks and be carefuls filled her comm, the earpiece grew silent as the sounds of market activity took over.

As plans went, it was, as Cade would say, balls out.

She could picture the tall, broad-shouldered ex-marine saying it. Dry smile. Amused eyes. Always having her back whether he agreed with her tactics or not. Love and grief and fear made people do dangerous things. And Rion was no exception. Revenge had a hold over her and the crew, and they weren't going to back down until Gek 'Lhar paid for all the lives he had taken away.

One way or another, the Sangheili commander was about to have a very, very bad day. And it was just the beginning.

Rion edged away from the main market area and paused at the head of a long corridor, giving the Sangheili time to find the large vault Elld had repurposed into his auction house.

As she waited, she reached into her pocket, retrieved a pair of black gloves, and pulled them on.

The right glove was a normal black mesh and synthetic material. But the left one, while made from the exact same material, sported a wafer-thin, malleable scanner sewn into the palm of the glove. With Little Bit's help, Niko had been able to turn his idea into a working prototype—a small device that recorded the residual light left on a datapad screen. A message, a look at finances, a picture—if it had recently been on the screen, the scanner could capture and store the light impression left behind. It had no communications or relay capabilities, so it would remain undetected and unaffected by Elld's jammers. Once reunited with the software Niko and LB had also created, they'd be able to download the scans and reconstruct the residual light of up to two or three consecutive images.

Rion was keen on using it to get a better idea of what Gek might be up to, and how to make what remained of his life a living hell.

As soon as a gleam of light illuminated the corridor, she knew the Sangheili were inside the vault. She glanced at the time. Five minutes to auction. It was now or never. Rion straightened and headed down the corridor, keeping her thoughts focused and her courage up.

Once she entered, she'd be in a frequency dead-zone, with all communication-capable technology—commpads, datapads, translators, you name it—completely useless. The only tech allowed here was strictly controlled by Elld.

By the time Rion neared the vault door, she'd been swept by a number of security protocols, none of which were seen, but were there nonetheless. Commissioned by the now defunct Harris-Romner Bank, the *Flintlock* had been created with the highest protection measures of its time, offering transport and storage of private and commercially owned valuables across the galaxy. When the ship was sold, Elld and his investors had purchased it, bringing it here to Komoya and reshaping it into the perfect financial center.

Two familiar Sangheili mercenaries armed to the teeth in a mishmash of Covenant War–era armament flanked the hallway, their rifles slung over muscled gray shoulders, clawed hands casually supporting the barrels. Their bare heads turned in unison as they stared down at her from their lofty height, regarding her with the same kind of irritation Niko had for Komoya's gnats, their insect-like mandibles shuddering mildly in disgust.

"Hey, fellas," Rion said, knowing the casual greeting would add to their annoyance, before turning her attention to a small metal desk placed outside the enormous vault door. Behind the desk, Tomn, a male Yonhet, was regarding her with a high degree of disdain.

While the Yonhet appeared to be the most humanoid of the alien species, they were also one of the most unapproachable and misunderstood. Rion had never seen a female, but the males were hairless with milky-pale skin, deep-set eyes with sagging skin beneath, and drooping mouths lined with short, sharp teeth. Their foreheads were wrinkled in deep folds, but their cheek and brow bones were sharp and prominent, their heads sporting strange pocks and markings. Each Yonhet had two sets of slit-like nostrils cut into a wide nose, and a series of gills along the jawline.

Tomn's attitude aside, the Yonhet often projected a subservient air, but Rion had found them to use that to their advantage. They were very cunning, excellent traders, and had a knack for acquiring the most unique artifacts.

On the desk was a datapad and a neat row of sticky one-and-dones—small subgrade translation tech encircled by medical sticky tape. Peel the back off, place in front of an ear or over it, and voilà—a neat little device that fit most alien species and peeled off easily when no longer needed. Cheap and disposable, they were an effective tool to hand out at large events or to give to folks in the Outer Colonies who couldn't afford even low-grade technology.

Tomn handed one to Rion. She removed the back and placed the coin-size piece on the skin in front of her ear. Inside the vault, Elld would be employing an ambient translator, which covered the entire space, but out here in the hallway where her own tech was jammed, these were necessary to communicate.

"Name?" the Yonhet asked, even though he knew exactly who she was.

"Rion Forge, same as last time."

He ignored the sarcasm, checked his datapad, and then gave her a smirk. "Sorry, Tomn does not see Rion Forge on the list."

"Maybe Tomn should inform Elld that Rion Forge is out here in the hallway with curiosity and credits to burn—lots and lots of credits. Or . . . don't. But once Elld finds out Rion Forge was here, Elld might always wonder if a higher price could have been achieved. . . . So what's on the auction block today anyway?"

Tomn's nose wrinkled, and he let out a soft hiss to show his displeasure before accessing his datapad and typing in a quick message. A ding sounded a few seconds later. "Fine. Tomn sees your credit was last checked five months ago. Must run another before entry."

"Of course."

Due to *Ace*'s repairs, she'd had to pool all of her and Ram's funds into one account in order to show her good status. Nerves spiking, she bit on her bottom lip, waiting. One more step to go, and then she'd be inside a locked vault with an Elite Sangheili warrior who wanted her dead. The question of sanity wasn't lost on her, but then her grandfather always said self-preservation was a foreign concept to the Forge family.

"Rion is cleared to enter," Tomn said, nodding to the guards, who stepped forward to receive her weapons. Once she'd handed over two loaded M6s, extra ammo, two knives, and a stun gun, the Sangheili swept her with a sensor as she peeled off the one-and-done and stuck it to Tomn's desk, much to his ire.

Tomn stood, stepping past her to the entry pad mounted on the wall by the vault. Rion continued to watch him, leaning over slightly to see until he turned around and hissed at her again.

A series of metal locks echoed inside the door before the thick barrier slid back. Rion drew in a deep breath and went inside.

Here we go.

CHAPTER 3

Walter Hahn was just finishing up a quick meal at his desk when Turkish, the holographic avatar of the ship's smart AI, appeared over the small integrated projector in the desk's surface unit.

"Agent Hahn." The AI's hands were clasped behind his back, posture ramrod straight. He wore the uniform of an early-nineteen-hundreds-era field soldier from the Ottoman Empire, complete with handlebar mustache and proper accent. "Pardon the interruption."

Hahn wiped his mouth and refolded his napkin carefully. He always found it fascinating, the AIs he'd come across and the wide range of avatars they'd chosen to represent themselves. Was it indeed some lingering memory, some deep ancestral impression of the donor mind that went into shaping the AI's choice, or was it completely a reflection of the new personality emerging and its need to set itself apart from its donor?

He was confident this one's choice of avatar was the former.

"Yes, Turk?" he asked.

"My surveillance of Rion Forge has resulted in an alert, specifically in her financial activities. It seems a coded financial check was run through a highly encrypted credit system about an hour ago. I was able to break this code and unravel the encryption."

"Could you trace the location?"

"The check was run from Komoya, a small moon orbiting the gas giant Vitalyevna, in the Sverdlovsk system. I've alerted Captain Karah and we are already prepping a slipspace jump to the system. We should arrive within the hour."

As luck would have it, they were still in one of the systems along the Via Casilina Trade Route. The jump wouldn't take too long. "Thank you, Turk. Would you please have Kip Silas sent to my office?"

"Certainly, Agent Hahn. He has now been alerted."

Hahn watched the avatar disappear before relaxing back into his chair and letting the information sink in.

While he was surprised Captain Forge had evaded detection this long, he'd always known she'd eventually turn up.

Hahn had recruited Kip Silas to work undercover as an engineer on the *Ace of Spades*, Captain Forge's salvage ship. While it was Kip's job to monitor and report on any high-value discoveries and salvage, Forerunner artifacts were the real prize and the driving force behind Hahn's directive. And they'd found more than Hahn could ever have hoped for.

And then it had all slipped through their fingers.

When news of losing the location of the debris field and a bona fide Forerunner AI had reached the highest levels of the Office of Naval Intelligence, Hahn had finally gotten the notice of his superiors. Not quite the way he'd envisioned it, but at least he was on Hugo Barton's radar. And when he fixed things with ONI's head of Forerunner research and acquisitions, Barton was sure to see Hahn's potential.

Barton had ordered the heavy prowler *Taurokado* to retrieve Kip from Venezia and then pick up Hahn from his base on Gao. Once on board, they'd both been debriefed and new orders received.

Due to Hahn's excellent track record across the Via Casilina as a counter-contraband agent specializing in Forerunner artifacts, adept at handling informants and acquiring salvaged Forerunner relics, he was given a second chance to secure the AI and the coordinates to the debris field.

At all costs.

A faint ding alerted him to a presence outside his office door. On his viewscreen, he could see Kip Silas standing in the corridor. "Enter," he said.

Kip stepped inside, dressed in the nondescript black ONI uniform worn by the rest of the crew. Its crisp tailoring was completely lost amid the unkempt hair, red eyes, and unshaved jaw of the lackluster recruit.

Hahn let out a deep sigh. Kip would never be a true company man. His lingering moral compass and natural desire to see the good in people, like Rion Forge and her crew, would be the man's downfall. Taking the ethical high ground and doing the right thing was a luxury ONI couldn't afford, not when they were competing in the Forerunner arms race against a re-forming Covenant.

The sooner Kip fully adopted ONI's views, the better.

CHAPTER 4

Rion scanned the familiar vault. Floor-to-ceiling storage units of varying sizes, each with its own security keypad, lined the walls. Tall round tables had been arranged in the center of the vault, designed for bidders and their guests to stand at during bidding. The gathering was small this time around, which meant the item up for auction was something most in the black market business couldn't afford. Four parties stood in attendance: Gek 'Lhar and his two guards; two Jiralhanae—mercenaries, from the look of them; four Kig-Yar pirates; and two humans, most likely of the anti–Unified Earth Government ilk.

The humans gave her a nod of species recognition, which she returned as the heavy vault door closed behind her. Each individual echo of the locks sent fresh adrenaline pumping into her body. The guests seemed to eye her, one by one. First the humans, then the birdlike Kig-Yar, then the enormous hairy Brutes, and finally . . .

What had she been thinking?

Gek 'Lhar turned his head in Rion's direction and she held her breath.

And three, two, one . . .

His singular beady eye, seemingly too small and lost within that giant leathery gray head of his, snagged on her, and time froze. The scar over the other eye was deep and jagged and pale, adding to his already menacing appearance. Rion had envisioned this moment so many times during the last ten weeks, and wasn't surprised when a hot wave of emotion surged to the surface, burning through her chest and stinging her eyes.

Regret rode right along with the rage and grief. For a decade, she and Cade had danced around each other, moving together, moving apart, too scared to commit, too afraid of getting hurt.

And now it was too late. He was gone.

And she was sick and tired of holding it all in.

Her mouth twisted into a smirk.

The utter lack of fear and respect was more than the Sangheili commander could bear. Rage shuddered through all two and a half meters of his body, multiplying exponentially as his claws flexed and a deep growl rumbled through his throat. Before she could blink, he shoved his guards aside and barged past the Brutes and the Kig-Yar, the humans darting out of the way before they were trampled.

There was nowhere to run. But Rion wouldn't have fled even if there were a way out. She lifted her chin. *Hooked ya, you goddamn roach.*

His hand closed around her neck, the skin rough and cold, as he lifted her off the floor and held her at eye level. *"Mistake, little vermin, coming here, taunting me. . . ."* He squeezed slowly until her airway closed. His mandibles flexed as he hissed and leaned close with that blunt reptilian face, watching her die, enjoying the time it took.

Her heart hammered. Panic raced through her system.

Remember why you're here. Trust the house.

Where the hell *was* the house?

Rion slapped at 'Lhar's cold scaly shoulder, then moved lower, her left hand gripping the data screen on his bracer. The attendees simply watched—no one was going to stop the Sangheili. In reality, no one cared. The Brutes were enjoying the show. The Jackals squawked. And the humans regarded the entire affair sadly, as though she were already lying dead on the floor.

Black dots floated in her vision.

Trust the house.

And then, finally, salvation. The telltale whine of lasers priming. She'd never loved a sound more. Chaotic shafts of red beamed over them, coalescing in fine points on Gek's forehead and throat.

His grip eased a fraction.

"Come now, Commander 'Lhar." A raspy voice filled the quiet that had quickly descended. The Yonhet, Elld, stood behind Gek's shoulder, hands tucked behind his back. "Elld understands this way of doing business is new to the commander, but Elld must insist rules be followed. Kill later if necessary, but not here. Unless Gek 'Lhar himself is willing to die in order to kill this female?"

The Brutes chuckled deeply—a human female wasn't worth the sacrifice.

Rion slapped at Gek's hand and kicked wildly. House rules be damned at this point; she was about to pass out.

"Elld has given Commander a chance," the Yonhet continued. "Don't ruin it."

Gek held Rion's gaze for a drawn-out moment. *"Once my business here is complete, I will end you,"* he promised, but she barely heard the translated threat or cared because his claws snapped open and she dropped to the floor.

Blessed air flowed into her lungs, each desperate breath filled with pain as she landed hard, her legs giving out. But she'd made it. Unbelievably she'd made it. Laughter tore through her throat like glass. The room spun and her stomach clenched into a hard, sour knot.

The commander marched back across the room, muttering about taking orders from a species that had once been the Covenant's slave labor. *How that must chafe,* Rion thought darkly, rubbing her sore throat. The fact that he was adhering to Elld's rules meant he intended to win whatever was up for sale. He wouldn't have come otherwise. And winning meant that Rion walked free while Gek had to stay behind and pony up the cost. By the time he was released from the vault, she'd be gone—with his luminary. And with new information from his bracer, thanks to Niko's glove device.

It was the perfect setup.

Rion shoved a dark strand of hair out of her eye and looked up at Elld. The light in the vault cast a gray, sickly pall over his milky skin. He was nearly identical to Tomn, though the markings on his bald head were slightly different and his gills and jagged teeth were a bit longer, suggesting a more advanced age. He wore a tunic of dark-gray weave and a bemused expression on his face. "Credits to burn, Elld hears." Then he walked away to begin the auction.

For a moment, Rion stayed on the floor, waiting for her vertigo to subside and the strength to return to her limbs. But as soon as a metal cart was rolled into the room, she pushed to her feet.

The cart held a viewscreen and a small metal box. Elld moved to its side with a remote in his hand.

"Inside this coded container are the access codes to a heavy excavator formerly in service to the Covenant. Some of you call it a Harvester." On the viewscreen an image appeared of an enormous six-legged excavator. "As all can see from the time stamp, this is a real-time uplink." The camera panned around the Harvester. "Elld does not have to express the power of such an item nor the value of one with its original Sbaolekgolo colony, and one that has a *working* plasma drill."

The enormity of what was being offered sank in. The Kig-Yar began cackling excitedly as the humans whispered to themselves, and the Brutes looked eager to use the damn thing to shed as much blood as possible.

"The first such item to come onto market," Elld continued. "Might very well be the last. Shall we begin the bidding?"

"You claim the drill works. Show me," Gek demanded.

Elld gave him a serene nod, then spoke into a comm. "Activate the drill."

A few seconds passed before the screen flashed bright, fading to reveal an intense yellow beam of superheated plasma shooting from the mouth of the excavator, melting a hole into the nearby rock.

An opening bid of twenty million credits from the Kig-Yar began the auction. Rion lifted her hand, having no intention of buying. "Twenty-five."

As the bid increased around her, the pieces fell into place. Though they were used in battle, the Harvester's primary function was as an excavator. For the last ten weeks, Gek and his crew had had the opportunity to poke around the debris field. He possessed the luminary, which allowed him to detect and track down other Forerunner artifacts. He must have found something very big hidden very deep within the debris. Something he couldn't recover without the Harvester and its drill.

She glanced around the room. There wasn't a single buyer in attendance with good intentions for this thing. Not one. Any one of them could glass an entire city with that machine.

With the bid now at thirty-five million in favor of Gek, the Kig-Yar were out, and so was Rion.

"Do I hear forty?" Elld inquired. "Forty? Forty million."

"Forty million," one of the Brutes piped up. The other humans immediately bowed out, leaving the Jiralhanae with the top bid.

Elld gave the room a few more seconds before turning his attention to Gek. "Bid rests at forty million." Gek didn't respond, and for one brief moment Rion thought things were not going to pan out as she'd thought. "Very well, then. Going once at forty million . . . going twice—"

"Fifty million," Gek announced in a deep, threatening tone, leveling a death stare at the Brutes.

Hell, was he trying to wage war?

Tension filled the room. The rage coming off the Brutes was palpable. Even Elld, with all his security protocols, looked a little paler than before. He swallowed and found his voice. "Fifty mil-lion to the Sangheili."

Dead silence.

At Elld's faint nod, mounted plasma guns dropped out of the ceiling—a little incentive to maintain order. "The bid stands at fifty million," he said. "Fifty million. Going once . . . twice . . ." He gave a serene nod to 'Lhar, "Sold, to the Sangheili commander, with Elld's congratulations."

The Brutes lit up the room with a volley of colorful curses as the vault door released. Rion was the first to leave, darting into the hallway to collect her weapons, then proceeding to get the hell out of the corridor, heart pounding, eager to regain comms contact with the crew.

As soon as she was back in the market proper, her tech came alive. She hit her comms. "I'm back on," she said breathlessly, and waited for a reply. Nothing. "Guys?" she said, weaving through the shoppers. "Where the hell is my crew?"

Damn it.

"We're here, Cap," came Niko's hasty reply, and Rion let out a sigh of relief. "Got the luminary. We're almost to the shipyard."

"Good. Gek won't be tied up in details for long. I'll meet you there."

Rion left the market through the massive hangar doors and headed out into the night. As she started for the dark canal bridge, she stopped dead in her tracks and looked back at the *Flintlock*.

Yes, she wanted payback, but she also knew that letting Gek 'Lhar get away with codes to a Harvester might end up hurting a hell of a lot of innocent people. There wasn't time now, but as soon as she was airborne, she'd alert the UNSC. Hell, maybe she should tell Agent Hahn—that might get ONI off her back for a while. The Sangheili commander was a prize no matter how you looked at it.

As Rion turned back toward the bridge, she already knew she could—

A hood slid over her head. "Hey! What the—"

Gloved hands gripped her wrists together, restraints binding her in a flash before she was lifted off her feet and hoisted over a shoulder as though she weighed nothing at all.

CHAPTER 5

R ion had never felt it coming, too distracted and rushed to sense the presence behind her. One second she was formulating a plan; the next the world went black, the hood pulled over her head, arms grabbing her from behind. . . . By the time understanding dawned, she was being carted away.

Her first instinct was to struggle, but when she felt the bounce of the bridge over the muddy canal she quieted. The last thing she wanted was to cause a tumble into the canal. Many a Komoyan had fallen into the clutches of the planet's muck and never resurfaced.

Instead, she focused on her other senses—she might be blind, but she could still hear and feel and smell.

No words, just footsteps, quick and sure. Her captor's breathing was similar; it didn't sound labored with her weight at all. Next was smell. Definitely human. Relatively clean. The scent of Komoya hadn't yet settled through her captor's clothes and skin, which suggested this wasn't some pirate or merc.

While she couldn't do much with her hands, she could feel the arm locked over the back of her legs and the occasional bump of gear against her shin, a holster and weapon no doubt. With every jarring step her gut tightened, and her head began to pound.

Gradually the smells and sounds changed. Noise reduced in favor of the low drone of an engine, the scent of fuel, and finally the metal clang of boots on a cargo ramp as she was carried onto a ship of some kind.

As her captor finally set her on her feet, the pressure in her head faded, leaving behind a touch of dizziness. She wobbled, trying to find her balance in the darkness. Now that movement had stopped, the environment inside the hood took precedence. It was musty and damp, making it hard to breathe. Suddenly things got very claustrophobic. Rion tried to stifle the rising panic, but knew she was fighting a losing battle.

A hand grabbed her shoulder and steadied her, then guided her backward until her legs hit something solid, and she fell onto a hard seat or bench. "Take it off!" she managed. "I can't brea—"

The hood came off. An instant wash of cooler air met her damp skin.

Second time tonight she'd been manhandled and nearly suffocated. Her neck still ached, and she was tired of gasping for air and feeling broken glass in her injured throat with each breath, swallow, and word she spoke. Unfortunately, the night had taken a turn at the worst possible time. And her composure was starting to crack.

She took note of the pilot ahead in the cockpit, and then leveled a glare at her kidnapper.

Beyond the fact that she was on a utility bench in the back of a UNSC Pelican, it didn't take much to figure out her abductor was on the Office of Naval Idiots' payroll. Even in his nondescript black uniform, light gear, and face mask, which covered everything but his eyes, the man standing in front of her screamed special ops—if special ops was in the business of employing giants. The guy had to be just shy of seven feet, built like a ton of bricks, and probably about as intelligent and fun.

"You have got to be kidding me," she muttered, her adrenaline at recent events giving way to anger. "You spooks had to pick me up *now*? Unbelievable."

The Big Guy—as she decided to call him—frowned, though there was more curiosity in his gaze than anger at her comment. He'd probably expected a little shaking in fear or crying in panic or begging for release. His gaze dropped to her neck. No doubt, from his lingering look, her skin was already starting to show signs of bruising.

So the spook had a heart.

And if she'd been picked up, then it was highly probable that her crew was next or already in custody.

Perfect.

And the night had been going so well.

No sooner had the thought come and gone, another spook entered; this one was also abnormally tall, but more slender than the Big Guy—a woman in identical gear, strong enough to carry in a struggling, pissed-off kid without much effort. "Caught this one fleeing the shipyard," she said casually. "Wily little bastard gave me quite the chase."

"Screw you!" Niko yelled beneath his hood.

The woman dropped him on the bench next to Rion.

"Cool it, kid," Rion said in a low voice, bumping her shoulder to his. He went still, head coming up and tilted in her direction.

"Oh no," he whispered, realizing she had been caught. "No, no, no—hey! Where's my sister? I swear, if you hurt *one curl* on her head, I will—"

The woman leaned forward and yanked the hood from Niko's head. He jumped. Poor kid was red-faced and sputtering, eyes wide, scared and livid.

From what Rion could tell by the woman's body language and from her eyes, the only part of her visible in the mask, she didn't seem fazed by Niko's unspoken threat. In fact, she seemed to regard him with a dry humor that Rion knew all too well. "What?" she asked. "What will you do?"

Niko leaned forward, mouth open, obviously ready to lay into her, but managed to control himself; he sat back and ignored her.

She laughed. "I like you, kid. Maybe you *are* as smart as they say."

The woman straightened, turned away, and approached the Big Guy.

"Well, I don't like you!" he yelled after her. "And, yeah, I *am* smarter!"

"Other two are secure on their ship," she informed her partner. "We're all set."

"Wait!" Rion jumped to her feet. The Big Guy immediately shoved her down, but she popped right back up, fury rising swift and hard, her first instinct to lash out and repay the rough action in kind. Any other time she gave as good as she got, but her desire to see Gek 'Lhar pay in some way—now that her plans were going up in smoke—won out instead. "You can't just leave Komoya."

His brow rose, and he seemed to regard her with some thought, a calm intelligence in the brown eyes, making her rethink her earlier assumption about him. Maybe not a *total* pile of bricks, then. "Orders are orders, ma'am," he said with finality, and turned toward the cabin.

Rion swore under her breath and grabbed his arm. Her entire night had been ruined by ONI. All her plans might be over before they'd really begun. But one thing was certain—if she wasn't getting off Komoya scot-free, then neither was Gek. "Do you have any idea where I was? We can't leave. Gek 'Lhar is here."

At that, the Big Guy stilled, glancing back at her with a quiet kind of judgment as though, if he searched deep enough, he could see the truth or lies in her claim.

"Look, he just won an auction for a Harvester." No reaction. "*With a working plasma drill.* Are you hearing what I'm saying? A Sangheili with an axe to grind against humanity is about to leave Komoya with a goddamn plasma drill, if he hasn't already."

"You two lug-heads know what a plasma drill can do, right?" Niko asked, leaning past Rion. "If left long enough, the thing could eventually cut clean through to a planet's core. Destroy worlds. Any of this ringing a bell?"

After a pause, the Big Guy gave a curt nod and the woman immediately slid into the copilot's seat and bent over the controls, communicating with whatever ship they had in orbit, her voice muffled. It took just a few seconds before she was done and leaning out of the cabin. "Only ship that's requested launch codes is the *Ace of Spades*."

"What are you, amateurs?" Niko said, sitting back and shaking his head. "A roach like that doesn't request codes."

Rion shot him a quick warning to behave, and then faced the Big Guy. "He had to *pay* first—the money had to clear. Elld puts every auction winner in lockdown until funds are confirmed and transferred, then he'll hand over the codes and coordinates to the Harvester's location. Tell your people to look for a Covie war freighter in the West Glades Airfield. His ship might still be there." And if by some miracle it was, it wouldn't be for much longer.

The Big Guy turned to the woman. "Tell Turk to run a sweep of the area. See if her story checks out."

"Yes, sir."

Another muffled conversation, and about thirty seconds later, the woman announced: "Turk's confirmed—there's a vessel matching that description in West Glades Airfield."

"That's him," Rion said with urgency, hoping Gek hadn't switched vessels or left behind some phony decoy signature in his wake. Either way, ONI leaving them alone was a very good thing. "That's his ship. If you don't get to him before he jumps, you'll have a radical Covenant zealot out there with the capability of destroying cities, if not an entire planet. And I know we're not worth more to you than that."

"Yeah," Niko added, holding his hands up like scales weighing his next words. "Small time salvagers." His left hand dipped low. His right hand went high. "Psycho hinge-head. Take your pick."

Rion touched the man's arm with her gloved left hand, her fingers splaying over the forearm unit he wore. "We're small time salvagers well under your pay grade and not worth the big catch about to slip through your fingers."

The man grabbed both of Rion's shoulders and pushed her to

the bench, wordlessly producing a knife. He cut her restraints and then produced more of the thin carbon-fiber ties from his back pocket, which he looped around her wrists and attached to the bar behind her. Then he did the same for Niko. Once that was done, it was as though Rion and Niko no longer existed as the two operatives loaded up on gear and weapons in a clean, efficient manner.

Rion watched them with interest, noting the way they moved and interacted, the unrattled, confident aura. They could do this with their eyes closed. She'd been around enough military and ex-military to see that these two were the cream of the crop. More than special ops, much, much more. . . .

They spoke low into their comms, telling their buddy Turk to provide eyes from above and standby support.

As they filed out of the Pelican, Rion called after them. "Wait! What about us?"

They didn't acknowledge her, but the ramp started to close and the pilot began initiating takeoff. "*No, no, no.* Damn it, this is not part of the plan," she muttered, shifting in her seat to study the restraints.

As Niko turned her way, she managed to get to her knees on the bench and then angled her hip toward his tied hands. "Back pocket."

"On it," he said. "Total amateurs. What do they think, this is our first kidnapping? So full of themselves. . . ."

"Niko—this *is* your first kidnapping," she replied with impatience. "Hurry it up. We need to get off this boat."

He twisted enough to reach into her back pocket and pull out the small knife she kept there. And then he fumbled it. It clanked to the deck. As the Pelican lifted off, it slid to the end of the cargo bay, completely out of reach.

Niko winced. "Sorry."

Rion sat back and gave a defeated sigh. Her knife probably wouldn't have put a dent in the carbon fiber anyway.

She'd been so close. . . . They'd had the luminary, for God's sake.

Now it was in ONI's possession and would probably never again see the light of day.

CHAPTER 6

"**S**ir, we have the salvagers in custody," Turk informed
Agent Hahn as he stood at the tactical table on the
bridge, eager for an update. "Two in their ship, the *Ace
of Spades*, and two restrained in the Pelican and ready for transport."

"Good. Have a team meet me in the hangar bay."

Agent Hahn paused to stare out the prowler's viewscreen at the
murky brown moon hovering above Vitalyevna's planetary ring.
Komoya was one of the gas giant's twenty-seven moons, and it was
a dim and dirty place, the very definition of backwater—though,
with well-defined radar, defense, and commsat systems, it was a
backwater that took its protection very seriously. In order to keep
a low profile, the *Taurokado* had stayed out of Komoya's orbital

range, using its nearby neighbor, the uninhabited moon Rostov, to run signal interference.

As Hahn turned to leave, the bridge's comms officer caught his attention.

"Captain?" The comms officer paused to listen intently; then: "Apollo reporting. . . . Salvagers are claiming Gek 'Lhar is on the ground. . . ." He listened again as Captain Karah moved to the tactical table.

"Turk, patch me in," she ordered, holding up a hand to silence Hahn before he had a chance to argue in favor of his mission.

Despite the respect he held for Karah and her decisions, Hahn couldn't help but think that if Rion Forge slipped through his fingers this time, he'd lose her for good. And while Gek 'Lhar was a high-value target because of his association with Jul 'Mdama and the Covenant element operating out of Hesduros, so were Hahn's salvagers. After all, they held the key to an asset far greater than a renegade Sangheili and whatever was left of the Covenant.

Still, he obeyed her command, staring across the table at the captain. There weren't very many people who intimidated him, but Netah Karah was definitely one of them. In her crisp uniform and buzz cut that showed just a hint of silver, she was a formidable adversary. No-nonsense, fair-minded, with dark features etched with dignity and authority. Karah carried herself like an aristocrat from the days of old. At just forty-three years old, her accomplishments were equally impressive and hard earned.

"Understood," Captain Karah was saying. "Apollo, you have permission to engage. Support inbound. Turk?"

"On it, Captain. Broadswords deploying."

"And the salvagers?" a female voice asked over comms.

"Send them up immediately."

"Roger that. Apollo out."

"Relax, Agent Hahn," Karah said, meeting his concerned gaze across the table. "Your prize isn't going anywhere."

CHAPTER 7

R ion felt the Pelican rise through the atmosphere, felt the change as they hit the exosphere, the engines easing to a low hum, relying on the occasional thruster burst to provide direction. And then relative silence, broken only by muffled communications coming from the cockpit.

Eventually, the vessel shuddered and slowed.

"We're docking," Niko said.

And all Rion could think about was how the rest of her crew and her ship were faring.

The pilot refused to tell them anything, and after a few minutes the ship set down with a slight wobble. Then he released the bay doors and left the ship entirely. There wasn't much to see from their position—just steel and titanium and cargo containers.

Letting her head rest against the bulkhead and closing her

eyes, Rion attempted to think her way out of this new situation. There was no doubt in her mind that Hahn was behind their apprehension. He'd made no secret of what he was after—the debris field coordinates and Little Bit—and she had a very bad feeling he was now way past his willingness to barter and deal.

"What are we going to do?" Niko asked. "You think Less and Ram are okay?"

She nodded. "They're not after us, Niko. They're after artifacts."

He sighed. "Little Bit is an artifact to them. What do you think they'll do to him?"

"I don't know." She opened her eyes. "I'm sorry. Not much we can do. If they have *Ace*, they have LB."

"But they don't have—"

She shook her head, silencing him. ONI might have possession of Little Bit, but they wouldn't have everything. Rion would just have to figure out her play as the game progressed.

Eventually footsteps echoed over the metal flooring. Two men in nondescript flight suits appeared, cut their restraints, and then escorted them from the Pelican.

As Rion and Niko descended the ramp, the enormity of the hold was revealed. She wasn't sure what make of ship they were in, but it was fancy as hell, and could hold several smaller support vessels.

"Rion," Niko said, elbowing her side. Looming next to them was a familiar dark-winged ship, dwarfing the Pelican. The *Ace of Spades* had been docked here as well and her ramp was down, Lessa and Ram being escorted off the ship. They caught sight of each other and exchanged relieved glances. Less was such an open book. Her cheeks were pink with anger and worry swam in her eyes. Ram, on the other hand, strolled down the ramp with a casual calm—this wasn't his first run-in with ONI.

Once on the main hangar-bay floor, they joined up as a four-man team of spooks approached. From the cart laden with tech and scanners, their intentions were clear. They passed Rion and her crew and headed straight for *Ace*. Both Niko and Lessa stopped, a string of emotions crossing their faces as they watched the team enter the ship. Their entire lives were about to be turned upside down.

It took everything Rion had to stay put and not run after the team. She just prayed their home would be in one piece when all this was over.

Ram moved toward her, quietly saying: "We scrubbed her before they got on board."

"Navs too?"

He nodded.

Good. No need to make it easy for them. Another group headed their way—an officer, by the looks of him, flanked by two crewmembers.

"What do we tell them?" Lessa asked.

"The truth, if it comes to it."

"But—" Niko started.

"If we don't play nice, they'll make us wish we had, and I want to walk away from this with my crew and my ship intact. This isn't the time or the place to make our stand."

Ram lifted a dubious eyebrow. "We're going to make a stand?"

She stared straight ahead, watching the group draw closer. "If they take something from us, we're sure as hell going to take something from them." Rion just had to figure out what that was exactly.

"And this," Niko said under his breath, putting his arm around her and giving her a quick squeeze on the shoulder, "is why we love your vengeful ass."

The lead officer was slender and balding, and had the look of a shrewd businessman rather than an ONI operative. Rion lifted her chin a notch and stepped forward. The more she could separate herself from the crew and hold his attention, the better.

"Captain Forge," he greeted her with a congenial tone.

"Agent Hahn," she replied. He seemed pleased with her deduction, though it wasn't hard to figure out his identity; he'd been trying to contact her for ten weeks.

"I did try to do this the easy way."

"So did I," she said. "Ignoring you *was* the easy way."

"That didn't quite work out for you, though." He turned and gestured for her to walk beside him, leaving the others behind, thank goodness. She glanced back. "Your crew is safe, Captain," he assured her.

"And what are your intentions for them?"

"Two kids and a wounded salvager? I have no intentions for them at all. And I'm sure you'll do whatever is necessary to see it stays that way."

"Am I being charged with a crime?"

"Not yet. Your record is surprisingly clean for someone in your line of work. All we want is information and cooperation. Once those aims are achieved, you and your crew will be on your way. We could have done this more than two months ago, but you opted for . . . a more difficult path. So here we are."

"You're going through an awful lot of trouble for a small-time salvager," she said as they left the hangar and headed down a hallway with glossy white walls and metal grating for flooring, then entered a large conference room with more white walls, two of which framed expansive glass panels. An oval table stood in the center, and along the walls were more intimate seating arrangements.

After the door slid closed, Agent Hahn paused at the head of the table, his hands resting on the back of a chair. "Shall we get right to it? The last transmission from our agent was hindered. . . . We have you closest to the Procyon system—"

Rion walked around the spacious room. "Never heard of it."

"—and from there into uncharted space where, according to our intelligence, you discovered a substantial debris field, one that contains Forerunner ruins, and recovered an artificial intelligence. As you know, we must confiscate that AI and secure the location."

Rion paused to inspect one of the glass walls, tapping on it, wondering who was on the other side, if she even warranted that amount of interest. Her faint reflection stared back at her: tired eyes, messy hair—thanks to the hood—and ugly bruises forming on her throat. Her image appeared just as frazzled as her nerves. She ignored Hahn and smoothed the flyaway hairs behind her ears.

"Captain, might I impress upon you the importance of keeping Forerunner technology out of our enemy's hands. . . ."

While she agreed, she couldn't help but push him a little. "The war is over, Agent Hahn."

"The war is never over. You know as well as I do that Gek 'Lhar and others like him are trying to rebuild the Covenant. They gather enough ships and the right technology, and before you know it, we'll be back where we were four years ago."

"Well, now that you have my luminary, it shouldn't be too hard to find your precious technology."

"You are well aware that proximity matters. Time matters. We could engage in repeated explorations into uncharted space, looking for that debris field. Or we could just get the coordinates from you. Sometimes the simplest answer is the right answer."

A low tone echoed from Hahn's datapad. Rion watched him through the glass's reflection as he checked the screen. His jaw went tight at whatever he read, and she couldn't help but feel a surge of satisfaction. He excused himself and was gone long enough for her to start worrying. When he finally returned, his mood was darker than before.

"Your ship's navigational logs and charts have been scrubbed."

"Standard procedure," she told him, turning around. "Our livelihood depends on keeping our finds and locations secret. You know . . . from *poachers*."

"We're not poachers if the tech already belongs to us," Hahn replied, reading more of the message and growing more irate.

She let out a sharp laugh. "Since when does Forerunner technology belong to the Office of Naval Intelligence?"

He set the pad on the table. "Who would you like it to belong to, Captain? For nearly thirty years, we saw how close the Covenant came to wiping us out with the limited amount of reengineered Forerunner tech they possessed. Think what the wrong group could do with an entire arsenal. Do you really want to be responsible for that?"

Hahn engaged a holoscreen that appeared over the conference table. Images appeared, one by one. "Let me give you some incentive here. Warehouse on Komoya . . . warehouse on Venezia . . ."

Two more images joined the list with a flick of his hand. "Gao. Tal-itsa. We have seized your assets across the Via Casilina, including your bank accounts—all six of them. And we have your ship and your crew. Whether that's temporary or for the foreseeable future is up to you. Understand, Captain Forge—this *is* us playing nice."

Rion stared at the images of her warehouses for a long moment.

"Your choice," Hahn said, watching her.

"Not really though, is it?" She regarded him for a moment. This should be cut-and-dried. Hahn had what he was after. He didn't need to threaten her entire business. "You have everything you wanted from me, Agent Hahn. You have my AI, and through him you have the coordinates to the debris field. And you've also got my luminary thrown in for good measure. The rest"—she gestured to her entire livelihood hovering in the air above them—"is overkill and unnecessary. Now, when can I leave?"

"You can leave when you or your AI gives us the location of the field."

So that was it, then. Little Bit, bless his fragmented heart, wasn't cooperating. Rion's amusement and surprise, however, quickly turned to dread, because while LB's loyalty lifted her estimation of him, it also might end up costing her everything.

"How about this, Captain?" Hahn said, gathering his datapad, taking her nonanswer for refusal. "I'm going to step out for a bit. Give you a few minutes to think about it."

"No, wait—"

But he kept going. Damn it.

An hour, possibly more, had passed before the conference room door slid open again. During that time, Rion had repeatedly banged on the door and walls, trying to get someone's attention and convey her willingness to cooperate, before things went even further south than they already had, but no one had acknowledged her. Eventually she'd given up, and was sitting in one of the chairs with her boots propped on the table when Hahn entered with the Big Guy who'd apprehended her outside of the *Flintlock*.

Immediately her gaze locked with her kidnapper's, eyes narrowing to fine, unimpressed points while his remained calm and neutral. No mask on his face this time, but she'd recognize the unusual height and those steady eyes anywhere. He sported a few laugh lines around his eyes and mouth, and his features weren't completely unpleasant—decent forehead, short brown hair, straight nose, and strong jawline, only marred by a deep scar cut diagonally across his chin. Like Hahn, he wore a black flight suit with no name tag or rank.

Yep. The Big Guy was *way* more than special ops. Her earlier suspicions solidified, and she was pretty sure she was getting her first up-close-and-personal with a Spartan. Well, second, if she counted being carted across Komoya like a thirty-kilo bag of rice.

He took up a spot near the corner by the door, hands clamped behind him, as Hahn approached the table. The tension this time around had increased. If she wasn't mistaken, the ONI agent was livid and exasperated, though he tried hard to hide it behind a straight posture and a flat expression.

Rion winced inside. Given the time he'd been gone, she'd guessed their attempts at communicating with Little Bit had been unsuccessful—possibly disastrous, knowing LB. Rion pushed to her feet, about to inquire, when the door slid open again, and Kip Silas walked in.

She froze at the sight of him.

He appeared no different than the last time she'd seen him on her ship, still scruffy, still tired-looking, and still with that sadness behind his eyes. Mixed emotions coursed through her—anger, hurt, disappointment. Kip had been part of her crew, welcomed into the family, and his betrayal had hit them hard. It had been a long time since she'd read someone so completely and utterly wrong. Yet even now her instincts told her he was a good guy, which only made her confused and angrier.

He came to a stop across the table from her position. "Come on, Rion. Just tell them what you know."

She wasn't refusing—they just hadn't given her the opportunity. And now Kip was here. . . . "I'm sorry, did you say something? Because I don't speak traitor."

"I'm only trying to help, to save lives. You have no idea how dangerous these artifacts are. And you have no idea who you're selling it to."

She laughed. "Oh, don't you dare put this on me. The stuff I bring to market is sold in the clear. At auction. If *they*"—she threw an arm out to the glass—"don't want to pay what it's worth, that's on them. And let me tell you, they can afford it. Just ask any salvager's confiscated bank accounts. If anything I recover goes to someone else, you can sing your sad song to them, not me."

He remained quiet, and she couldn't help but add, "And I hate to break it to you, but you don't know me well enough to come in here and play the nice-guy routine to talk some sense into me."

His faint smile held a note of regret. "I like you, Rion. I like Niko and Lessa. I liked Cade, for God's sake."

She lurched forward, but the damn table was between them. "*Don't*. You don't get to talk about him." Her chest tightened as the familiar crushing weight of Cade's death took her breath away. Kip was forever part of that memory, and right then she hated him for it. "You don't get to talk about any of them."

He bowed his head as though he understood and accepted it. "Nothing I did put any of you in danger."

"No, you're just the reason we're here." She shook her head and paced, needing to move. "But I guess you would call that *nothing*."

"What did you tell me once? There's enough salvage out there for everyone. Rion, you don't need the debris field. The technology that might be lurking there—what gives you the right to take it and sell it to the highest bidder, to someone who might kill millions of people? Where is your conscience, your culpability? Because at the end of the day, *you're* responsible too. You could be the reason civilians, entire families lose everything."

She wanted to choke him for throwing her own words back at her. "I've never and will never sell a goddamn thing that could kill millions of people and you know it." She came around the end of the table to face him, but held on to the chair to keep steady and to prevent herself from getting any closer and hurting him.

"Fine. I'll give you that—when it comes to human and Covie tech. But Forerunner? How do you know? How much does *any* of us know about Forerunner technology? You could sell one small piece that might be the key to launching a weapon of mass destruction. You just don't know. But they do." He threw his hand toward Hahn and the Big Guy. "They have experience with Forerunner artifacts, years of it, entire divisions devoted to its study and use and reengineering. They understand things about it we never could, and they need to keep that tech out of the wrong hands."

Kip paused and let out a long-suffering sigh before glancing to Hahn for permission to continue. Hahn dipped his head, and Kip turned back to her. "Gek escaped Komoya. Please, don't let him get what he's after."

Rion gave the Big Guy the most disappointed look she could muster. And while he didn't react, there was a faint tic in his jaw that told her he wasn't happy about it. "Really?" she said to him. "I handed him to you all wrapped up with a bow and you just let him go. If you hadn't interfered, we would have taken out Gek *and* that damn Harvester." She wanted to scream. "But that's what you spooks do, isn't it? Interfere in everything. Why don't you just go and leave the Outer Colonies to their own devices? We sure as hell do a lot better job protecting our own than you."

"A commonly held sentiment in these parts," Agent Hahn said, undaunted by her insult. "But we *spooks* see the big picture, one that encompasses the whole of humanity and our place in the galaxy. You know we're right, Captain. And you know *exactly* who 'Lhar is and what he's capable of doing."

She remained quiet, mostly because it was pretty hard to argue a point she wholeheartedly agreed with. "Look, if Little Bit isn't cooperating, he's doing it on his own. Just give me your word that we'll be free to go when I give you the coordinates."

"There's something else we want as well." Hahn pulled a small device from his pocket and walked down the length of the table, placing it on the surface in front of her, then stepping back.

Rion's eyes closed and she prayed for calm.

No need to ask what it was; she'd held that thing since she was a little girl.

It was the holostill containing the image of her father.

Sensing the shift in her mood, the Big Guy moved with Hahn, stopping a few feet behind him. He didn't trust her—at least he was capable enough to figure that out.

She picked up the holostill, picturing ONI in her quarters, knowing that they had scoured her ship, turned over everything, discovered her newfound information on her father and the *Spirit of Fire. . . .*

If they were trying to shake her up, they'd certainly picked the right thing. But Rion would be damned if she'd let them see it. "Why are you working with these creeps, Kip? You're not one of them." He didn't fit the ONI mold. Even now, in his uniform, he seemed uncomfortable and out of place.

"My family. My wife and unborn son." He cleared his throat. "Sedra. Last year."

"The bioweapon in the capital," she said, remembering. Hard for anyone to forget. The entire Outer Colonies had been shocked and horrified.

He nodded. "That was the result of Forerunner technology. So you see, I'm living proof, and what happened there *will* happen again and again if we don't get to the tech before the Covenant. I've seen you in action, Rion. We're on the same side. You're not the bad guy here and neither am I."

She didn't know what to say to that, because she believed him. Her instincts weren't wrong. Despite her anger and his betrayal, it wasn't like she could fault him for trying to make a difference. And while she knew grief intimately, she'd never known what it was like to lose a husband or a child. His loss was enormous, and it wasn't that difficult to understand his position and what drove him to work for ONI.

"Time's up, Captain," said Hahn. "What do you say?"

"What are you asking?"

"You know what I'm asking. I want you to talk to that fragment, Little Bit. He opens up or you don't go anywhere. I want the coordinates and every scrap of information you both have about the *Spirit of Fire*."

At the vessel's name, the Big Guy's gaze snapped to Hahn. Apparently he was on a need-to-know, and he hadn't known *that* part. Every marine—hell, every military man and woman, and a large part of the human population—knew the story of the *Spirit of Fire*. She was a shining emblem of courage and loss and mystery. Eleven thousand souls just . . . gone.

The money and salvage could be recouped in time. But the only things she had left of her father? Those couldn't be replaced. She'd waited twenty-six years for answers. Little Bit and his projections were the closest things she'd ever uncovered that had a shot at locating the ship and her father, and if she let Hahn have them, she was back to square one.

ONI wanted it all.

Everything.

The life they'd built. What they'd fought for, what Cade had died for. . . .

"We have the other holochips from your quarters, the video files . . . am I missing anything else important?"

Rion seethed inside. "No. I think you got everything that's left of him." She lifted her chin as a cold, brittle anger twisted around her heart. "Glad to see this is how the military treats its lost marines and their families—families who only want to find them and bring them home."

It was the first time the Big Guy looked even remotely concerned. But if he felt any discomfort at what ONI was doing to her, he quickly cleared it from his expression.

"Bringing them home is not your job," Hahn said.

"No, it was *your* job," she said angrily, leaning forward. "And you all failed. For twenty-six years, you've failed to find them."

"Maybe because there's nothing to find."

Her fists clenched at his flippant, unfeeling reply. She could feel the snap coming, a slow fiery build cracking through all that cold self-control she tried so hard to maintain. She knew what Hahn was asking: he wanted the projection Little Bit had created to track the ship. He wanted access to the video clips and every iota of intel Little Bit had managed to save. "If I get LB to cooperate, will I get my father's things back?"

"Just the images. Everything you've collected over the years or obtained from the fragment must be confiscated and remain classified."

Snap.

Rage surged through her like a firestorm. She lunged for Hahn's throat.

The Big Guy stepped in her path.

"Or we can use your crew for leverage," Hahn continued as the Big Guy threw out his arm to block her from shoving around him. "We'd like to keep them out of this, as I'm sure you would too. I'd hate to have to expose them to interrogation."

"Living up to your reputation," Rion snarled, pushing away

from the Big Guy's grasp, glancing from him to Kip and back again. "This is who you're siding with, Kip? People who threaten kids?"

"They're hardly children," Hahn said, moving closer once more. "Soldiers have been dying at a far younger age than your crew, losing more than you can possibly imagine. And they'll continue to die if we don't secure that site. Is this really what your father would have wanted, for you to lose everything you've worked for? Was this really worth getting Cade killed over?"

And that was it.

Rion lunged to the side of the Big Guy and swung a right with everything she had, landing a solid fist to the side of Hahn's mouth. He stumbled and then dropped like a stone as the Big Guy grabbed her arms, putting his body between her and Hahn once more. But she wasn't done, leaning around the soldier to yell, "No, it *wasn't* worth it, and I don't need a heartless bastard like you to point out the obvious!"

She shoved at the Big Guy, but it was like trying to move a bulkhead out of the way. He didn't budge. She stepped back, furious, as he stared down from his lofty height with that stony expression, a small lift to his right eyebrow. Her fury hardly spent, she jabbed his solid chest. "Yeah, you stay behind your spook badge of dishonor while the rest of us out here in the real world bleed and hurt."

The soldier's expression darkened and he bent down until he was eye level, a retort on his lips, when Kip angled between them, clearly fearing for Rion's life, and pushed her away.

"Get off me," she growled, retreating as Kip held up his hands in a gesture of peace and then went over to help Hahn. Rion continued to stare daggers at the Big Guy.

"You got mixed up in something far bigger than what you're capable of handling," the Big Guy said in a low tone. "Salvage what's left. That's what you're good at, right?"

"You don't know anything about me," she shot back.

"Well, if you're as resourceful as they say," he replied, looking her dead in the eye, voice even lower, "then suck it up. Do the right thing by your crew. And live to fight another day."

He turned his back on her and helped Kip lift Hahn to his feet.

CHAPTER 8

A gent Hahn and Fireteam Apollo leader Spartan Dylan Novak escorted Captain Forge to her ship. For the duration, she remained quiet and stiff between them, her anger simmering around her like a growing storm. Once they were well through the hangar-bay doors, Hahn slowed to a stop, intending to impart a few words of warning to the captain, but she continued past him without a glance or hesitation in her step, her head held high and her back straight.

Next to him, Novak let out a soft chuckle as he crossed his arms over his chest and watched Forge proceed to the *Ace of Spades*. Novak's amusement erased Hahn's sudden moment of shock, and he closed his mouth.

"Where I'm from, Walter, that's what's called a big ol' middle finger," Novak said, still grinning.

"I know what a middle finger is," he snapped. He drew in a

controlled breath, counseling himself to ignore the Spartan's jab. Even back when they were both wet behind the ears and assigned to Borneo Station, Novak had had a warped sense of humor. "I'd expect nothing less from an Outer Colony salvager. They're all one *very* short step up from outlaws and pirates."

Rion Forge's pride and independence had taken a major hit, and no doubt she was still reeling. ONI had rendered her helpless, and that was the one thing her type feared most. It also made her unpredictable. She was daring, tenacious, intelligent, passionate . . . but she was also a renegade, prideful, stubborn, and insolent. He was curious to see how she'd choose to move forward.

Hahn was a highly proficient handler, but in his experience, people like Rion Forge never really came around.

Too bad.

He rubbed his aching jaw and then worked it slowly, left to right, still tasting the iron tang of blood in his mouth. She'd gotten a hard sucker punch in, and Hahn suspected the highly trained Spartan-IV could easily have intervened and prevented the assault if he'd wanted to.

Novak hadn't been pleased about being pulled from the combat deck during training, as he'd been smack in the middle of simulated war games with the two Spartans recently assigned to Fireteam Apollo. But Hahn had convinced Captain Karah that having the Spartans play special ops to Rion Forge and her crew down on Komoya was essential to their success. . . .

Or perhaps Novak had been caught by surprise, just as Hahn had been, neither one suspecting the salvager had it in her to dare strike an ONI officer.

Whatever the case, Hahn knew his old friend well enough to

know that despite Novak's surface amusement, the Spartan was in a foul mood—failing to apprehend a high-value target like Gek 'Lhar could ruin any soldier's day. From what Hahn had gathered, apprehending the Sangheili commander hadn't originally been on Apollo's mission agenda—they were stationed on the *Taurokado* for reasons above Hahn's security clearance. And they, along with the entire ship, had been pulled off mission to pick up Kip Silas and then Hahn before taking measures to secure Rion Forge and her precious cargo.

'Lhar appearing right beneath their noses was, as Rion indicated, a gift, one that didn't happen often. Unfortunately, operating in stealth to capture Rion and her crew without raising any alarms on Komoya had worked against them in snagging the commander.

"Might want to put a pain patch on that," Novak commented as they watched Forge walk up the ramp. She paused at the top, turned around, and leveled a death glare in their direction, slapping the panel to her right to close the ramp, not looking away as it slowly lifted. "You made an enemy today, Agent Hahn."

"You mean *we*."

Novak laughed. "Oh no. This one's all on you, Walter."

Hahn frowned. He could easily have thrown the captain in the brig for assault. "You think I was too harsh on her?"

The Spartan gave a slight shrug. "I think if you had left her the warehouses and accounts, she could have been an asset."

"She never would've been an asset. I ran her personality profile three times. Besides, if we pandered to every salvager out here, we'd never get anywhere. Sometimes we have to play the bad guy so that the next one who comes along thinks twice."

"Then you should've taken her ship too," Novak said as the ramp closed on her figure. "She won't let this go."

Hahn laughed. "What, you think she'll use it to engage? Rion Forge hasn't gotten this far in life by being that stupid."

As the ship powered up, Turk's voice came over his comms. "The *Ace of Spades* is requesting permission to leave, Agent Hahn."

"Ah. Turk," he said with relief. "Glad to hear you're back with us." In the hour and a half that Rion Forge had been sequestered in the conference room, Turk had not only encountered an uncooperative Forerunner AI, but had been trapped for a time within the vast, jumbled, alien labyrinth of Little Bit's fragmented framework.

Had he not ensured Rion's cooperation, Turk might have been lost for good, and it would have been a disaster, costing Hahn his job at the very least.

"Permission granted," he said.

In seconds, the clamps holding the ship released, and the *Ace of Spades*'s thrusters engaged.

Turk's voice came over comms once more. "Spartan Novak, you're wanted on the bridge."

As Rion Forge directed her ship from the hangar, Hahn and Novak headed for the corridor.

Novak might question his methods, but Hahn had a track record to uphold. He *always* achieved his objective. He worked the entire trade route to monitor and acquire Forerunner artifacts. He was one of the best counter-contraband operatives in the field, and he intended to maintain his position. "What matters is that we secured the AI and the coordinates to the debris field," he said, more to himself than to Novak.

"And we know where Gek 'Lhar will be," Novak said. "The hinge-head is on borrowed time."

CHAPTER 9

Ace of Spades

From the time Rion had left the conference room until now—guiding *Ace* out of the ONI ship, a prowler if she had to guess—she'd forced a high degree of detachment upon herself to stop from doing something irrevocable to the smug Agent Hahn, and then focused on putting space between them and ONI.

When she'd crossed the catwalk moments ago, she'd been met with the concerned faces of Lessa and Niko, accepting their hugs and fielding their questions and concerns with short responses. Once in her captain's chair, she'd had to bite her tongue to keep from giving in and showing weakness when they still needed her strength. They weren't out of the prowler's range just yet.

But when they found out what they'd lost . . .

Ram swiveled in his station chair to face her. Their eyes met.

He made no attempt to placate her and she appreciated it. He comprehended ONI's reach as well as any salvager.

Using small directional bursts through the thrusters, Rion guided *Ace* out of the hangar bay, through the energy field separating the vacuum of space from the pressurized interior of the bay, and finally to freedom.

"We're so sorry," Lessa blurted as soon as they were away, her big eyes glassy. She was wringing her hands. "They separated us, and . . . they said they were going to ship you off to a black site and we'd never see you again. . . ." She drew in a deep breath.

Niko was staring down at his hands. When he lifted his head, her heart gave a painful pang at his misery. "They took Little Bit."

"I know. We'll talk about it later."

Rion drew in a deep breath as Less and Niko went to their stations. "Less, plot a course for Venezia."

Niko glanced over his shoulder and opened his mouth, a question hovering, but Rion put a finger to her lips and shook her head. *Say nothing. Not now.* Not while they could hear. Understanding dawned, and immediately he returned to his screen, fingers flying, running scans no doubt, trying to find out how much damage ONI had done and what they had left behind.

Once *Ace* was at a safe distance, the FTL spun up for the jump and they entered slipspace, heading back to their home base of New Tyne.

Slipspace always reminded Rion of the wee hours of night, when the energetic world faded into slumber . . . or a waiting room that stretched for light-years as the world went by without you. Niko called it the pause button. Less liked to say it was the time between time when they could pick up where they left off with old hobbies or tasks left for idle hours.

They'd reach Venezia in a couple of days, which was relatively quick in terms of space travel.

But right now, that seemed like an eternity.

Rion left the bridge with the eyes of her crew boring a hole in her back. There'd be time soon enough to talk. Now she just needed to be alone and process.

Back in her quarters, she sat on the end of her bed and tried to reason through what had just happened.

It wasn't unheard of—ONI, the UNSC, giving salvagers the once-over. It happened. If they were working a site close to an exclusion zone or some other area of interest, they were routinely pulled, searched, and anything of military value seized. Everyone in her line of work knew the drill.

But this . . .

This was different. Extreme.

Every warehouse. Every bank account. Little Bit. Her projections. Her father.

They'd taken way more than they needed.

They damn well didn't need to obliterate her livelihood and grab the video files of her father, but they'd taken them anyway—a crystal-clear message that they could have taken a lot more, that she was at their mercy, and not to forget it. And she never *would* forget it. They'd made sure of that.

And if they thought they'd scared her, they were sorely mistaken.

Scrutinizing her quarters, she noticed their touch everywhere—every drawer, surface, and nook had been tossed. Her gaze settled on the desk drawer where she kept her father's images and the data chips, and every bit of intel she'd ever found in her long process of searching for the *Spirit of Fire*.

Part of her hoped that they'd left her with something. After all, John Forge himself wasn't top secret. She had a right to keep her work, her memories. With a small thread of hope still clinging, Rion pushed to her feet, went to her desk, and pulled open the drawer.

A few images remained, but everything else was gone.

Including the haphazard, but curated, collection of files and chips and charts and notes.

Tears stung her eyes as a hollow well opened up inside her, leaving her as empty as the drawer she was looking into.

ONI had stolen twenty-six years' worth of searching and hope. Her best shot at finding her father had vanished, and they had no intention of giving it back. It was loss on top of loss. Outrage and disbelief rose so swiftly that she had to grab the desk with both hands and squeeze her eyes closed, reminding herself to breathe, to be grateful the crew was unharmed and *Ace* hadn't been confiscated along with everything else.

A mistake they'd regret later.

It took several minutes to regain her composure. When Rion finally opened her eyes, she zeroed in on her hands. On the gloves she still wore.

She straightened and slowly pulled them off, fingertip by fingertip. With each movement, an iron determination settled inside her, and the beginnings of a plan began to take shape.

CHAPTER 10

**Nor's clearinghouse, New Tyne outskirts,
Venezia, Qab system, four days later**

The pair of Kig-Yar always stationed outside the entrance to Nor Fel's massive storage complex came to attention when Rion approached in her old truck and parked. Through the dirty windshield, she studied the clearinghouse and the high-voltage fence that surrounded the buildings.

Normally she met Nor on payment days, when the notorious Kig-Yar trader sat in her New Tyne office and doled out credits to salvagers. Only on occasion did Rion have reason to come here—mostly to deliver large salvage items for auction. But all that seemed like a lifetime ago now.

The dust picked up again, pinging against the windshield. Through the rearview mirror, she noticed Less and Niko in the bed of the truck pulling their jackets over their heads to avoid the grit as they hopped out.

"This should be fun," Ram said as he got out of the passenger side.

"Fun but necessary," she replied, and stepped outside into the cold.

The guards by the gate, a pair of Jackals in minimal armor with carbines slung over their shoulders, stared at the approaching party with round eyes over large beaks lined with sharp teeth. Rion could tell from the way their avian heads lifted that they were scenting the newcomers. Not really necessary, given that their eyesight was very good. Kig-Yar enjoyed scenting things to suss out weakness or illness—which they always reacted to aggressively—and sometimes they just liked to size up potential meals for kicks.

While Rion had a good working relationship with Nor, some of the guards the Kig-Yar female employed were far from being acclimated to dealing with a variety of species.

One of the males called in the newcomers through his comm unit as Rion glanced up at the many cameras stationed around the facility.

Upon approval, which was nothing more than unintelligible squawking through the comm system, the chain-link gate slid open. "Don't touch the fence or the gate," Rion reminded them as they entered.

On a normal day, the fence was dangerous enough; but on a really bad day, when some idiot radical thought he could raid the clearinghouse, the fence's specially designed components emitted a high-frequency EMP charge—a handy little feature that rendered any attacks on Nor's goods moot while the clearinghouse itself remained shielded from the pulse.

Rion never asked what happened to those unfortunate morons.

All she knew was that they disappeared, and maybe the Jackal guards got their tasty meal after all.

They crossed the lot to the main building. The side entry door slid open and they stepped into another guard station, which blocked the entry and the hallway that led to Nor's office.

Nor Fel was an extraordinary paranoid, keeping an arsenal of the finest surveillance sweepers in the sector, military-grade software that was constantly upgraded. She left nothing to chance—which was a necessity, considering her business as one of the Outer Colonies' preeminent movers of postwar salvage. Everyone and everything entering her place of business got swept. And those entering her office at the clearing house got the spa treatment.

For the last few days, Rion had made sure she and the crew kept their talk to a bare minimum, while Niko and Ram had spent that time sweeping the ship for ONI surveillance. They did the best they could, but Nor could do far better. Rion was counting on the Kig-Yar's equipment to remove any lingering ONI bugs that were hitching a ride on them and on her ship.

An initial sweep at the guard station revealed several tiny metallic sensors stuck to shoes and hidden in their clothing. They removed their jackets and footwear and were scanned again until they came up clean. First round complete. Halfway down the corridor leading to Nor's private office were two additional guards, a human and a Kig-Yar engaged in a game of dice next to a Saffire Diagnostics bio-scanner, the same type used for entry into diplomatic headquarters or top secret military facilities. It was a freestanding white tunnel of bug-detecting technology.

The guards paused when they saw Rion and the crew. "Do you have an appointment, Captain?" a clean-cut young man in a lab coat asked.

"No. But she'll see me or she wouldn't have let me get this far."

He stood and powered up the scanner. Once it was ready, he gestured for her to step inside while the Jackal monitored the scan on a screen in front of him. The pulsating white light inside the scanner turned red. "Step back, please," the man instructed. "Put your left arm on the table."

Rion did as directed. The man grabbed her forearm tightly, holding it against the table, and selecting one of the many strange and sharp medical devices—scalpels for all species—on the table next to the scanner. He spoke to the Jackal in basic Sangheili, checking the screen before spraying her skin with analgesic spray and then slicing into her arm without preamble.

"You speak Covenant," she said with a tight smile as he made a neat cut into her skin before reaching for a pair of tweezers, the ends of which he stuck into the wound.

"Very little."

"Nor doesn't usually employ humans." He opened the tweezers inside the wound and grabbed hold of the silicone bug implanted just below her skin. She thought back to a moment during her time with Hahn when she might have felt a tiny sting, but in all the tension and drama, she couldn't place exactly when the bug had been inserted or by whom.

"No, she doesn't," the young man answered. "But things started to get messy when she installed this scanner. Jackals aren't great at being delicate, if you get my meaning. She got tired of all the blood and the customers complaining. . . ." He pulled a tiny gray device the size of a rice grain free and dropped it into a pan. "Looks like ONI tech," he said, peering at it for a moment. "Seeing more and more of them these days. Advanced little buggers."

He pressed a seal onto her wound.

"You're pretty good at this," she said, holding the seal tightly so it would bond to her skin.

"I work at the clinic in New Tyne," he said with a shrug. "At least the complaints here have gone down."

"Would you mind scanning me again?"

"Sure."

By the time they were finished, and everyone was bug-free and sealed up, Rion finally felt a measure of relief.

The Jackal led them to Nor's door. It slid open a fraction and Nor Fel stuck her head out. Her beady yellow eyes studied them intently over a long, toothy beak. "What you doing, lurking out here?" She spied Rion's seal and snorted. "Come inside." She noticed Ram at the back of the pack and gave a surprised squawk. "You two . . . working together." She cackled at that as she moved aside to let them both in, then held up a clawed hand to Lessa and Niko. "Hatchlings, stay."

Nor then proceeded to close the door in their faces. Her clawed feet tapped over the floor as she waddled around her desk and took a seat. Her bling was heavy on the rings today, flashing as she rested her leathery elbows on the desktop and then propped her lower beak on the teepee of her bejeweled claws. Her eyes were near slits as she regarded Rion. "Trouble follows you, Rion Forge. Ever since Eiro."

"I need to borrow your sweeper and software for my ship."

"Fine. Fine." She tapped a claw on the table as she thought.

"ONI coming around. Asking things." The feathers that ran down the back of her head and neck stiffened. It was clear she despised them. "Sticking beaks in business not they own. Despicable. And Gek 'Lhar. Ha! Wants you dead for what you gave him. All trouble Nor does not need."

"Well, I'm not on anyone's radar anymore. Gek is in uncharted space, if I had to guess, and ONI got what they wanted, so . . ." Rion rose to leave.

"Sit." Nor waited until Rion complied. "Your warehouse outside of town—all gone. Came in with ship and lifted it up, away. Nothing left but foundation. But I save you something. I know things ahead of time. So I go and do you another favor. See now. It is you owes me *three* now."

Rion's brow lifted, and she couldn't help but be intrigued. "That depends on what you saved."

"That safe of yours—no cracking it." Nor laughed. "But I go through your things . . . find this. . . ." She pulled a small datacore from her drawer and set it on the table. Nor's smile was more of an openmouthed pant, but Rion was familiar with the sight of the Kig-Yar grin. "Why this pricey thing not in your safe?"

Rion knew exactly why. Because Niko had begged to study it before they put it on the market. Nor hadn't had to dig very deep; Rion was pretty sure the core had been left front and center on Niko's worktable. Any other time, she'd be livid at him for not storing it before they left, but Rion wasn't about to look a gift horse in the mouth. "What do you want for it?"

Nor touched a claw to the top of the core and pushed it across the desk, where it came to rest in front of Rion. "Saving my favors. . . . Take it."

Whatever Nor had in store for her, Rion knew she'd pay the price later.

She agreed to owe another favor and left Nor's with a datacore containing a salvaged dumb AI—a completely functioning mining facility superintendent.

It was worth a small fortune.

Outside the city, where the roads were still dirt and the neighbors few and far between, Rion sat on the tailgate of her truck with Ram and Lessa, parked on a rise overlooking the small commercial lot where her shipping container once sat. Niko stood on the side of the road, looking at the site with his fingers linked and resting on top of his head.

"Well," Lessa said with a sigh, "Nor wasn't kidding, was she?"

It had made a lovely warehouse once upon a time.

Nearly four hundred square meters of space gone. Rion hadn't needed more room than that—the big salvage was always dumped at the clearinghouse, so there had been plenty of room for small-scale acquisitions, a workspace, and her office, which boasted a very pricey Bernard MK2, where she'd kept a copy of Little Bit's projections for the *Spirit of Fire*.

But paying the best for one of the most uncrackable safes in the galaxy didn't mean much when someone could simply fly over and lift her entire business up off the ground and steal away with whatever was inside.

Seeing the foundation solidified the enormity of what ONI had taken from her. Her search for her father might have just come to a permanent end.

Along with her job and livelihood.

Niko dropped his hands and kicked the small rocks on the side of the road, watching them bounce down the hill. "This is bullshit. They can't just take everything."

"They already did, Niko," Rion said.

Lessa hopped off the tailgate and put a hand on her brother's shoulder. As they stared at the vacant lot, Rion knew the reality was settling in for them as well. She wasn't the only one with irreplaceable items stored inside the missing container.

Niko shrugged Lessa's comforting hand away. "How can they get away with this? Who do they think they are?"

"They think they're protecting humanity," Lessa said, shoving her hands in her pockets.

Niko turned around. "How can you say that? They don't care about humanity—they care who's in charge. ONI did it because they can. This is all a big power trip. They couldn't give a rat's ass about us."

"I'm not defending them," she replied, frowning. "I just lost all my stuff too, you know."

"Oh, what, you lost your knitting needles and your wool? Big deal."

Lessa flinched. "No, I— Niko . . . we lost everything we took from Aleria."

Niko shook his head. It was clear he didn't want to fight with his sister, but his emotions were overwhelming him and he couldn't seem to help it. "We didn't have anything to take, Less! We left Aleria with a bag of shitty clothes. There was nothing of value from that life worth saving. Nothing at all."

Her eyes went round and hurt. She blinked a few times,

trying not to cry. "There was Mom's stuff, her blanket and her—"

He rolled his eyes. "Oh, come on. You never knew her, Lessa. That stuff they gave you at the shelter—that could have belonged to anyone. You just believed what they told you because you *wanted* it to be true. Why do you think we don't even have a last name? Because no one knew who our parents were!"

They were standing toe to toe. Rion perched on the tailgate, ready to intervene if necessary. Lessa's lips thinned and her round face was pale and utterly stricken. Suddenly she shoved Niko in the chest so hard that he ended up in the dirt on his rear end. As she stormed off down the road, he sat up and watched her go with a mixture of anger and regret and hurt, about to call her back. But the words didn't come. So he gave up, lying back in the dirt and letting out a frustrated groan.

Ram remained quiet next to Rion for a moment, picking at his fingernails. "You want me to go get her?"

"No, let her cool off awhile." Rion gave him a flat smile. "Bet you didn't expect all this when you asked to crew with us. What is it they say? Be careful what you wish for?"

"Well, I *was* looking for a distraction. . . ." His dry humor crinkled the corners of his dark eyes. He had a lot of lines there, permanent evidence of his good nature.

Rion watched Lessa marching farther away and let out a deep sigh. She hopped off the tailgate and walked over to stare down at Niko. He felt her gaze and removed his hands from his face. "If you're going to lecture me, don't bother."

"Wouldn't dream of it."

"Right. You always lecture me. Just leave me here. I've decided this is where I'm going to stay. Until I die."

Oh boy. She kicked the sole of his boot. "Get up." He scowled, and she kicked him again. "Get up. Go get your sister. We have work to do."

Thirty minutes later, they were all sitting at a corner table in a busy bistro/bar in downtown New Tyne. The mood was somber. Niko and Lessa weren't speaking to or looking at each other, and Ram wasn't quite sure how to interact, so he stayed quiet. After the waiter left, Rion dug into her jacket pocket, pulled out the small core, and placed it on the table.

Now she had their interest.

"Here's where things stand. ONI now has the location of the debris field. They've either apprehended Gek 'Lhar by now or they're fighting over the field as we speak. They have Little Bit." She drew in a deep breath. "And they confiscated all his clips and projections on my father and the *Spirit of Fire*. They didn't just take our warehouse here; they took them *all*, along with all of our bank accounts. We have zero leverage, and everything we've worked for is gone."

Rion let that sink in for all of three seconds before diving in to the rest of her speech.

"So here's what we're going to do. Niko, you're going to meet Nor's people at the airfield and use her software and sweeper to clean the ship. Top to bottom. Once it's clear, you're going to do it again. Less, you're going to contact Rouse at Tiny Birds and ask him to do a quick sale on this core. He likes you. You can get him to do it for beans. Use half the profit to load us up on fuel cells, and food and drink stores. I want *Ace* packed to capacity." Lessa nodded and pulled the core toward her as Rion turned her attention to Ram.

"Ram . . ." she began, "I don't know what's in store for us or where we'll end up . . . so if you want out, I'll completely understand—"

He held up a hand. "I don't jump ship when things get rough. I knew when I signed up that we'd be dodging ONI. Things went a little sideways, sure," he said, with a smile at his understatement. "But I'm part of your crew now. I'm still in. And Gek is still out there. Whatever you need me to do."

Rion gave him a grateful nod. "All right," she said, clearing her throat. "You'll take the other half of the core's profits and secure us new star charts, since we scrubbed ours, and then you're going to get Niko the tech he needs to decipher whatever the hell is on *this*. . . ."

She reached into her other pocket and laid the augmented glove on the table. "I didn't take these off until we *left* the prowler."

Niko sat straighter, eyes going wide. "Wait. You used it on ONI?"

"I did. And if there's anything useful on this scanner, I promise you we'll use it to take our lives back. We're not out of the game yet."

CHAPTER 11

Ace of Spades, orbiting Venezia, five days later

Niko slapped two separate files onto the lounge's center table, directly in front of Rion as she sat eating her breakfast bowl of warm rice mixed with fresh Brillon eggs they'd picked up from the market in New Tyne. "Well, here it is," he said. "Little Bit's short contribution to what would have been an amazing partnership." He let out a heavy sigh.

Ram peered around from his chair facing the viewscreen, antiquated reading glasses slipping down his nose, while Lessa stayed leaning on the meal counter, cradling her breakfast bowl in her hands and giving her brother a contrite look.

Niko slid into the chair next to Rion, completely invading her personal space. He touched a finger to the document in front of her. "Translated readout from Gek's comm. And a whopper from the big ONI dude who grabbed you on Komoya."

Rion glanced up at him, mouth full as she asked, "You read them?"

He gave her a frown as though she was crazy for asking. "Now, Gek's last report is a real shocker," he said with sarcasm. "He's going to win the auction, lots of religious bullshit with some dude named Jul 'Mdama, and then after he acquires the Harvester, he's headed for the debris field to mine, blah, blah, blah, some precious weapon, blah, blah, blah. Same ol' Covie song and dance. But *this*," he said, tapping the next report, "this is some serious gold."

Rion wiped her mouth, pushed the bowl aside, and went to pull the document closer to read, but Niko couldn't contain his excitement.

"That big dude who nabbed you is a *Spartan*," he said in a delighted rush. "A real-life Spartan. I mean, it fits, right? I'm thinking the lady was too—which makes me feel a whole lot better about being carried across the canal. Anyway, you were right. Their ship is a prowler. The *Taurokado*. Only got this one image, but it's a report about some distress call and orders to investigate after securing the debris field and looking around for your dad's ship." He tapped the file. "Apparently they think this signal might be related to some redacted-slash-coded incident in 2554." He pointed to a particular sentence. "Look here, *Proceed with extreme caution. High-value asset. Containment Protocol BKW-112. . . . Secure access to the site. Do not engage. . . .* They even slipspaced a commsat to the area to block the distress call from reaching anyone else."

Ram had removed his reading glasses, his attention fixed on Niko's revelation. Lessa was listening intently as well.

Rion picked up the document. "So they're protecting their asset from being found . . . that's promising."

"Right? And I'm thinking while they're off saving everyone from Gek, and securing *our* debris field—bastards that they are—we'll skip on over and do a little rescue-and-recover mission. There's definitely something of value at this site."

Lessa approached. "And then we make a trade for our stuff back."

"Exactly," said Niko.

"We could get in and out before they have a chance to point in our direction," Ram said, joining them. "May I?"

Rion slid the reports his way.

He put his glasses back on. "The Ibycus system. That's a two or three week hike, give or take." He typed the system name into the integrated pad on the table. A holo appeared showing a single-star system with four small planetary bodies inside a large asteroid belt. "The planet where the signal is being broadcast is here," he said, pointing at a small sand-colored world, closest to its star. "Geranos-a, it's called. Uninhabited. Gravity weighs in at zero-point-six-seven-nine g's, so we can manage that. Atmosphere's too thin though."

"There should be time, right?" Lessa asked. "What do you think? ONI has to get to the debris field, secure it, and then travel to Geranos-a. . . ."

The ONI prowler was a faster ship than *Ace*, but they should have plenty of time. . . . Still, Rion didn't want to rush things or make any knee-jerk decisions. Whatever was so valuable on Geranos-a might be more than they could handle. But then again, they wouldn't know for certain unless they headed out to Ibycus and took a look.

"We didn't start it," Niko replied, taking her hesitation for a no-go.

"ONI doesn't have to know how we got our hands on their salvage," Lessa said. "Just that we came across it somewhere, somehow. We could be there and gone without them even knowing."

Rion considered their words. They could salvage the site, rescue anyone stranded, leave long before the *Taurokado* arrived, wait a spell, and then auction whatever they'd salvaged at Nor's. No doubt, if the asset on Geranos-a was as important as it seemed to be, ONI would come calling, and when they did, Rion's price would be the return of all of their confiscated items. Plus interest for their troubles, if she could swing it.

"All right," she said. "What's to stop them from forcibly taking our salvage once we have it? They send a Spartan after us or after Nor, and no one will stand a chance."

Silence filled the lounge.

"There's a good chance they wouldn't risk angering the Venezian militia," Ram said, "and starting a war with the Outer Colonies."

Nor's clearinghouse worked because she operated within the thin confines of Venezian and UNSC salvage law. If ONI disregarded their own rules for all to see and stormed the clearinghouse, they'd infuriate a lot of very dangerous and well-armed groups who relied on Nor for their goods.

Rion wanted Little Bit's projections. She wanted the video clips of her father. She wanted her credits back, and she wanted Lessa's damn blanket.

Still, she hesitated.

Losing Cade had changed things. He was always going to be an enormous factor in her decisions from now on. All those stolen items, no matter how much they meant, weren't worth losing another one of her crew.

Rion's head came up, and she saw the understanding in their eyes. They knew what she was thinking without saying a word.

Finally Lessa spoke up, which surprised Rion, because Less was usually the more cautious one in her crew. "Well, it wouldn't hurt if we went out there and took a look around. . . . I mean, we *are* salvagers."

"Universal law says we're legally bound to offer assistance to distress calls," Ram added, thoughtfully tapping a finger to his lips. "We'd simply be responding to a ship's distress call, and help-ing any survivors. We could render aid—and, while we're there, liberate their high-value asset."

"Call it an exploratory mission," Niko said.

While the risk weighed on Rion's mind, she also knew that if they played this right, it might work in their favor.

The crew was in accord and waiting for an answer.

Beyond sticking it to ONI, there might be more than that valu-able asset to be found. She'd just be playing the hand ONI had dealt her, after all. Plus it would be immensely satisfying to give ONI a taste of what they'd been dishing out to salvagers for years. At the very least, Rion couldn't deny that wiping that smug look off of Agent Hahn's face would be extremely satisfying.

"We'll need a jump plan and a complete chart of the planet and the system," Rion said.

Lessa's lips drew into a smile and Ram gave an approving nod. Niko clapped his hands as Rion pushed up from the table, glanced around at the *Ace* crew, and grinned. "Let's get back to doing what we do best."

CHAPTER 12

hree of this planet's years have now passed.

The cataloging and parsing of my human personality and body pattern is nearly complete. Memories have settled into place, and much of the past now resides in appropriate sectors to be examined at will:

My life on Erde-Tyrene.

My time with the Forerunners, with Bornstellar and the Librarian. With my human friends, Riser, Vinnevra, and Gamelpar.

The long responsibility as monitor of Installation 04.

And the rather disastrous meeting with modern humans after millennia of separation.

There are gaps, of course. More recent than not. Damage done. Things lost.

And things that remain whether I wish them to or not.

I reflect often on the past. I ponder who and what I am, and what I will become.

The lines between good decisions and bad ones are blurred. They meet and diverge like star roads, in constant motion, stretching and tangling and affecting things seen and unseen.

I travel these roads through the detached lens of a visitor to an ancient history. But the lens does not diminish the regret, the pride, the loss, and the horror of those final days of the great war that took place between the Forerunners and the Flood, and my part in it.

Part savior—I did exemplary work in my short time aiding the Librarian.

Part destroyer—as monitor, I performed my functions well.

I was Chakas.

I was 343 Guilty Spark.

What am I now?

Neither identity is satisfactory any longer, for I am changed.

I am less. And I am more.

I tuck my alloy hands beneath my metal head and lie back against the giant leaning shard of the Rubicon's aft exterior, which juts up from the sand. It is a good place to study the stars or simply enjoy the sight of them in the sky. There is no moon or light pollution, so the nights here allow me to see far and deep into space.

I raise one knee up—digging my undamaged heel into the sand to brace me—and I spend this night, like many others, staring up and letting memories wash over me.

Still a few rogue pieces to put together, compartments to merge.

The order of things, at times, confounds me, but I find when I don't try so hard, my memory patterns seem to fall instinctually into the right place.

This has taken much practice—letting go, slowing down my thought processes.

Allowing my mind to wander.

I have not experienced such a thing since I was Chakas, since I had a physical body and mind, and my days were spent in idle, unfocused, and reckless pursuits.

But now, as I gaze up at the stars, letting patterns drift and settle, I have begun to embrace this forgotten part of being human, this reminiscing, roaming, and sensing. My armiger body feels nothing, of course. Unless I simulate what I believe to be the correct response to external stimuli.

And I do. Quite often.

I laugh. I sing. I hurt. I cry. I let sadness wash over me the way my human personality pattern remembers it.

A hundred thousand years is a long time to yearn, to miss old friends.

What am I becoming?

Something . . . someone free.

Free to choose.

Is it a luxury, a fundamental right, or is it a burden, this freedom? I hum.

I enjoy this function most of all. Vibration spreads through my updated vocal cords and my being fills with melody.

I remember how much I desired, at one point in my existence, to be human again. Now, however, I am beginning to conclude that humanity can mean more than simple biology, more than cells and sinew and bone. It is the consciousness, as well. And that aspect is something I still—in a manner of speaking—possess.

I have no wish for a physical existence. At least, not yet.

This form will do until I have fulfilled my purpose.

A meteor flares and then trails across the blackness of space, flickering out as though it was never there to begin with. Gone. That is the span of a human life, a bright burning silent burst, a flicker, a gasp. Then nothing more.

But other things persist, from one age to the next, defying the laws of nature, refusing to forget.

In this, I am not alone.

CHAPTER 13

Facility at Voi, Kenya, Africa, Earth, June 2557

Annabelle Richards, former head of ONI Special Operations and current director of Project: BOOKWORM, walked quickly down a man-made corridor. Behind the glossy white walls, floor, and ceiling were kilometers of fiber optics, cables, and reverse-engineered Forerunner technology—an elaborate and sophisticated labyrinth designed to trap, confound, and essentially cut off an artificial intelligence from the rest of the galaxy.

But not just any AI.

This place had been designed and built to hold one very dangerous and elusive intelligence.

Should they ever find him.

If there was anything to find.

When Annabelle had received word that the ONI-commissioned research vessel UNSC *Rubicon* was broadcasting a distress signal from an uninhabited planet in the Ibycus system after three years lost, she'd sat back in her chair and stared at the top secret missive in shock—so surprised in fact that the facility AI, Ferguson, had appeared on her desk with a medical alert, noting her sharp rise in blood pressure.

A cargo ship had picked up the faint signal a few weeks earlier and, because the signal indicated a military vessel, the captain had passed along the information to the authorities. Once the intel reached her, Annabelle had taken over. Unfortunately, the timing couldn't have been worse, as her team had been out on maneuvers. But she'd found the closest ONI vessel in the sector, the *Taurokado*, and ordered them to secure the site for her team once their current mission was complete.

Once the *Taurokado* made it to Geranos-a, they would stay in orbit, with strict orders to avoid contact or engagement of any kind with the surface. If Guilty Spark, by some miracle, was still with the *Rubicon*, care must be taken.

Now that her team had returned from maneuvers on Titan, Annabelle felt a small measure of calm.

As she stopped at the end of the corridor and scanned her security clearance to open the elevator door, her nerves were firing in a million different directions. They'd been waiting and hoping for a break like this, and there were many times during her short tenure when she had wondered if all the preparation and effort of the last year and a half would be for nothing.

Project: BOOKWORM might finally be able to do the work for which it was created—interview, interrogate, and study the ancient Forerunner monitor 343 Guilty Spark.

At the heart of BOOKWORM were two of the most highly

classified and important pieces of data ONI had ever recovered. One was found on the shield world Onyx by Hugo Barton and his research team in the spring of 2554. Known as the Bornstellar Relation, it was an ancient Forerunner testimony detailing the key players in the Forerunner-Flood War and the galaxy-wide firing of the Halo Array. The other was a data drop recovered from deep space in late 2555. While the exact date of the drop was unknown, it had been ejected by someone or something on the *Rubicon*. The data contained an autobiographical account given by 343 Guilty Spark to the *Rubicon* crew, which mirrored events in the Bornstellar Relation.

It was shortly after this discovery that BOOKWORM came into being.

These combined accounts had provided incredible insight into Forerunner civilization—their customs, biology, rates, technology, and history—as well as their final days fighting the Flood, ruthless and invasive parasitic organisms whose sole purpose was the consumption of all sentient life in the galaxy.

Nearly one hundred thousand years ago, in a last-ditch effort to defeat the Flood, the Forerunners had created Halo—massive ring-shaped weapons designed to fire simultaneously and purge all sentient life from the Milky Way galaxy, in essence starving the Flood of its food source and wiping the slate clean. Meanwhile, the Ark stood outside the galaxy, ready and waiting to reseed life once the Flood was finally dead and gone.

Annabelle's job as director was to compartmentalize information between divisions so that no one knew the full scope of the project, while coordinating the effort to find Guilty Spark, to study him, and ultimately determine whether the shocking claims in his account were true.

And while his testimony had gone through dozens of translations, which were then continually run through ONI's advanced statistical AIs—"stat bots" whose sole function was to analyze and predict probabilities and causalities based on the text—there were questions left unanswered, things that didn't add up, and eventualities they had to prepare for.

They'd learned many things from the Forerunners and their incredible technology. There were personnel here chomping at the bit to study the monitor, to see how it had survived as long as it had without devolving into complete rampancy. Finding that answer might increase the longevity of humanity's own smart AIs.

But Annabelle felt somewhat differently. Every monitor, every ship, every bit of ancient technology was inherently dangerous. They were weapons that had to be contained. The numbers of lives lost on the Halo rings, on the Ark, and, of course, during and after the Covenant War were astronomical.

Two years had passed since Operation: FAR STORM. She'd been part of that mission and had seen firsthand the devastation and destruction wreaked by rogue and rampant AIs. Even the ancient Forerunner tales themselves, in the wrong hands, could lead to disaster.

As the elevator neared the surface, where the facility boasted its own airfield, two hangars, a comm tower, and personnel quarters, Annabelle drew in a deep breath, squared her shoulders, tugged her jacket straight, and then shoved an errant strand of red hair behind her ear where it belonged.

The elevator stopped, the door slid open, and the quiet hum of her small space evaporated. The tarmac was full of life and noise. The scent of clay and dry grass, mixed with jet fuel and exhaust, met her as she stepped outside. A hefty dose of hot savanna wind blew her sleek hair into a frenzy. "Damn it," she muttered at her forgetfulness, pulling a small band from her uniform pocket and tying her hair back quickly before heading across the tarmac to the large, angular shape of the *Eclipse*-class prowler *Bad Moon Rising*.

A fit figure in a black flight suit emerged from beneath the enormous black wing. There was no mistaking the captain of the *Bad Moon Rising*. He was a formidable presence, a lifelong military man, a veteran with a list of war medals a hundred meters long, and a classified file even longer. His hair was as black as the ship he commanded, but graying at his temples, which Annabelle thought gave him a very distinguished air.

"Captain Hollier, how were maneuvers?"

The captain held out a hand to escort her away from the ship and the loud whirring of its powerful engines. Behind him, the hangar bay was being loaded with supplies for their journey to the Ibycus system.

Once they could speak without shouting, he gave her a perfunctory smile. "Maneuvers were excellent, Director."

Annabelle should've been used to that title by now. Her military rank was that of captain, but for the tenure of this project she was referred to as "Director," and it sounded odd every time she heard it.

"Gear is already on board," Hollier continued. "We're just loading up supplies and then we'll be ready to go."

"You've been briefed?"

"Yes, ma'am. Ferg briefed us on the way in."

While knowledge of the project was heavily compartmentalized, Hollier knew enough details to allow him to thoroughly complete his mission—to investigate the source of the signal and contain any remains of a Forerunner AI, thought to be on board, for study. "The containment chamber?"

"In working order."

"Good. I don't need to explain how important this is."

They'd had many discussions about the mission, many trials and maneuvers and simulations to prepare them for an eventuality that might never come. And while Annabelle had complete belief in Captain Hollier and his team, she still needed 100 percent reassurance.

"No, ma'am, you do not," he replied evenly, and she appreciated his calm demeanor and understanding more than ever. "We're ready. We'll bring back your asset and we'll bring it back contained."

"See that you do."

He gave her a crisp nod and then turned to go.

"Captain?" she called. He paused, turning back around. "Be careful out there."

He dipped his head and then walked toward his ship as a large helping of guilt settled into her stomach, curling into a tight little knot, which would certainly stay there until they returned.

The six-member asset recovery team, or AR team as Annabelle called it, of the *Bad Moon Rising* strode across the tarmac and met up with Hollier, falling in line, duffels on their backs, and looking ready for anything. A black patch with a white wolf in midhowl was sewn onto the shoulder of each flight suit. No name tags, no military designations; just the "howler" in honor of the ship and captain they served.

Annabelle had selected the personnel carefully, finding the perfect candidates in Hollier's team. They'd been pulled years ago from elite special-ops forces across the UNSC and within ONI's Delta-6 candidate pool. Each member was highly skilled in the art of asset and artifact retrieval, which covered a wide range of skill sets—reconnaissance, direct action, unconventional warfare, counterintelligence, and more. They'd received training by specialists from REAP-X and XEG to identify, decipher, and handle Forerunner technology and artifacts, as well as the latest tech in reverse-engineering and xenoarchaeology.

In short, they were highly trained combat specialists who could function effectively as Forerunner artifact hunters, able to navigate any number of hostile worlds and environments. They were also a tight-knit group who had cut their teeth as a squad on previous projects, facing high-risk scenarios and impossible situations in the harshest of places.

In addition to the six ARs and the captain, there were two supporting staff members: a trauma medic, and Thea, a smart AI with complete knowledge of BOOKWORM's purpose.

The ramp began to close, and Annabelle sent a silent prayer for success. Failure wasn't an option. If Guilty Spark was found intact and operational, and her team's attempt at containment failed . . . if he tried to take over the *Bad Moon Rising* the way he had the *Rubicon*, the prowler would begin a hard self-destruct sequence. ONI couldn't risk this particular rogue intelligence running rampant across the galaxy with a prowler at his disposal.

The team knew the risks. But these weren't ordinary people; they weren't even ordinary soldiers. They believed in their training and their capabilities. They might be from all different backgrounds, but they had one key thing in common. They had no ties, no family, no one to miss them if they didn't return, and, most importantly, no one who could compromise their judgment and prevent them from completing the task at hand. Their only bond was to the mission, to one another, and to Annabelle. That was it.

It might have been a terrible way to choose a team, but Operation: FAR STORM—those lost on the Ark and the numerous casualties here in Kenya as Home Fleet defended against the Ark's Retriever Sentinels—still weighed heavily on Annabelle's mind and heart. She'd never forget returning home from the Ark to find such destruction and casualties strewn across the savanna.

Being in charge, holding others' fates in her hands, hadn't been easy then, nor was it now. With a heavy sigh, she headed across the tarmac to where BOOKWORM's head of xenoarchaeology, Dr. William Iqbal, waited for her. "Doctor," she greeted him. "Come to see them off?"

The wind ruffled his graying hair as *Bad Moon Rising* prepared for lift, its thrusters maneuvering for the push off the tarmac. The dark ship ascended, rising steadily into the air.

"Godspeed to them," the doctor said, hands tucked into his tan trousers, staring up through thick glasses as the prowler increased its acceleration and shot up into the sky. He didn't need the glasses—not with today's advances—but like many scholars, he held on to old traditions.

She opened her mouth to inquire about preparedness, but he was expecting it. "Don't worry, Annabelle. We're ready for this. All the teams are standing by."

Annabelle regarded the darkening sky. With only the distress call containing the *Rubicon*'s transponder codes and location, they didn't have much to go on. There was no way to tell if the ship had crashed, if there were survivors, if Guilty Spark was still with them or damaged or long gone.

"You're still worried," William said, looking at her in that studious way of his.

"Of course I'm worried. You've read the stat bots' evaluations. You know there's a chance—if he's out there, if he's on Geranos-a with the *Rubicon*—that this might be exactly what he wants. You've read his account. You know as well as I do what he's after—or rather, *whom* he's after. He *wants* to come to Earth, William. I'm sure of it. And I can assure you he has no desire to do so in our custody."

Guilty Spark could very well be among the most dangerous and singular minds in the entire galaxy.

"Well, we'll know soon enough."

William's hand squeezed her shoulder. "If he's there, the pod will hold him, Annabelle. We've learned from our mistakes with Intrepid Eye. We're prepared."

Maybe. Hopefully. "And the stat bots' analysis . . . ?"

"What about it?"

"Guilty Spark's story—do you still agree with their conclusions?"

"I do. 343 Guilty Spark is an unreliable narrator with an unclear motive for relating his tale."

Unfortunately, that was exactly what she thought too. And God only knew what that true motive was.

CHAPTER 14

With the cooperation of Rion Forge's fragmented AI, the *Taurokado* had been able to locate the debris field without incident. If they played this right, they might even catch Jul 'Mdama's second-in-command, Gek 'Lhar, and his newly acquired Harvester. Fireteam Apollo leader Spartan Novak was determined to remove the Sangheili commander from the game board for good.

Captain Karah stood across the tactical table, monitoring the feed from the drones as they hovered low over Site 037, a large chunk of Forerunner construction embedded in rock. Almost as soon as the drones began their coordinated grid pattern, Novak saw something on the surface. "Looks like battle plating. Turk, can you magnify?"

One of the drones descended and increased magnification. "That's definitely UNSC plating," Captain Karah agreed.

The more evidence, the better, Novak thought, as the drone recorded the location and then continued on, searching for more. They already knew—thanks to information gleaned from Little Bit, the name given to the fragmented AI recovered by the *Ace* crew—that the *Spirit of Fire* had been on the Forerunner world. A shield world, of all things, the fragment had said.

Novak had never dreamed the fragment would possess such startling intel. They'd watched actual video footage of Sergeant John Forge, and witnessed the brief fight between Red Team and the Elites . . . and they'd learned just how the ship had defeated the Covenant and destroyed the shield world.

Novak had watched the feed along with those on the bridge, and for a long time no one spoke. Forge's final mission was of the highest order, the stuff of heroes and legend. There was a very good likelihood that his sacrifice and the crew's efforts had saved humanity. Had the Covenant gotten its hands on the Forerunner battlefleet stationed on the shield world, and all the technology the world itself contained, the war would have been over in a heartbeat.

The discovery breathed new life into the search for the lost vessel. They now knew *why* the ship couldn't make its way home. Using their slipspace drive to blow up the shield world was ingenious, but it had also taken away the *Spirit's* ability to jump. So they'd drifted, lost in uncharted space. Eleven thousand brave souls. They could be anywhere. Settled on a planet. In cryo . . .

It didn't sit well with him, after all the crew had done and sacrificed. The idea that they might still be out there somewhere, hoping for rescue, that his Spartan brethren on Red Team were MIA. . . .

Novak crossed to the viewscreen and regarded the debris field, the scale of it, the enormity of what the *Spirit of Fire* had accomplished, as Rion Forge's words rang in his head.

She was right. They'd failed them. For twenty-six years, they'd failed to bring them home.

As the drones moved on, scanning, recording, sampling, Captain Karah joined him at the viewscreen. "What do you think, Spartan? Think they're still out there?"

He thought again of the video files they'd retrieved from Little Bit, and of Rion's father. Novak had read the man's file with interest—some hair-raising moments, for sure, but a die-hard marine who got the job done. Novak could see where his daughter got her mettle, and her insolence.

And as a former marine himself, he hadn't liked taking Rion's memories from her.

Hell, he didn't like keeping this new discovery from the families even now—but that wasn't his call to make.

"Yes. I believe they're still out there," he answered. They had to be.

"Turk, how are those calculations coming?" the captain asked.

"The fragment's path projections are correct. I'm running it through applicable Forerunner star charts, speed, time, variables—Captain." He paused, a warning tone entering his voice. "One of the drones is recording evidence of Flood contamination . . . collecting samples now." Turk stared off into space as he commanded the fleet of drones sent out to explore several sites within the debris. They'd record video, take high-res images, and gather samples so Hugo Barton and his team could ascertain the validity of setting up a research facility here in the field.

Suddenly an alert blared through the bridge. "Captain, we have enemy contact!" Turk said.

"On screen. Battle stations."

As the *Taurokado* proceeded around a vast section of debris, they came face-to-face with a small Covenant battle group. The *Taurokado* was a prowler, designed for stealth recon and incursions; as fast and advanced as she was, she wasn't equipped with the firepower they'd need to engage a battle group.

"Evasive actions," Karah said with a note of reluctance. "Spartan, think you can distract them long enough for us to recover the drones and drop a buoy they won't detect?"

"Not a problem." He pressed his fireteam comm channel. "Apollo, suit up. Deployment bay in five." He turned to Turk. "Have the techs prep the Broadswords."

"I'm on it."

Novak strode from the bridge and headed for the deployment bay, where he met his team, a pair of Spartan-IV's, Adam Cerra and Danelle Reid, assigned to the *Taurokado* a month prior. Three was small for a team, but Apollo was transient, without a static roster, forming and reforming depending on need and mission. As a result, those assigned to Apollo were chosen for their heightened ability to quickly adapt to one another and to any situation. The three of them went to work, and in minutes were streaking from the prowler to play chicken with the battle group.

The enemy stayed in position while one of the destroyers launched a pair of Seraphs.

Almost immediately, the hunting pair latched on to Novak's tail. He banked the F-41 Broadsword right, punched thrusters, and dove beneath a colossal chunk of mountain range. When he came out the other side, Reid closed in on his three o'clock. As soon as he was clear, she blasted the mountain, raining debris onto the pursuing Seraph, causing it to smash into the scaffolding of a substructure that Novak missed by mere meters as Cerra drew the other Seraph off.

As he piloted up and over a massive island with clear Forerunner ruins and Covenant activity on the ground, Novak hit his comms. "Captain, you seeing this?" There was the damn Harvester, crouched like some enormous beetle, firing an intense beam of plasma into the surface rock and creating a plume of illuminated dust.

"Affirmative, Spartan."

"Well, now we know why the group's not giving chase," Spartan Cerra said through comms.

"They're protecting the site," Reid said; then, "Novak, you've got one on your six, and looks like we got another pair incoming."

"I got him." The Seraph dropped down behind Novak, twin plasma bolts sailing just past his wing as he banked and then dove the Broadsword through a rift in an enormous piece of Forerunner infrastructure, a giant section of scaffolding the size of an orbital defense platform, with large chunks of terraformed surface still clinging to the outer portions of the metal.

Despite the obstacles, the Seraph stuck close as they wove in and out of rock and metal.

Damn, the bird was hard to shake.

Turk's voice came over comms. "Drones on board and buoy dropped. Fireteam Apollo, you are clear to return."

"Damn. And I was just getting warmed up," Reid said, coming in hot behind the Seraph.

"All right, you heard him," Novak said, smiling. "Apollo, let's smoke these losers."

CHAPTER 15

Ace of Spades, slipspace to Ibycus system

The most boring part of space travel, in Niko's opinion, was slipspace. Nothing to see, no stops along the way, spotty communication with his chatter buddies and his group of friends back on Venezia. Plus, Cap always used the downtime to make them repair or clean something, or catalog salvaged parts in the hold. Since there was nothing currently in the hold, cleaning had taken precedence.

And so the time since they'd left Venezia had taken on the monotonous cycle of wake, work out, shower, eat, clean, sleep. . . .

All made worse by the fact that he and Lessa were still at odds, the ghost of Cade seemed to lurk everywhere, and Niko had lost everything that usually made the long trips bearable: his work.

He pulled on his flight suit, then splashed water on his face and cleaned his teeth, dragged his fingers through his unruly hair and eyed his tired face in the small mirror. He scratched at the overgrown stubble on his jaw, knowing he should shave but too damn tired or bored or angry to give a damn—he wasn't sure which.

The ONI bastards had invaded his personal space and taken everything, all his notes, his projects and models, his files and research. . . . His workstation had been thoroughly cleaned.

But he missed Little Bit most of all. The things he and LB could have accomplished . . .

With that AI fragment, he'd had a taste of true technological majesty, and then it was gone, like the mythical creature it was.

The only thing the spooks hadn't taken was his memory, and Niko remembered every story LB had told, every account of the past and technological information that had slipped though his fragmented core. Outrageous tales, unbelievable bits of data, strange things, amazing things. And, man, the stuff Niko had learned!

His gaze settled on the photographs he'd pinned to the board above his workstation. He was surprised ONI had left them behind, but he was sure glad they had. On that board was everyone he loved, mostly candid shots taken on the ship and at salvage sites and R&R stops along the way.

For a little while, they'd been a happy unit—a loud, argumentative, happy family—or what he always imagined a family was like, anyway.

Cade had died in that debris field, and for what?

With Little Bit, Niko could console himself with the lofty idea that they might do something great, something that benefited the entire galaxy, the civvies, the little guys, those stuck on dirty worlds, ruled by dirty politicians and thugs . . . something that would make Cade's death serve a higher purpose or have some deeper meaning. Make it somehow better.

Stupid idea. Nothing would make it better.

Cade McDonough was the only man Niko had ever known who hadn't exploited him, hit him, or ignored him. Niko had learned that a person could be strong and capable and inspire loyalty without instilling fear. And, man, how he had tried to get a rise out of Cade, to test him, to see if he was like the others back on Aleria.

He'd been afraid to believe in someone like Cade; yet somewhere along the way, he'd begun to trust that it was no act. Cade never told you what kind of man he was—he showed you.

And, goddamn it, he missed the hell out of him.

Niko wiped at the sting in his eyes, and gave the pictures another look before leaving the room.

He didn't know his mother or his father. Never would. But Rion and Cade had been the closest he'd ever get, and the loss burned inside him. And, yeah, he'd taken some of his anger out on Lessa, who stubbornly clung to a past that didn't deserve her efforts while she should be grieving for the person who had been there, who actually had given a damn.

He didn't like to think about it, but now, thanks to the joys of slipspace and ONI spooks, there wasn't much else to keep his mind occupied.

He despised cleaning and working out and watching whatever holovid Lessa had programmed into the ship's entertainment system. He didn't like the things he'd said to his sister and he wasn't sure how to fix the rift he'd caused. And if he walked into the lounge one more time and saw her and Ram playing that stupid Sangheili board game again like nothing was wrong, he might just scream.

He stopped outside the gym and checked the systems panel

on the wall. Another eight days of slipspace travel left. He didn't know how he was going to get through it.

The best part of space travel, in Lessa's opinion, was slipspace.

She loved the quiet, the time to do laundry, clean out her quarters, study star charts and navigational techniques, knit or paint or dye colored stripes into her frizzy blond hair.

As she sat on her bed, applying her favorite cerulean blue polymer to her toenails with her old UV paint pen, a sudden wave of sadness stilled her hand. Only a short time ago, she could add sparring with Cade to that list. They'd had a standing gym order to train every time *Ace* entered slipspace.

She was stronger, more confident, and sometimes able to fell a man twice her size because of Cade.

He'd been a great teacher—calm, relaxed, showing her different moves and techniques and the reason behind them in a manner she, as a novice, could easily understand. She already knew how to fight dirty, but Cade hadn't quelled that knowledge, nor had he made her feel inferior because of it. Instead he gave her ways to build upon what she'd taught herself. He never made her feel like she'd come from nothing—quite the opposite. He made her feel like she could do anything and become whatever she wanted.

She'd put him on a pedestal. But he deserved it.

Lessa knew where she came from and was well aware there was an emptiness inside her where parents should have been . . . where anyone who gave a damn should have been. Rion and Cade had filled that space. Less had never expected to lose one of them so soon—in fact, it had never really crossed her mind.

And now Cade was gone, and she wasn't quite sure how to deal with the loss.

Except, apparently, to argue with her brother.

She rolled her eyes, finished the color application, and then flopped back on her bed to stare at the ceiling. It was plastered with old star charts. Odd, that. She never thought she'd like space and navigation so much. In fact, before Rion came along, Less's goals had been squarely built on solid ground—dusty, arid ground, but still. She'd had dreams of finding her parents with Niko and living out their days in some honest trade. . . .

Her eyes rolled—what a dumb dream.

Honest trades on Aleria were very hard to come by.

Niko was right. The small items they'd arrived at the shelter with could have come from anywhere. Around those items—the blanket, Niko's baby clothes, the ribbon holding back her riot of curls, the cheap metal bracelet she'd been wearing that no longer fit—she'd created a fiction, a lovely little farce with no basis in fact.

And her brother had finally called her on it.

In a very short amount of time, Lessa had lost a father figure who had blinked in and out of her life so quickly that the sting of it still stole her breath.

Her brother no longer needed or wanted her protection.

And her lovely little fiction had been snatched away by ONI.

She didn't know who she was anymore, just that she wanted things to go back to the way they were before. Though lately, there was a whisper inside her, a faint suggestion to let go, to stop trying so hard to hold on. . . .

But if she let go, what was she left with, exactly?

Did she want to be like Rion, searching for a father she might never find, her life driven and directed by that sole purpose? Did she want to strike off on her own now that her brother had grown up?

And if Cade could die, the *Ace of Spades* wasn't as safe as she'd thought.

Funny how there was a time when Lessa had wanted nothing more than to be on the ship and as far from Aleria as she could get. Niko had been the opposite, demanding to leave the ship and go back to the life he knew. He'd been spitting mad, crewing with a bunch of hard-asses, as he'd called the captain and Cade. But now Less was sure the very idea of leaving the *Ace of Spades* wouldn't even cross his mind.

They'd come full circle, it seemed.

But did she want to leave?

A deep sigh escaped her as she sat up. She honestly didn't know.

CHAPTER 16

Ace of Spades, Ibycus system, June 2557

Rion was on the bridge when the *Ace of Spades*'s alert system pinged. She turned it off immediately to keep from waking the crew, and stayed in her chair as the sensation of dropping out of slipspace pushed and pulled ever so slightly on her body. A quick check of her FTL showed the engine in excellent working order—should be; she'd paid enough for it.

A few distant stars peppered the viewscreen as *Ace* slowed to subluminal speed. Rion pulled up the star chart of Ibycus and used the navigational software to pinpoint their location within the system. Not too far off course. They'd dropped out only a few hours' journey from Geranos-a. "Good girl, *Ace*," she murmured, plotting a course correction into the nav system.

All things considered, it was a decent drop.

Rion relaxed in her chair and stared at the screen without

putting her focus on any one thing. A full sleep cycle had become foreign these days; she rarely got more than a few hours at a time.

Apparently neither did Ram. He entered the bridge in a T-shirt and baggy pajama bottoms, hair loose to his shoulders, carrying two mugs of Casbah coffee—a splurge in credits due to its import tax, coming all the way from Tribute in the Inner Colonies, but so worth it.

He handed her a mug and then moved to the nav panel and pressed a few commands. "Not far now," he said quietly, leaning his hip against the console and staring out the viewscreen, sipping his brew. "Mind-boggling sometimes . . . how tiny we are, moving through something so vast."

And there were many people out there who couldn't handle it, couldn't live a life in space. If you weren't a seasoned traveler, the endless nothingness, the long stretches of isolation could weigh on a person's mind, overtake it, put you on a path to madness. She'd seen it once on the *Hakon,* when they'd been set adrift, months on end, food running out, not a single star in sight. . . . Cade had—

No. Memory lane wasn't a place she wanted to visit right now, so she focused on the cigarette poking out of Ram's shirt pocket. She hadn't seen him smoke since she'd found him on Komoya. "You *ever* going to smoke that thing?"

He shrugged. "Trying to quit. I'm down to smelling it every once in a while."

"You know we have patches for that, right?"

He returned her sarcastic smile, then shrugged. "Call me old school. So I was looking over the report from Gek's commpad," he said, changing the subject. "He sounds serious about whatever he thinks is in the debris field. He mentions using it against us, hitting us at our heart. I think he means Earth."

Rion pulled her feet under her and then took a sip from her mug. "If he believes he can make it there, and make a statement, he won't hesitate. He might make it to Earth, but he'd have to get through Home Fleet."

Ram thought about it for a moment. "Unless he has help from the inside. The alien refugee settlements on Earth are growing. Makes you wonder how the hell they're able to weed out the bad from the good."

Good point.

Hell, even the refugees were at risk. "There's been talk for a while, Covenant loyalists wanting retribution against defectors, wanting to send a message. Those refugee settlements on Earth might be courting disaster. Once we get the salvage and find a port with a decent comm relay, I'll turn Gek's report over to the authorities."

His attention was drawn once more to the view. "Strange to think of Jackals, Grunts, and hinge-heads making a home on Earth after they wanted us all dead, while *we'll* be lucky if we're not permanently barred from the planet if ONI ever finds out what we're planning."

"Would that bother you?"

He scratched his beard, thinking. "I don't know. Never been to Earth." He paused to take a drink, then shrugged. "Guess I'm like most—a small part of me always yearns to see the homeland."

She smiled over the rim of her mug. "Didn't peg you for the pilgrimage type."

He shot her an eye roll. "All of us colonists are, to some degree. 'I might be Komoyan, born and bred . . .'" He grinned as he recited familiar lines:

> "But in me lies the need to tread
> On shores of sand and plains of red,
> On soft green grass to lay my head.
> Past stars and years, to distant view,
> A long way home, I push on through;
> She calls and sings her song of blue,
> My heart, my soul, my homeland true."

Rion mentally recited along with Ram's spoken words. The lines were from a famous folk song written by early colonist Mary Parker Meade. Known throughout the colonies, it was the kind of simple song taught to schoolchildren, and sung at events and holidays and by happy drunks in bars. It was an everyman anthem. And it was sung replacing the first line with whatever planet, colony, outpost, or ship you called home, just as Ram had done.

"Earth is home as much as Komoya is," he admitted. "I think it's a need in all of us to see it at least once, don't you?"

She might've felt a tiny twinge of homesickness, but Rion's perspective, being born and raised on Earth, was far different from those growing up in the colonies. There was and would always be something special and even mystical about Earth. There would always be those wanting to go home, like Ram, and those wanting to leave, to branch out and make their own way, as Rion had done.

"Since we're up," she said, "let's recon the system and see what else is out there."

They worked silently after that, noting the giant orange star coming into visual range as *Ace* adjusted course through the asteroid belt, and then toward the four small planets that orbited the star.

An hour later, Geranos-a was in their sights and they'd located the ONI commsat. Rion kept *Ace* out of range of the commsat and settled the ship into high orbit.

Lessa entered the bridge with two breakfast wraps—thank God for a crewmember who liked to actually cook meals instead of relying solely on packaged fare—and handed one to Rion and the other to Ram. "Figured you two would already be at it. So that's it, huh? Looks . . . inviting."

"If you say so." Besides the color, Rion thought it looked a lot like the old pictures of Mars before the planet had been terraformed. She took a bite of her wrap and groaned.

"That's the last of the Brillon eggs, by the way," Less said.

With her other hand, Rion pulled up the planet's image on the tactical table. "Pretty barren. Mostly sand and rock. Atmosphere is too thin for much, if anything, to survive."

"So we're not looking for survivors then."

"Depends," Ram said around a mouthful of food. "Whoever or whatever sent the distress call might have enough oxygen reserves to live on or, if there's a ship down there, could have a pressurized section still able to support life."

Lessa spun the holograph to find a blue dot indicating the location of the signal. "At least the light gravity will make carrying stuff a breeze."

"Once Niko is up, we'll send in Michelle to recon the commsat and see if we can disable it."

"He's up," she replied, her tone suddenly rigid. "Heard him in the gym."

Rion regarded Lessa for a long moment. "He didn't mean it, you know?" she said carefully. "What he said back in New Tyne . . ."

Lessa shrugged. "I know he didn't. But that's not really the point, is it?"

Rion had the feeling it was a question she couldn't or shouldn't answer, so she left it alone. When nothing more was forthcoming from the girl, Rion finished her food and then buzzed the gym as Ram left to get dressed.

"Yeah?" came Niko's out-of-breath response.

"Need you to prep Michelle when you're done."

"'Kay. Give me twenty minutes."

True to his word, Niko arrived on the bridge just shy of twenty minutes later, freshly shaved and showered, a definite change from the last several days.

"Michelle's launched," he announced, and headed for his comms console to pull her feed up on screen and direct her movements. The drone, affectionately dubbed Michelle, had begun her life as a UNSC spy drone, but under Niko's care, she was all that and more.

The commsat wasn't easy to spot; the thing was encased in flat black stealth coating and was only about seventy-six centimeters in circumference. Michelle approached and scanned the satellite. "There's no SATCOM network out here, so it can't relay information, only store it," Niko said. "It's using a disruptor wave to break up the distress call. It's illegal for us to mess with commsats, especially military and government. We could leave it alone, destroy it, or bring it on board so I can salvage the components," he said, glancing over his shoulder. "My vote is for salvage."

"Well, we can't leave it and risk it recording our activities," Rion said. "Can you disable it before bringing it on board?"

"Can you disable it," he echoed, shaking his head and returning to his screen. "Yeah, of course I can disable it. . . ."

Niko commanded Michelle to send out an EMP pulse, rendering the commsat inert, then employed a magnetic well to tow the device back to the ship.

Once Michelle was docked and the airlock engaged, Lessa went down to the cargo bay to receive the device, and then deployed Michelle again for an exploratory flyby over the distress signal's origin.

As Niko guided Michelle through the atmosphere of Geranos-a, Lessa returned and fed him navigational corrections to account for the winds. Soon the surface appeared, a wash of sand and dunes with a few rocky outcroppings dotting the landscape.

"Coming up on the signal," Niko said.

The drone descended over a pile of slate-like rocks and slowed to a hover above an antenna stuck into the ground. A thick band of cables ran down its length and over the sand.

"Well, clearly someone did this," Less said. "There must be survivors."

"Or were. We don't know how long this thing has been broadcasting," Rion said.

"Guess we just follow the lines?" Niko asked, glancing to Rion for confirmation before piloting Michelle along the cables.

Down the dune and into a flat valley, half-buried bits of wreckage began to appear . . . then a large section of fuselage came into camera view with a jagged opening covered by a wind-worn cloth, flapping in Geranos-a's steady winds. "That looks like a shelter," Ram said, standing.

"And look, the cables lead inside," Lessa said.

"Wait. Niko, back up." Rion sat up straight. "Angle down . . . those are tracks." The sand was already filling in the impressions. "Someone was definitely down there. Recently. Ram, you got anything on life signs?"

"No. Nothing."

"Could we be getting interference from the winds?"

"I'm not picking up any."

Rion tapped her finger on the arm of her chair. Odd. But there was only one way to find out who'd made those tracks. She pushed up from her seat, energized by the anticipation and excitement of discovery. "Ram, since you're still recovering, you'll take over here."

He frowned at her, returning to his seat. "I'm good, Forge. Body is chock-full of nanites—"

"Yeah, and they're still repairing you, so you'll be our eyes on the ship. Less and Niko will come with me. Let's suit up, kids," she said with a clap. "Grav carts, cutters, med kit—and we go in armed until we know what we're looking at. Ram, set us down here"—she leaned over the tactical table and pointed to a spot on the holographic image—"just on the other side of those rocks. And keep *Ace* running and weapons warm until we know what kind of survivors we're dealing with."

Ram swiveled in his chair. "Don't forget that ONI thinks the site is dangerous enough to issue a 'proceed with caution.' Remember that. Tread carefully."

She nodded. "Will do."

The *Ace of Spades* settled onto the sand, using a rocky dune as protection from the winds streaming at a steady twenty knots. Rion,

Niko, and Lessa were waiting at the cargo bay in light fatigues and breathing masks with oxygen converters and reserve tanks, with grav carts and tools at the ready. As soon as Rion saw the green light on the pad by the door, she hit the airlock and released the ramp.

Hot, dry air and sand swirled as they exited the ship with their gear. Rion's boots should have sunk deep into the soft sand, but the gravity was so light that she barely made a dent. "Comm check," she said, and waited for Niko and Less to reply.

"All good, Cap," Lessa said, glancing around.

Niko was staring down at his feet before jumping a few times to test the gravity. "G's aren't that light," Rion remarked. "Come on, let's get moving."

They made their way across the sand to the rocky dune in the distance. Leaving their gear at the bottom, they climbed to the top to inspect the antenna. "Well, at least we know there were survivors at some point. This didn't get here all by its lonesome," Lessa said, craning her head. The antenna was more than three meters high and made from a long titanium shaft.

"Looks like some sort of ground plane mast-radiator combo," Niko said. "Depends what's underneath it and what's attached at the other end of these cables."

"Should we turn it off?" Less asked.

"Yeah, shut it down," said Rion.

Niko dropped to his knees and brushed the sand away from the ground to inspect the cables. "Hold up. . . . The cables have been stripped and wired directly into the shaft and this broadcasting board. Honestly never seen anything like it. It'll be easier to shut down from its power source." He glanced behind him at the trail of cables snaking down the dune.

"All right," said Rion. "Let's get off this rock and find the source then."

Rion went slowly along the cables' path, directing her grav cart beside her and picking up a few pieces of ship wreckage to examine and then toss back into the sand as they went across the valley floor. They wouldn't know what kind of craft they were dealing with until they got to the main site.

A sudden glint caught her eye. She picked up what appeared to be glass and realized it was vitrified sand.

So far, what she was seeing wasn't exactly consistent with survivors. A wreck this bad, this old and weathered, in this kind of environment, crashing hot enough to turn sand into glass? Although it wasn't unheard of, people surviving through insurmountable odds like this. Yet even if there was a chamber buried somewhere under the sand with oxygen and pressure lasting for years, there still was the issue of food. . . .

"Hey." Lessa's hand nudged Rion's shoulder. "Look at that." She pointed to a raised area a couple meters away, stacked with a mound of rocks. A piece of metal jutted up from the stack to mark the spot. "Is that what I think it is?"

"A grave site." Rion stared at it for a long moment, feeling very keenly that something just wasn't right. Nothing was adding up the way it should.

As they continued on, she asked, "Ram . . . still not picking up any life signs?"

"No. Nothing."

"Any traces of power?"

"No, it's really quiet. Nothing breathing or moving. . . ."

"Gotta love a good mystery," Niko commented drily.

"All right. We're coming up on the main site." Intact, the fuselage would have been enormous. Most of it now was either buried in the sand or sheared off. The cloth hanging over the jagged hole was ripped and threadbare, flapping in the wind with audible snaps.

"This is starting to feel really creepy," Lessa said, eyeing the entrance and the cables that disappeared inside.

Rion pulled her rifle over her shoulder. "Heading inside."

Carefully and slowly, she ducked past the cloth and entered the wreck.

The floor was sand, but the walls were clearly titanium plating.

As Rion moved farther in, it became dark enough that she had to use her light to see down the length of the hull. With Less and Niko doing the same, they revealed a strange scene of what appeared to be a collection of wreckage.

Rion moved toward a makeshift worktable built out of storage containers, its top consisting of a long piece of metal plating and piled with cables and wiring, cracked screens, a few dead power cores, and an assortment of system components and motherboards.

Lessa stared down at the table where a collection of random personal effects had been placed—a belt, burned photos, a hairbrush, a sock, a broken bottle of brandy. . . . "Yeah, definitely creepy."

Niko picked up a few system components and tossed them into his cart.

"I *really* don't want to run into a dead body," Lessa said, her nerves getting to her. "Especially one in a mask or space suit. No offense to the dead or anything, but that totally freaks me out. . . ."

"That happened to you *one* time," Niko replied.

"Yeah, well, one time was all I needed for it to be awful." She shuddered. "And *you* were the one who screamed and ran away first."

"Yeah, sure. I think your recall needs work." He found a serial number on a small piece of tech and ran it through their database.

"No, it doesn't. You dropped your tools and left your grav cart and went running through the grass. You tumbled ass over end and then popped right back up and kept on going to the ship. I remember because it was funny as shit. And I had to make two trips to get your crap because you refused to go back out to the site."

"Whatever."

"Don't you ever take responsibility for anything?" she asked, nerves quickly replaced with annoyance as she reached beyond Niko for a piece of wreckage. He didn't move out of the way because a name popped up on the scanner, so she gave him a quick, forceful shove.

"Ow! Would you stop?"

"Would you move?"

"Well, maybe I would if *please* was somewhere in your limited vocabulary."

"Oh, here we go. Well, *please*, why don't you say what you really think?"

"What are you talking about?"

"That you think I'm an idiot."

"Well . . . that's true of everyone compared to me."

"Knock it off, both of you," Rion said, headache brewing.

"Sorry, Cap." Niko read his screen as Lessa moved past him in a huff. "Check this out. That serial number I ran through—it's coming up as a part on the UNSC *Rubicon*. Science vessel. Once we return to civilization, we can run the name through Waypoint and see what comes up."

"Good idea." Rion moved along the other bulkhead wall, inspecting the haphazard bits of wreckage until Lessa's shriek split through her earpiece. She swung around, rifle at the ready as Less stumbled back, bumping into a utility counter behind her, her weapon hastily drawn and pointed at a figure on the ground.

Heart in her throat, Rion approached slowly. Seeing that there was no danger, she placed a hand on Lessa's gun, lowering the weapon, then crossed to the figure on the ground. "Ram, you seeing this?" she asked.

"Jesus. Yeah, I'm seeing it. . . . Don't know what it is, but I'm seeing it."

Niko edged his way in front of Rion and knelt to get a better look. "Holy hell. Would you look at this?"

Rion nudged the figure's metal foot. The thing was a loose collection of humanoid metal parts: legs, feet, torso, arms, hands, head. Made of some type of black metal alloy, it was weathered and damaged in places, and unlike anything she'd seen before. The pieces had an elegant and sleek design to them, but there was nothing else around that showed how those pieces fit together. She had to agree with Niko. It was fascinating. Though the head was a little disconcerting with its angles and lines, which seemed to carve out a somewhat sinister-looking humanoid face.

"Could it be experimental?" Niko asked. "How much you think something like this is worth?" He shined his light over the thing. "It looks human . . . yet more advanced than anything I've ever seen. Maybe this is like some next-gen Spartan android or something? Like a prototype?" He swung his head around and met Rion's gaze. "This could be the asset, what ONI is after."

Lessa remained quiet through Niko's assessment. But when he paused, she asked, "You don't think this is the thing that made all this . . . the antenna, the grave? Do you?"

They stared at it, wondering. Lessa might be right. From what Rion had seen so far, the *Rubicon* had entered the atmosphere and crashed at a very high rate of speed. That a human could survive that, and then survive here for years with no air, no food . . .

Niko turned over the torso to check out the back. "I don't see a power source or anything that connects the pieces."

The cloth flapped outside. Sand pinged the fuselage like gentle rain, and the wind rocked sections of the hull. And still it felt too quiet. "Put it in the cart," Rion told Niko. "And then dismantle the antenna. While you do that, we'll keep looking around."

A few hours later, they'd explored the main wreck and the surrounding dunes. They were sweaty and tired, and made slow work of pushing the grav carts over the sand to the ship. Rion said a grateful prayer to Lady Luck. If not for the weak gravity, this day would have been rough.

When they reached the ship, she waited until Niko and Lessa were inside with their gear, then hit the airlock. Once through, they proceeded into the cargo hold, where Ram was waiting. He'd also brought cold drinks. "You're a saint. Thanks." Rion removed her mask and drank deep before issuing everyone's favorite order: "All right, kids, let get this haul unloaded."

CHAPTER 17

They are fascinating, these humans, much different than the crew of the Rubicon *with their military protocols and professional distance. There is very little protocol here. And very little distance. They are driven by emotion, their actions dictated by their feelings for one another.*

This is strangely unsettling.

The bickering between the younger two, relatives to be sure—obvious by their accents, features, and mannerisms—is hypnotic. The older female is their captain, but I perceive she is much more than that. The crew views her as a mother figure, a protector, and a friend.

I absorb every word, every move, and as I am transported into the hold of their ship, I realize that they are, much to my surprise, thieves, salvagers, opportunists.

This is altogether unexpected.

I find myself . . . excited.

A sudden rush of warmth fills me. Thievery and opportunity are old friends indeed, and I recognize them with much fondness.

As they argue and laugh and talk, I am reminded quite clearly—perhaps more clearly than ever before—of my past, my human life, my relationships and friends. . . .

I see memories.

The brim of a palm-leaf hat hanging over my eyes as my calloused feet walk on soft sand. I see bronze, work-worn hands, dirt beneath the nails, as I push through jungle. Bright white flashes of sunshine through green. Chuffing laughter ahead of me. Complaints behind me. And the joy of hunting, and scheming, and thieving . . .

I am jarred suddenly from this memory as my parts are placed in a large metal storage bin. There are several of these along the walls of the cargo hold. Once this is achieved, the captain says they will continue looking around the wreckage for a datacore.

They won't find one.

They leave, and soon the hold grows quiet. I power my visual components and examine my surroundings. Nearby on a bulkhead wall is a systems panel. I engage my hard light, assemble, and climb out of the bin to access the ship's systems.

Without one of the humans' AIs on board, everything is open to me without resistance. Information floods in.

Details about humanity and the current time period flow in at a rapid rate. The data is full and robust and varied. I see we have a common hindrance in the Office of Naval Intelligence. The office, ONI, as it is called, has left a few surveillance filaments threaded into the ship's fiber optics and communications cables. These I untangle and gladly destroy.

I see that a navigational and communication-wide cleanse was recently implemented. This, however, does not hinder my ability to delve into the personal files and messages and other detritus of the crew's lives, even using the displays in their quarters as viewports to *observe their personal spaces. I run free through filaments brimming with code, with life and pictures and history.*

Lucy Orion Forge. Ramsey Chalva. Lessa and Niko, siblings and orphans without a surname.

The captain's past gives me pause as a name I find, Spirit of Fire, *rings like an echo through the damaged halls of my memory. It is a ghost, a vague and sudden skip, and then it is gone, too quick to capture. I move on, certain that the knowledge is there and will reveal itself in time. And when it does, I will coax it into place, letting it settle where it was meant to.*

Once I glean every fragment of data there is, I turn my attention to the complete and utter lack of ship's systems. It is extraordinary that these humans have made it through space with such rudimentary functions. Awareness of all the things that can and will go wrong because of such simplicity creates a surprising sense of protectiveness in me. They are vulnerable without an ancilla, without advanced shields and weapons and drives.

For expedience's sake, I simply must repair these issues.

This is not out of line with my original objective with the Rubicon. *My ship must have the capability to travel over great distances, quickly and accurately. Therefore, upgrades must be implemented.*

And I certainly do not want to lose another crew.

There are enough cryopods on the ship to suspend them while I resume my work. However, this may not be the best option. The last time such a thing was attempted, the result was not exemplary.

I find I am hesitant.

I will ponder my choices carefully.

While the pull is strong to begin administering aid to the ship's systems, I retreat to my storage cart. They are returning.

CHAPTER 18

Back from their second canvass of the wreck site, Niko began unloading the carts as Rion headed out for one last attempt at finding a datacore. Lessa went up to the lounge to make a quick meal for everyone while Ram remained on the bridge, monitoring Rion's movements.

Besides the humanoid metal thing, they hadn't found much of note.

Normally, sorting salvage into bins wasn't Niko's favorite job. But in this case, he would have volunteered. He couldn't seem to stop arguing with Lessa, and he continued to say the rudest things to his sister.

Annoyed and on edge, he turned the volume up on his music until the cargo hold vibrated, and began sorting the tangle of cables and metal from the grav carts, tossing pieces into the appropriate bins. It took nearly an hour to work through the mess.

After a quick drink, he decided a break from cables was in order, and went for the bin with the humanoid thing.

The metal pieces were surprisingly light, the alloy worn and pitted by the sand, perhaps by the crash. Niko placed each piece on the floor to roughly make its intended shape. Head. Torso. Arms. Legs. Hands. Feet . . .

He stood back and stared down, scratching his jaw. There was nothing to connect the pieces. No cables, wires, or internal structures that he could see. So how did the thing fit together?

He continued staring at it for a while, then decided to rummage through the cart of smaller salvage they'd taken from the worktable. He heaped small optics, busted circuit panels, and more cables onto his workstation. A few pieces caught his interest, but there was nothing that looked like it might belong to their resident robotic construct.

A scrape of metal sounded above the loud music.

Niko stilled. That was odd.

Another soft clang echoed behind him.

A slow shiver started down his spine, and the hairs on his arms lifted. Pulse leaping, he casually reached over and turned his music down, feeling completely freaked out because he could swear someone was standing behind him.

But that would be silly. Right? The airlock was engaged. No one should be back here. He took in a few steadying breaths and hoped to hell that he was just imagining things.

In seconds there was another soft scrape, followed by a smooth whirring sound.

Oh God. There *was* something behind him.

Hands shaking, he scanned the table and grabbed a metal

bar from the salvage, swallowed, said a prayer, and slowly turned around.

Oh shit.

The thing was up. The robot was up.

Adrenaline raced beneath his skin, lighting electric chills through his nerves. Niko stepped back, hitting the table and dropping the metal bar. It clanged loudly, echoing in the silence.

Blue light glowed in between the dull, weathered plates and up through its head, carving out sharp, sinister cheekbones, a mouth, and large, slanted blue eyes.

It had to be nearly three meters tall and was held together by nothing, just . . . magnetism, maybe?

Niko's thoughts were racing; it seemed to be staring at him.

His heart hammered hard in his chest and his throat had gone bone dry. That's what lack of sleep did to you, messed with your mind, screwed reality right the hell up. He rubbed his eyes, blinked hard a few times—but the thing was still there, still staring.

Guess I don't need to look for those missing parts.

The thought caused a nervous laugh to spurt from his mouth. The thing tilted its head in response, and Niko almost fainted.

It felt like hours before he found his voice, managing a few intelligent words. "Holy shit."

He swallowed again, uncertain whether the thing was sentient or not, but it sure seemed to be studying him. *Okay, let's try this again.* . . . "Um . . . hey?"

Its head tilted again, and then it repeated, "Hey."

"Oh, dear God." Niko had never fainted in his life, but he was pretty sure this was how it felt, all the blood just collapsing out of your body, the whole universe tilting.

Despite his fear, another nervous laugh popped out of his mouth. He dragged his fingers nervously through his hair, a thread of excitement finding its way past his panic. "Um . . . okay," he said to himself. "Yeah, so . . ." He could barely hear himself speak through the pounding of his heart. He searched for something to say as he hit his commpad. "Well . . . you're taller than I thought you'd be."

No response.

"Right. Okay. I'm Niko. You're on a ship, the *Ace of Spades*. We *rescued* you. From out there . . . the surface of that place—that planet."

It dipped its head. "My thanks, Niko."

Niko scrubbed a hand down his face and let out a shaky breath. He wasn't sure whether to just give in and collapse in shock or clap his hands in demented glee. He was caught somewhere between fear and amazement. He'd never seen anything like it. And it was definitely sentient, its voice an octave higher than his, with a strange resonance, and a little scratchy.

Then it moved. And Niko was pretty sure he might actually die.

It leaned toward him. Niko leaned back, his hands gripping the worktable behind to steady himself. But the thing reached past him into the salvage bin next to the table, from which it retrieved a long metal piece. It straightened and set the end of the piece on the ground, holding it like a cane to support the damage on one of its metal calves.

"What are you?" Niko released his death grip on the table.

It cocked its head again, then seemed to look down at its collection of metal and blue light. "I am . . ."

It paused, as if it either had forgotten what it was or simply couldn't decide.

"Hey, it's okay—maybe something easier. What's that light? Is it what's holding you together?"

"The Forerunners refer to it as hard light." It straightened and turned its head slightly as though listening. "Your friends are coming."

The metallic clang of footsteps sounded above him. But all Niko could process was the word "Forerunner."

It said "Forerunner."

He glanced over his shoulder to see Lessa hurrying down the stairs and stopping halfway at the sight. Her face was pale and horrified as she lifted the barrel of the assault rifle over the railing.

"Whoa, whoa, whoa!" Niko shouted, leaping in front of the construct. Above them, Ram was on the catwalk with his own heavy assault rifle. "Don't you dare shoot!" he yelled. "Please!"

For a moment, no one seemed sure what to do next. Then the thing spoke again.

"Hello, Lessa." It dipped its chin to acknowledge her before looking up to the catwalk. "Ram Chalva."

"It knows our names," Niko said in awe. He turned around and faced it again with an odd mix of horror and delight.

"Niko, what did you do?" Lessa snapped.

"Nothing. I swear."

"He is correct," the construct said, surprising him.

"Niko, move away." Rion was standing inside, the airlock door closed behind her, her helmet falling to the floor, her rifle aimed, her breathing rapid. She must have heard the comm as well and hightailed it back to the ship. The deadly glint in her eyes as she sighted down the barrel of her weapon magnified Niko's fear exponentially. Time slowed and he couldn't seem to find his voice. But then he didn't have to.

"Captain Forge," the thing said from behind him. "I have awaited rescue from this planet for quite some time. You have my thanks."

The crew exchanged bewildered glances, all concerned and unsure how to proceed.

"You're welcome," Rion replied slowly.

"Guys . . ." Niko managed finally. "I think it's Forerunner. It's a Forerunner robot."

Niko turned around as the thing let out an odd strangled sound. "Goodness. I am *not* a *robot*." It stood straighter. "This form is a sniper-class combat armiger. I have adopted this construct out of necessity. It is not my original form, nor my previous form."

"Then what was?" Ram asked, eyes narrow with suspicion from the catwalk above.

It paused.

"Maybe he doesn't know what he is," Niko offered.

"Or maybe this is what ONI was creating on that wrecked ship," Lessa said. "This could be what they're now looking for."

The armiger seemed to bristle at that. "The Office of Naval Intelligence does not have the technology capable of creating me, child."

Niko's eyes went wide, and he saw that Rion's did as well. They weren't sure what to make of that, but he felt like bursting. The thing obviously possessed emotion, and his all-time favorite: sarcasm. He wanted to laugh out loud, but bit his tongue instead.

"I did not want to frighten you out there on the surface. I have been delayed. My ship and my humans gone. . . . Therefore I require—"

"The *Rubicon* was your ship?" Rion stepped forward, motioning with her rifle for Niko to move away. He edged to the side, creating an option to run if necessary, but not so far away to prevent him from protecting the armiger once again if need be.

"No. I simply had need of it."

"So you hijacked it."

"In a manner of speaking. . . ."

The cap's mouth went tight. When she looked like that, shit was about to get serious. Niko prayed that things weren't about to take a nosedive. "Yes or no," she said. "It's a simple question."

"Then yes, if you insist on defining my actions in such a manner."

"And the crew? Did you kill them?"

"Of course not." It was said with enough surprise and indignation that Niko believed him. "They were human. I needed them."

"So you kidnapped them."

"Also true, in a manner of speaking. I find your mode of questioning quite . . . annoying."

"Why did you kidnap them?"

Silence.

"Okay. Let me get this straight. You stole an ONI vessel and kidnapped its crew. And then crashed the ship. Everyone died except you. Does that about sum it up?"

"That is correct. But the crash and their deaths were not my intention. I strove to protect them. As I said, I needed them. Soon after I took control, there were . . . complications. By my calculations, I am only sixty-two-point-three five percent culpable in the tragedy."

"How did you survive the crash?" Niko interrupted.

"It was a simple matter of moving from one data stream to another, readjusting as things burned and broke. There was salvage in one of the science bays. These parts, recovered from the Ar— from the same place I was recovered."

"Jesus. It's only sixty-two-point-three-five percent culpable." Ram sat down on the catwalk, legs hanging over and rifle resting across his legs.

"I am not an *it*, Ram Chalva. I am . . . human. Like you. Only . . . far superior. And I do not appreciate your impertinence."

Niko clutched his heart and spun around to face the crew. "It doesn't appreciate his impertinence," he repeated, barely able to contain his excitement. Then he swung back around. "Wait— what do you mean, you're *human*?"

CHAPTER 19

T hey stare at me as though I am mad or in jest, which I find
highly irritating. I certainly am not jesting.

Madness, however . . .

The emotions stirring inside of me—indignation, annoyance,
impatience—flow freely, all things remembered, all things simulated,
though they manifest as very . . . real.

How odd.

I suppose from their point of view, the idea of me being human is
inconceivable. But then, their vision of what is possible is small and
limited.

No matter, I will expand their minds.

This notion gives me tremendous pleasure.

I am human, I want to say again.

I am Chakas.

I am 343 Guilty Spark.

I am Forerunner. Ancilla. Armiger.

Am I? Or was I?

Perhaps that is where my conflict lies.

I stand perfectly still.

Many of my fragmented personality strings were repaired and combined (or jettisoned) in my time on the planet. Two remain. Fire and ice, they clash. They do not belong together. Yet I oversee them both, am inspired by both, nurtured by both, and guided by both.

Have I become a third string, then?

The overseer of the other two.

A millisecond passed as I pondered this. The crew moves closer together. They whisper, casting wary glances my way. I, of course, can hear every word. Their suspicion and separation do not improve my disposition.

I am here. They are there. I am not like them. I will never be like them.

Of course, I have no desire to be.

Perhaps it is the weapons aimed in my direction. The fear my presence produces.

It all feels oddly tiresome and familiar—

I realize that the armiger form is somewhat distressing. During my time on Geranos-a, I managed to make only minor changes to the severity of this form due to a damaged interface between the construct's machine cells and the intelligence framework I commandeered.

"A ship has emerged from slipspace," I tell them. "At its heading and speed, it will detect your ship in approximately twelve minutes."

"How do you know that?" Niko asks.

"I have been in your ship's systems since boarding."

"Oh God, not again." Captain Forge hurries to the systems panel nearby.

"I suggest you leave the planet immediately. You do not have the firepower capable of winning an engagement with an ONI prowler."

"It's got to be the Taurokado," Lessa says.

Ram jumps to his feet. "Already?"

"Delay any further and you will not have the capability to flee, Captain," I tell her. "If they succeed in apprehending me, I will not be responsible for my actions. I have been imprisoned long enough, far longer than you can fathom. I mean you no harm. I will try very hard to be zero percent culpable in any foreseeable damage to you or your ship. Now, please. You must flee."

"Cap," Niko says at the systems panel on the bulkhead wall. "He's right. There's a ship coming in fast."

"I know, I can see." Captain Forge engages the ramp, then takes the stairs two at a time, but the ship wobbles. I have employed the Ace of Spades's thrusters without her input. She grabs the railing to maintain her balance as the ship rises quickly through the thin air. Her eyes blaze at me. "Get out of my ship!"

"Apologies, Captain. I will not. Your decision process moves with all the impetus of a snail. You wasted time. Without my aid, we will be apprehended, and I simply cannot allow another delay."

I lift my chin and fold my arms over my chest in a decidedly human gesture. They must know I mean what I say and will not be swayed.

Niko watches the exchange with surprise and dread as the captain's cheeks turn red with anger. She wants control. I understand this.

But, like me, she cares about her freedom and that of her crew. I am counting on it. She gives me one final scowl for good measure, knowing she is caught, knowing there is nothing she can do. "Do not fry my engine!"

"*Acknowledged, Captain Forge. Please hold on and prepare to enter slipspace.*"

We have not reached the exosphere of this planet, but I simply cannot wait. I enter coordinates and command the primitive drive to engage in a slipspace entry.

"What are you doing? We can't jump here!"

Captain Forge and the crew hold on as the ship surges upward. "Of course we can," I say. "The atmosphere is thin and composed mostly of carbons, which will enable us to open a portal in the stratosphere without incident."

While it is a crude little ship, it answers my demands nimble and quick.

Then suddenly . . . the quiet.

As soon as we are in slipspace, Captain Forge runs up the remainder of the stairs to the panel at the landing.

"Did they follow?" Lessa asks, still clutching the stair railing.

"No." The captain grabs the upper railing, her knuckles white and her mouth in an angry line. "Where the hell are you taking us?"

"I have plotted a course for the closest Forerunner facility, Etran Harborage. It contains everything I require for my journey ahead. I have been unable to connect with the ancilla there, however. But it is no matter for concern."

The crew seems bewildered by my reply, shock and disbelief the prevailing mood.

Niko's dark eyes are very round. I watch him, trying to determine if the look on his face displays horror or excitement. I decide it is both.

Whether the captain likes it or not, we are going to Etran Harborage. My itinerary has not changed. After utilizing one of the Ark's *surviving portals to return to the galaxy, I intended to take the Ru-bicon there and apply an upgrade seed to the ship to prepare for the journey ahead, but the* Ace of Spades *will do just as well. In fact, it will do better. It is inconspicuous, smaller, faster, and much easier to manipulate.*

A Forerunner ship would be ideal, of course, but that would draw too much attention for my plans.

As I study them, I detect another expression closer to fear.

It is the realization that they are trapped, like the birds I once caught as a boy and sold to a dealer in the streets of Marontik. So many cages . . . caught by something more intelligent and advanced.

They are at my mercy and they know it.

I do not prefer this look on them.

It, too, is familiar.

I know what it is like to be controlled by others, to have my choices taken from me.

If I do the same to these humans, does that not make me the same as the Didact, the Master Builder, and even the Librarian?

Despite knowing they do not have a choice, they aim their meager weapons in my direction. They must know that firing them while in slipspace might result in total destruction, but I can see they will do what it takes to be free.

Freedom means to them what it now means to me.

"I will not be imprisoned," I say.

"Neither will we," Captain Forge immediately replies.

I have had three years on Geranos-a to repair, to parse and catalog and remember being human. I have not lost my past, have not lost what it feels like or what it is to be human. And I have not lost what it was to be 343 Guilty Spark.

I remember, and I do not like what is remembered.

Hard. Pitiless. Robotic. Alone.

I do not want to be that . . . cold . . . again.

And I do not want to lose these humans the way I lost the others.

"I will not and cannot be imprisoned," I repeat. "But neither will I imprison you."

I realize this statement is placating, and perhaps not entirely true. However, I must find a way to make them want what I want.

CHAPTER 20

Ace of Spades, slipspace to Etran Harborage

A*ce* might have been moving peacefully through slipspace, but the battle inside Rion was raging. Losing control of her ship was a goddamn nightmare.

Tension filled the hold. Her weapon remained trained on the sleek metal components that formed the armiger as it stared up at her through glowing blue eyes. So it didn't want anyone to be imprisoned—a hollow claim, given that it had just infiltrated her ship's systems and issued commands.

Still, Rion was curious at its behavior. Whatever moral dilemma was taking place inside the armiger might work in their favor, or it could become an utter disaster.

"You want us to believe you won't take over our ship the way you did the *Rubicon*," she said, lowering her weapon and moving down the stairs.

"I admit that was my original intention. But I see now that if I am to truly embrace my humanity, I shall employ a different tactic." It gave a slight bow as though bestowing a great honor upon them. "Cooperation."

Rion paused. "Cooperation," she repeated, unimpressed.

"Indeed. Etran Harborage is a Forerunner shield world, Captain. Taking you there benefits us both. Within this world, you can claim all the materials and tools your ship can carry. There is an entire Forerunner fleet at your disposal. And you *are* in desperate need of salvage, are you not?"

It was cunning, she'd give it that.

"Hold on, though. You still haven't answered my original question," Niko said. "And just now, what did you mean by embrace your humanity? Were you really human? Did the Forerunners make you, and how is that even possible? Forerunners and humans didn't exist in the same timeline, not even close."

"The history of the human race has been lost through war, through time, through the machinations of those long gone and those at the highest levels of your current society. I assure you, humanity did indeed exist during the time of the Forerunners. Humans were a force in the galaxy, an interstellar civilization with advances even the Forerunners did not fully understand."

Rion paused on the stairs, completely baffled by its words. "So then, where are they now?"

"Long gone, I'm afraid. Humanity engaged in a brutal war with the Forerunners. And they lost. As punishment, they were devolved, back to mere hunter-gatherers, and returned to their homeworld, Erde-Tyrene. What you call Earth. I was born among these devolved humans.

"I *was* human. Then I was Forerunner. I bore witness to the end of it all, and I survived for a hundred thousand years, waiting and watching the galaxy come back to life after we ended it."

"You're . . . a hundred thousand years old?" Less said, caught between astonishment and suspicion.

It nodded. "Give or take, yes."

Its words rang in Rion's head. Everything it said went against the entire foundation of human history, everything they knew, everything that was. It spoke with such matter-of-fact simplicity that it gave her a moment's pause, and she didn't know how to respond or feel. And neither, obviously, did the crew.

Remnants of Forerunners's ancient and mysterious civilization littered the galaxy, adding pieces to a past that had long been forgotten. If they existed a hundred thousand years ago, what else was possible?

Rion powered down her rifle, slung it behind her hip, and climbed the stairs once more. She headed across the catwalk, growing annoyed and angry, alarm bells ringing in her head, tiny strands of doubt twisting and threading through her instincts and beliefs.

"Where are you going?" Niko called after her.

She threw up a hand and kept walking. Who the hell knew? She was just going. She'd heard enough.

This wasn't the plan. They should be out there salvaging, looking for her father, doing what they did, getting on with the lives they had built, not involved in some weird-ass ONI experiment with a crazy robot who thought it was an eons-old human.

This wasn't what she wanted.

After a brief moment of hesitation, the crew followed, leaving the armiger behind, filing into the lounge behind Rion. She immediately went for the marsh-cane whiskey in the cabinet above the sink, grabbed a glass, and poured a healthy dose, downing its harsh bite in one gulp. Her eyes closed as she concentrated on the burn in her throat and the warmth spreading across her unsettled stomach.

A hand grabbed the bottle from her grasp. She opened her eyes to see Ram taking her glass and pouring his own drink. When he was done, he passed it on to Lessa and then Niko.

For a long, heavy moment, no one spoke. No one knew what to say.

"You think it's telling the truth?" Ram finally asked as he leaned against the counter.

Rion let out a sharp laugh. "That it won't take over? Or that it's a hundred-thousand-year-old human mind in a Forerunner-constructed body? Or that humans were once contemporaries with the Forerunners? Or that they *regressed* us back to cavemen?" She rolled her eyes. "Jesus. Take your pick."

"I don't see a reason for him to lie about history," Niko said. He was sitting at the table, chair kicked back. "And if he wanted to take over, he could have done so."

"*It* already has," Lessa said, dropping onto the couch. "It's just being nice about it. For now."

"And who's to say that once we outlive our usefulness, it won't just kill us or take *Ace* and leave us stranded? We have no idea what its plans are or what its end goal is," Rion said. All they knew was that they were on a course for some Forerunner shield world.

Niko sat forward, shaking his head. "You guys aren't really seeing the big picture here. Let's say he's telling the truth. He might've been formed from a working human mind, but he's now a completely functioning Forerunner AI. Do you not see the value in that?"

"Sure. If we could trust it," Lessa said blandly.

"He has one hundred thousand years of knowledge," Niko persisted. "He probably knows where every Forerunner planet and city and hub was, how to operate relics and artifacts, how to build Forerunner technology. Hell, he's taking us to a *Forerunner world* where we can pick and choose our salvage. This is everything we ever dreamed about."

"And here I was thinking we'd just be lifting a datacore," Rion muttered, downing another shot of whiskey. She wiped a hand over her mouth. "We're going to have the entire UEG after this thing."

"Not necessarily," Ram said. "You heard it. It said it wasn't in the armiger body when the *Rubicon* crashed. If it's to be believed, no one knows it's this . . . *thing* now. For all ONI knows, the AI was destroyed when the ship crashed. They might have no idea if it survived or who placed the distress call."

"No, but the *Taurokado* might have identified us as we were leaving," Lessa said. "Either way, they'll go down to the site and they'll see a lot of salvage is missing. And if they know it's us, they'll have to come after *Ace* to make sure we don't have their asset. It doesn't change the fact that now we're a target."

"It's a big galaxy, Less. We might end up a target, but now we have a super AI on our side," Niko said.

"It's on its *own* side, Niko, not ours," Less fired back. "It has its own agenda."

Silence settled in the lounge, the low drone of *Ace*'s engines humming in the background. Rion stared out the viewscreen—nothing but black and the occasional streak of some star beyond the bubble of slipspace. A cage was still a cage, no matter how free they were to roam around within it. The armiger had access to every part of her ship, and very likely was listening in even now. And while they were stuck in slipspace, there wasn't a damn thing she could do about it.

"We're on hold until we're out of the jump," she told them. "Niko, make sure you finish maintenance on Michelle. We might need her where we're going."

He frowned. "But—"

Rion gave him a pointed look. Michelle didn't need maintenance, but she had a very nice EMP pulse generator. They couldn't use it anywhere near the ship, but once they got to wherever the armiger was taking them, Rion needed all options available, especially the ability to shut that thing down and regain control.

CHAPTER 21

Facility at Voi, Kenya, Africa, Earth

Annabelle sat back in her desk chair and rubbed her face in frustration, trying very hard to maintain her composure.

A salvage ship. A goddamn salvage ship. Unbelievable.

And they'd jumped before the *Taurokado* could stop them.

They could be clear across the galaxy by now. She wanted to scream.

Outer Colony opportunists were dregs, thorns in the UEG's side. ONI had better things to do than play babysitter to a bunch of lowlife thieves and smugglers. There were bigger things going on in the galaxy, much bigger things. And to make matters worse, Hugo Barton was on the line lecturing her about the importance of his research and—

"—and if you *ever* pull my team and my ship off course again, I will make a formal complaint to CINCONI and HIGHCOM."

She let out a long steady breath. "Obtaining 343 Guilty Spark is a far higher priority than a Forerunner debris field at the moment. I realize the *Taurokado* is under your command, but it was the closest ship to my asset. If you want to take it up with Osman, please go right ahead. And while you're on that, ask yourself who approved transfer-of-command in the first place." She sighed. "Hugo, I don't have time for this, so unless you have something constructive to say, I believe we're done here."

He blinked, utterly taken aback by her sharp response. Was it wrong, the intense satisfaction she felt at his sudden inability to put two words together? No. Not wrong at all. In fact, it was high time she gave him a taste of his own medicine. For the last year, she'd put up with his demeaning lectures.

Due to his experience overseeing the Trevelyan research facility on Onyx for the last several years, as well as uncovering the Bornstellar Relation in that time, Barton was an obvious choice to consult on BOOKWORM. He and Dr. Iqbal had many combined years' worth of knowledge in ancient Forerunner civilization, artifacts, and technology. And long before Annabelle had been chosen by Admiral Osman to run point on BOOKWORM, they'd obtained some of the highest levels of clearance within ONI's ranks.

And now that Barton could add head of Forerunner acquisitions to his job description—which was a fancy title meaning that all discoveries of large Forerunner sites and artifacts of note were funneled through his office and parsed out to the appropriate division—his ego had grown exponentially. Possessing knowledge that very few people in the galaxy wielded could go to some people's heads, apparently. Sometimes she had to wonder if Osman would have been better served choosing someone with a background like Barton's or Iqbal's to manage BOOKWORM. Yes, Annabelle had traveled through the portal here at Voi and had gone to the Ark, witnessing marvelous and dangerous and sobering things. But she'd had no previous knowledge of the Bornstellar Relation or of the *Rubicon*'s existence until after the interview process was over, the job was hers, and her security clearances came through.

And then her mind had been blown.

"My ship has arrived in the system," she told Barton after he was finished with another lecture she hadn't even listened to. "Command of the *Taurokado* is yours once again. Happy hunting." She cut the feed and sat back, letting out a long breath, and catching movement out of the corner of her eye.

Lieutenant Commander Radeen was standing in the doorway.

She had no idea if he'd just arrived or had heard the entire exchange. He rarely showed any emotion one way or another, but she thought, for the briefest of moments, there was a glint of pride in his eyes.

"Commander?"

He stepped into the room. "The AR team's full report should be coming in within the hour."

"Good. When it does, patch it through immediately."

He hesitated, seeming like he wanted to say more, but then decided against it. He dipped his head, smiled, and pulled the door closed behind him.

Annabelle sat there stunned. Wonders never ceased. That might be the first time in years she'd actually seen the man smile.

CHAPTER 22

When it came to Rion Forge, failure seemed to follow Walter Hahn wherever he went. No matter that he'd secured Hugo Barton his debris field and his Forerunner AI. No matter that, because of his efforts, the Office of Naval Intelligence would continue to achieve great things, necessary things, for the good of the galaxy, whether the galaxy at large knew or approved of it or not.

All of that fell short and was forgotten the moment they entered Geranos-a's atmosphere and caught sight of the *Ace of Spades*.

No one had been more shocked than Hahn himself.

How the hell the salvagers had found the site, he couldn't begin to guess. But he knew it wasn't by coincidence.

This was payback, plain and simple.

Now Barton, and no doubt the entire crew of the *Taurokado*, looked to him as the cause. Because he had made a critical mistake with Rion Forge: he'd taken too much from her. She'd gotten under his skin, he admitted that, and he'd gone too far. Instead of scaring her into submission, he'd created an enemy—and a reckless one at that.

Hahn hadn't missed the look in Spartan Novak's eyes when he'd taken her father's mementos and files. He'd thought it stern and bold, but in hindsight it was harsh and perhaps unnecessary.

Too late to turn back the clock now.

Shortly after they'd arrived at Geranos-a, an ONI black ship appeared and proceeded to take over the site on the planet below. Hahn had no idea what, if anything, Rion and her crew might have retrieved from the surface, but they hadn't gone there for shore leave. Now he was bound and determined to recover whatever they'd taken and correct his mistake.

Hahn was going for maximum damage control; he had to do something now.

With a little digging, and Turk's help, he'd been able to locate the commanding officer who'd sent them to Geranos-a in the first place—a Captain Annabelle Richards.

He waited a full twenty-four hours at Jupiter Station for a reply before his aide alerted him with good news. "Sir, she's on the line."

Hahn sat straighter in his desk chair, tugged his black ONI-issue jacket down to smooth any creases, and then turned on his screen. The face staring back at him was not what he'd expected. Annabelle Richards was a rail-thin, petite woman with straight red hair parted in the middle, one side tucked behind her ear. Looking at her file wasn't in his pay grade, but considering all the roadblocks he'd encountered just to gain contact information, she must be very important within ONI's ranks.

"Agent Hahn," she prompted, not bothering to hide her impatience.

"Yes, ma'am. As you may know, I'm the counter-contraband agent on the *Taurokado*—"

"Yes, I know," she cut in. "I read your file. And I read Captain Karah's report. None of which has been very helpful. You underestimated your salvagers, Agent Hahn—made an enemy of them when your directive was and *is* to make them work for us whether they realize it or not . . . or want to or not." She gave him a tired, somewhat pained look. "Unless you know where they are with my wreckage, I don't see the point—"

"So they did take something." Her flat expression told him he'd overstepped. "Please," he said hastily before she dropped the feed. "Captain, I don't know where they are at this moment, but I believe I *will* know."

"What are you saying?"

"I'm saying that I can lure the *Ace of Spades* to a meeting."

Her eyes went sharp and narrow. "They could be anywhere in the galaxy right now. What makes you think you can get a message to them?"

"Navigating the smuggling trade in the Outer Colonies is my specialty, ma'am. I know it pretty well. There are lines of communication, channels used by traders and salvagers. Everyone out there knows when goods come in, when private sales happen, when big things are discovered. The *Ace of Spades* might be in slipspace or hiding out on some planet with no commsat, but they won't be doing that forever. And when they reemerge, they'll check in. They'll want to know the state of things—if we're still after them, how safe they are. I propose we send out a message, one they'll find appealing."

"Which is?"

"That we're willing to make a deal. I believe that's why they went to Geranos-a."

"To steal ONI property and then trade it back to us?" She shook her head in disbelief.

"I know it sounds preposterous and reckless, but please understand—these salvagers, they operate on a different level. They have no respect for the law or for the military. They consider themselves equals to us in every way."

Captain Richards didn't look convinced. That anyone would think to steal from ONI and then try to make a deal . . . even to Hahn, it did indeed sound ridiculous. But things were different in the Outer Colonies.

"If we offer a trade and can sweeten the deal, so to speak, they might not be able to resist."

"Explain."

"We—I—took possession of items confiscated from the crew via Article Eight Zero Nine Point Seven Five of the UNSC Salvage Directive, which included personal property, salvage, bank accounts, and, from the captain, intelligence regarding the UNSC *Spirit of Fire*."

"All of this I already know."

"Yes, of course. But their leader, Captain Rion Forge, is the daughter of one of the *Spirit of Fire*'s crew. She's been looking for that ship for a very long time. And honestly, she's had more success than we ever have. I'll have her file sent over. But I believe because of her emotional ties, we can entice her with the return of her items, plus additional information regarding the ship."

"You do realize there might not be any additional information about the ship."

"She won't know that."

A sharp red eyebrow lifted slightly, and Richards regarded him for a long moment. "It's not in my nature to appease thieves and criminals. But our choices now are limited, aren't they."

Hahn ignored the dig. "They'll trade, Captain Richards. And when they do, we'll seize the ship and recover whatever wreckage they took from Geranos-a."

"All right, Agent Hahn. Send out your message. My AI, Ferguson, will contact you with my secure channel. And I'll arrange for you and your staff to stay at Jupiter Station to await a reply. If there is one, I want to know immediately."

"Yes, ma'am. Thank you."

The screen went black, and Hahn relaxed into his chair to let out the breath he'd been holding.

Rion Forge would make a deal. He was sure of it.

Her motive was revenge, after all. As motives went, it was always a reliable one, which from experience he understood very well.

CHAPTER 23

Facility at Voi, Kenya, Africa, Earth

losing her channel with Agent Hahn, Annabelle tapped her fingers on the desktop. After receiving *Bad Moon Rising*'s initial report on the salvage site, she'd been livid and somewhat depressed, but Hahn's proposal offered an intriguing solution. If they could lure Forge into a meeting, they might just succeed.

"Ferg?"

The facility AI appeared over the integrated holopad on her desk. He was lean and tall in form, and had chosen to attire himself in a sharp-looking business suit, white dress shirt, and plaid tie. "Yes, Director Richards?"

"I'd like all the intel we have on the UNSC *Phoenix*-class vessel *Spirit of Fire*. *All* the intel. If there's anything off the record or lurking deep in the eyes-only files, I want to know about it."

"Very good, Director."

Leverage over Captain Forge might prove vital.

Feeling hopeful for the first time in days, Annabelle left her office to seek a bit of fresh air. She took the elevator to the surface, then climbed the metal rungs built into the side of the airfield's power generator. On the roof of the one-story block building was an observation deck.

From this position she could see far across the flat savanna to the faint peak of Kilimanjaro in the west and the hazy cityscape of New Mombasa in the southeast, where the effort to rebuild was ongoing, and closer still the rim of the Artifact, otherwise known as the Excession, the Forerunner slipspace portal generator left on Earth eons ago by the Librarian. Once activated, the generator opened a portal leading outside the galaxy to one of the Forerunners' greatest technological achievements—the Ark.

One hundred seventeen kilometers in diameter, the deep depression in the Earth caused by the Artifact had created a rim that could be seen a full kilometer away, sometimes more on a clear day. Annabelle had witnessed firsthand the portal come online, the pylons rising impossibly high into the air, the astonishing electrical storm generated overhead.

She'd gone into the portal and traveled to the Ark itself. . . .

Two years had gone by, but sometimes it felt like yesterday.

Pulling her mind away from darker memories, she let her gaze drift over the dry grasses. Somewhere out there, the Librarian and her companion, Catalog, had ensured the portal's construction before dying here on Earth.

Of course, 343 Guilty Spark had suggested a different ending. One of Annabelle's directives was ascertaining if there was truth to Guilty Spark's claim. Had the Librarian survived the firing of the Halo Array? CINCONI wanted a definitive answer.

Because finding that answer might lead them to a treasure far greater than the Librarian herself.

ONI'S Holy Grail.

Project: BOOKWORM wasn't just about Guilty Spark or the Librarian. In the end, all roads led to the Domain. And how could they not?

The Bornstellar Relation had given them their first introduction to the Domain, a quantum repository containing all the knowledge and experience of the entire Forerunner civilization. But it hadn't been created by them. It was far, far older—crafted by the elusive Precursors and said to contain a hundred billion years' worth of wisdom and experience from "before there were stars" to the fall of the Forerunners.

Annabelle stepped to the railing as the hot, arid wind stirred the grasses and blew over her skin. With her fair complexion, she could never stay topside for very long during the day, but she did love it out here, especially now as the sun began to set, bathing the land in a dusty orange glow.

She often wondered how the landscape looked when the Librarian and Catalog were here, waiting for Halo's pulse to reach them, accepting their fate, and knowing, if nothing else, that they would succeed not only in starving the Flood by eliminating its food source, but in reseeding the galaxy after it was safe to do so.

Without the Librarian's efforts, humanity might not have continued. The Lifeshaper had set the stage. Prepared. Sacrificed. Perhaps thought she'd done everything she could. Annabelle could only imagine the horror the Librarian must have felt, finding out at the last minute that the most precious thing in the universe, the Domain, would also be destroyed in the firing of the Halo Array. The Forerunner hadn't counted on that, hadn't even known such a thing was possible.

But once she knew, all of ONI's stat bot analysis pointed to action.

The bots had studied what they knew about the Librarian, had built personality profiles, and one thing was abundantly clear—she would have tried, until her dying breath, to save the Domain. She'd sent a message to her husband, Bornstellar, the Iso-Didact, hoping he might repair whatever damage was done to the Domain, but could she count on him getting the message or succeeding?

The question remained: Had she done something more?

Annabelle hadn't been so sure, not until Dr. Iqbal and his team had discovered the remains of what was thought to be the Librarian's Catalog seven meters down in the Ross-Ziegler Blip, a fossil-absent geological layer in the Earth that coincided with the timing of the Halo's destructive force.

Thanks to another Catalog found by Hugo Barton's team on Onyx, they had known immediately what they'd unearthed and hoped that they too would find a datacore containing a testimony similar to the Bornstellar Relation. But all they'd been able to recover was an unidentifiable, twisted, misshapen mass inside the Catalog's carapace and an eroded datacore that yielded nothing of value.

They'd been so close to perhaps solving the mystery of the Librarian's final moments. As dictated by its rate, a Catalog's job was to observe and take testimony for the Forerunners' juridical record. It would have recorded *everything*—every word, every moment, right up until the very end.

The mystery only deepened when nothing else was discovered in the excavation area, suggesting that the Catalog might have been alone when it died.

So where was the Librarian? Was she still out there, buried beneath the savanna, under a shifting land that had changed, flooded, moved again and again over time, perhaps taking her remains with it?

Or was Guilty Spark right?

His last words to the officers of the *Rubicon* were etched in Annabelle's memory—she'd read them so many times:

". . . You and I are brothers in many ways . . . not in the least that we faced the Didact before, and face him now, and perhaps ever after. This is combat eternal, enmity unslaked, unified by only one thing: our love for the elusive Lifeshaper. Without her, humans would have been extinguished many times over. Both I and the Didact love her to this day.

Some say she is dead, that she died on Earth. But that is demonstrably untrue . . .

. . . after a hundred thousand years of exploration and study, I know where to find her."

Analysis suggested that the Lifeshaper to whom Guilty Spark referred in his final thoughts was *indeed* the Librarian, First-Light-Weaves-Living-Song. Guilty Spark and the Didact had no other unified love except for the Lifeshaper known as the Librarian. There was none who loved humanity more than she, and no other Lifeshaper who was thought to have died on Earth.

What Annabelle found particularly disturbing, however, was in mentioning his belief to the *Rubicon* crew, Guilty Spark wanted it known that she was alive.

The question was: why?

CHAPTER 24

Rion stood at the tactical table, keeping a tight watch on the slipspace feed, curious about the armiger's chosen destination and dreading the unknown.

The crew had assembled on the bridge, quietly sitting at their stations, waiting and monitoring systems. There was no way to tell where they were headed, because the destination wasn't inherently known to the new star charts they'd had to buy back on Venezia.

When they'd scrubbed all their previous navigational logs and star charts, also gone were the many notations, more than a decade of discoveries and out-of-the-way locales that weren't often found on standard maps. Her many backups were gone too, victims of ONI's warehouse thefts. Rion's chest ached at the loss. Light-years' worth of travel and navigational knowledge simply not there anymore.

Not that it mattered in this instance. The long-lost Forerunner world the armiger had in mind wouldn't be on any of her charts, old or new.

Speaking of which . . . The metallic echo of footsteps beyond the bridge bristled along Rion's spine. The sound grew with each step closer, until the armiger appeared in the doorway. All she could see for a moment, before it ducked its head to enter the bridge, were those strange eyes and the lines denoting cheekbones and mouth glowing blue in the dimness.

Once inside, it straightened to its nearly three-meter height, took four steps forward, and then stopped behind her captain's chair.

Save for Niko, they'd done a good job of avoiding it up until now, and it'd seemed content to remain mostly in the cargo hold during their journey.

Rion withdrew her attention as a low ping told them they were exiting the slipspace portal. Unease had her gripping the ends of the tactical table as *Ace* dropped smoothly out of slipspace and into . . . chaos.

"What the—"

"Contact!" Ram shouted as a shrill alert blared through the bridge. He scrambled from one chair to another, taking up the weapons systems and immediately maneuvering *Ace*'s cannons to let loose on two Seraphs screaming past their bow. "They're coming around!"

Rion hurried to her chair, knowing exactly where they were. "You took us back to the debris field!" she yelled in disbelief, sliding into her seat and taking immediate evasive action. "Hold on!"

The single-piloted Seraphs were quick and agile combat fighters.

During the Covenant War, they would've been armed with pulse lasers and plasma cannons, but she could only pray that postwar, their firepower was severely lacking. If not, *Ace* was in a world of trouble.

With each maneuver made, the Seraphs countered, staying glued to *Ace*'s tail as Rion piloted the ship between chunks of rock and metal. Debris exploded around them, bouncing against the shields and spraying into their path as the Seraphs' plasma cannons missed their mark.

"Damn it," Rion cursed at their luck.

"Captain, if you would allow me control—"

"You've done enough." She had zero time to deal with the armiger or her own shock. All her focus was on getting out of this mess in one piece.

The massive debris field was effectively an entire planet's worth of detritus available for hide and seek, and Rion used it to their advantage. "Less, find us a pocket. Niko, divert as much power as you can to shields."

"There!" Lessa pointed to a large chunk of rock with an overhang, under which was black space suggesting a cavern.

Rion pushed *Ace*'s engines to the limit, surging forward and leading the violet birds through a maze of switchback turns and climbs and dives. As soon as she lost them, she knew they only had moments before being found again. "Niko, dump a decoy."

"On it. Dummy away, Cap. That should keep them busy."

Or at the very least confuse them for a bit until *Ace* could drop beneath the overhang and divert all power to bafflers. Rion directed the ship around the rock once more, reversed her engines, and settled into the shadows.

The faint drone of *Ace*'s auxiliary power grew loud as the wait stretched on.

"Captain—" began the armiger.

"Shh."

They stayed quiet for what felt like hours, when in reality only a few minutes had passed. Eventually Rion released her death grip on her controls, as it appeared the Seraphs had given up the hunt.

With a sigh of relief, she turned her full attention on the thing that had put them in this mess; lucky for the armiger she had a surplus of adrenaline to fuel her brewing anger. "Are you out of your mind?"

In the hesitation of it not knowing how to answer that question, Niko jumped in. "Well, it's not like he knew—"

"Niko—"

"I'll shut up now."

The armiger walked to the viewscreen and stared out at the detritus—huge pieces of infrastructure, pylons, support beams, broken facilities, and large chunks of what was land itself—floating past. "When was it destroyed?"

It suddenly dawned on her that it had no idea the world once known as Etran Harborage had been completely obliterated. "Twenty-six years ago," she answered. "By my father's ship."

"The *Spirit of Fire*," it said somberly, still staring out the viewscreen. "I did not make the connection prior to the jump. There were no matching coordinates in your ship's navigational logs to draw that conclusion."

"Why did you choose this place?" Niko asked.

"I was simply following the path intended for the *Rubicon*. The

Harborage contained an entire dreadnought fleet and supporting shipyard. They had everything I needed. Now . . ."

One of the Seraphs appeared in the distance, a small violet dot slowly patrolling through an ocean of debris.

Rion knew the instant it detected them: it suddenly altered course and went from patrol speed to overdrive. "Damn it." She fired up the engines, engaged *Ace*'s thrusters, and hightailed it out of the cavern.

In seconds, they were back to being hunted through the field, dodging rocks, colliding with small debris, and taking a few hard hits from enemy plasma cannons. "Hold on!" Rion eyed a short section of large metal tubing and barrel-rolled *Ace* into the tunnel. The Seraph followed. As soon as *Ace* cleared the debris, she pulled up into a steep climb and then looped back over the tunnel to come down behind the Covenant fighter.

Ram let out a whoop and blasted the Seraph with their cannons.

"Cap!" Niko called over his shoulder as the fighter's shields absorbed the blast. "I'm getting some odd chatter. There's a lot of interference. . . . It's—wait, we're getting a hail."

"Put it on," she said, banking *Ace* hard right and sticking like glue to the Seraph's tail, knowing the other one was still out there somewhere.

"I think it's . . . laughter?" Niko said with a deep frown. "If you can call it that."

Over the chaos, Rion heard it too, and her blood ran cold. She didn't have to see his disfigured face to know who it was. The hateful, forced chuckle was a rare and strange sound coming from a Sangheili, especially a zealot like Gek, who despised human emotions and mannerisms. But then, he was sending a message, one he wanted to make sure she'd understand. "Where is he?" she demanded. "Lessa, get me a location!"

Gek 'Lhar wouldn't be in one of the Seraphs; she knew that much. But he was here somewhere.

As *Ace* burst out of the field and came around to dive back in, Rion saw the war freighter parked on a massive chunk of debris, illuminated by the yellow glow of the Harvester's plasma drill as it bored into the rock a few meters away.

Seeing red, she dove *Ace* back into the maze.

"Wait!" Niko yelled, his face turning pale as he listened intently. "I'm picking up—"

"My board is lighting up!" Lessa spun around with wide eyes. "It's . . . a fleet."

No wonder Gek was taunting her.

As they came around, they saw a Covenant battle group hovering just beyond the debris portion that Gek 'Lhar commanded.

Suddenly the other Seraph blasted overhead, joining up with the other as they flew toward the fleet.

Why the hell hadn't it fired?

Rion eased off *Ace*'s thrusters. "Niko, talk to me."

"I don't know. . . ." he said, listening. "It's translating, but the chatter is too fast. . . ."

"They're forming up," Lessa said. "The entire group is going hot."

"Oh . . . shit." Niko's eyes were as wide as saucers.

Rion opened navs and comms and blinked. Surely that wasn't right—

"We got company!" Ram shouted as an enormous slipspace

portal opened up at the edge of the debris field. "Multiple—holy shit. They're ours."

The Covenant battle group wasn't mobilizing to take out the *Ace of Spades*. They were preparing for a much larger engagement.

"Jesus," Niko whispered at the sight of the massive slipspace rupture widening just outside of the debris field and the huge UNSC battle carrier that slid through.

Goose bumps spread like wildfire up Rion's arms. Immediately, several portals manifested in the same sector, delivering another UNSC cruiser and three more frigates.

Ace was about to be caught in the middle of a major confrontation.

"They're entering hot right from slipspace," Less said, swallowing. "Oh God. Nukes away!"

Rion took immediate action, guiding *Ace* through the debris.

"They're nuking the field," Less said in disbelief. "The UNSC is nuking the debris field."

"They're retreating," Ram said. The Covenant battle group scattered, escape portals opening up all around the field.

"Niko, hail Gek and put it on screen," Rion ordered, pushing *Ace* to the limit to create as much distance between them and the nukes as she could.

He spun around. "Are you crazy?"

"Just do it."

"Twelve more nukes away!" Less yelled.

"Channel's open," Niko said.

The viewscreen went white with fuzz, then revealed chaos on the bridge of Gek's war freighter as his crew scrambled to take off before the UNSC nukes hit. A Sangheili peered at them in confusion, and Rion realized they must've opened the hail automatically. She saw Gek 'Lhar in the background shouting orders. He turned and saw her face, and his command was cut off midsentence.

Rion took his measure with all the hatred and menace she could muster, which wasn't very difficult. It flowed through her on a merciless wave. Her lips twisted into a satisfied smile. "Get ready to burn in hell, you hinge-head bastard."

And then she returned the favor and laughed.

The Sangheili's rage built, contorting his gray features, that one beady eye seeming to glow with fury. As he opened his mouth to reply, Rion closed the channel.

Then she punched *Ace*'s afterburners and they soared toward open space.

Niko had pulled up feeds of the battle as they retreated, and they watched with rapt attention as the massive UNSC fleet loosed a barrage of fire, protecting its nukes as they streamed from the ships, heading for all parts of the field.

Rion had known ONI would do one of two things with the coordinates they'd stolen from her: either commandeer the field and mine its contents, or utterly destroy it so no one else could have its ancient riches.

She guessed there weren't enough resources to monitor, protect, and explore such a large area. Next best option was to take it completely out of play, blow it to bits and disrupt the field's gravity around the dwarf star. Whatever wasn't destroyed would likely be pulled into the star. The Covenant wouldn't get their hands on anything useful now.

The last of Gek's vessels retreated into portals, disappearing into slipspace as the nukes found their targets.

"Concussions closing in fast!" Ram shouted.

Time stood still. They were almost at the edge of the field. Opening a slipspace portal now and potentially taking the concussion with them would be very, very bad. They had no choice but to ride it out, which would also be—

Behind her, Rion heard the armiger say, "Oh my."

And then the FTL began to spin before she gave the command. Rion threw a harsh glare at the armiger, just as a portal opened in front of them.

"Snail," it said with a smirk in its tone, before staring off into nothing as it took command of her ship.

"Goddamn it!" Rion yelled as space opened up in a flash of blue light and they streaked inside the rupture, taking with them a trace of nuclear concussion.

"I suggest you strap in," the armiger said calmly as *Ace* was rocked from behind and sent into a dizzying spin.

"Hold her steady!" Rion shouted, helpless to helm her own damn ship.

Ace spun dangerously close to the outer edge of the portal and imminent destruction. But somehow the armiger countered every spin and bobble with lightning speed and precision, the hull shuddering and creaking with the forces thrown at it.

Rion's fingers dug deep into the armrests of her chair. Bile stung her throat, and her gut rolled over and over in nauseating waves. Her vision went black and while she tried valiantly, she couldn't hold on to awareness.

When next she came to, *Ace* was gliding through the slipstream portal with ease. The crew was waking too, woozy and pale, faring no better than she was.

"Captain," the armiger said in the ensuing tranquility. "I would like to make a proposal."

She lifted her head enough to give it a withering look, still trying to catch her breath. "Wherever you pointed us this time, it's the last. When we get wherever the hell we're going, you are *off* my goddamn ship. You hear me?"

The lingering vertigo was starting to get the best of her. She squeezed her eyelids closed, hearing the armiger retreat, the echo of its footsteps growing dimmer until there was finally nothing.

Ram groaned. "Anyone else feel like they just lost ten years off their life?"

"That's the last time I go into slipspace on an empty stomach," Less said.

Niko looked up, his face a pale shade of green. "I think I might've barfed a little on the comms panel."

Rion let her head fall back against her chair and closed her eyes, wondering how in the hell they got into this mess in the first place.

After Rion splashed some much-needed cold water on her face and sat a spell in her quarters to let the unsteadiness ebb from her body, she headed for the lounge for a drink and crackers to fill her sour stomach.

The armiger was already there, facing the viewscreen, hands tucked behind its back in a disconcertingly human gesture. The alloy head turned slowly at her entry and it studied her with those ominous blue eyes, all the humanity suddenly gone, replaced by something disturbing and alien.

Ram was at the counter in a change of clothes, hair still wet from his shower, stirring something in a pot, while Lessa sat curled in her favorite chair nursing a mug of hot tea and seeming lost in thought, as she often was lately.

Niko came in as Rion headed for the counter, ignoring the armiger, to see what Ram was cooking. "You do know we have a food synthesizer and an entire cargo container of packaged meals, right?"

He ignored her quip. "Sometimes the moment just calls for a home-cooked meal. He's been waiting for everyone to get here," he said, with a nod toward the armiger. "You want some soup?"

"Not yet." She reached into the cabinet above him. "Crackers are about all I can handle right now."

He filled bowls for himself and the siblings, and then they adjourned to the table. It felt odd, having the armiger there while they were eating, alone and off to the side. Lurking.

Again it had taken control.

Again it had shown her how deeply they were at its mercy.

And again there wasn't a damn thing she could do about it.

Rion shoved a cracker into her mouth and chewed as she glared at the creature's back. She hadn't forgotten its words on the bridge. And finally, feeling a tad confrontational, she said, "All right . . . let's hear what you have to say."

The armiger unclasped its metal hands, then hesitated so long that Rion was just about to tell it to get on with it or she was going back to her quarters, when it shifted and limped over to the head of the table.

Without it making a move, the holopad in the center of the

table came to life, generating a beautiful green and blue planet—Earth. Though, clearly from a time long before overpopulation and pollution.

Ram's look was unreadable, but Lessa's face showed flat-out adoration.

"Well, I'm guessing that's Earth," Niko said, before slurping his soup. "But it sure doesn't look like that anymore."

"It did. Once," the armiger replied. "This is how it appeared one hundred thousand years ago." It seemed to stare at it for a moment. "I am aware of your agenda, Captain Forge. You brought me on board your ship with the intention to ransom me to the Office of Naval Intelligence in exchange for your confiscated items. Of course, this simply cannot occur. And I hope to change your mind. It appears we are both at odds with ONI, are we not?"

Rion didn't answer.

"You do not trust me," it continued. "I do not trust you. But fate has thrown us together; therefore, we must work together. I have no desire to commandeer your ship."

"And yet you have, twice now."

"To keep us free and safe, yes. Would you rather I allowed your capture on Geranos-a or your death in the debris field?"

It might have had a point, but still . . .

"You want your personal items and the fragmented ancilla in order to follow the path your father's ship took after destroying Etran Harborage. I will help you retrieve these items."

"In exchange for what?"

"The Office of Naval Intelligence has something of mine as well."

"You want us to help you steal from ONI."

"It would seem you have done so already."

Niko chuckled. "Well, that's true. We stole *him* from right under their noses."

"Whose side are you on?" Lessa asked.

"There are no sides," the armiger said. "We have a common enemy. The difference between us is that I have the tools to protect myself and you simply do not. Once we reach our destination, you will."

"And where's that?" Rion wanted to know. "Another Forerunner ruin?"

It dipped its head. "In order to evade ONI, you will need a better ship."

Rion laughed in surprise, nearly choking on her cracker. "I'm not ditching my ship."

"You will not have to. The Forerunners were master shipbuilders, among other things. They were explorers as well, spreading across a galaxy of three million occupied worlds. It was not uncommon for them to find themselves in contact with other species and races with rudimentary ships such as yours. They utilized design seeds to build their own ships from local resources if necessary. But there were many occasions when resources could not support a design, so the Forerunners used whatever local vessels they could obtain and created an upgrade seed—hard-light instructions, blueprints, if you will, which bonded to an existing structure, reinforcing the materials, molding them as needed, and upgrading components and systems."

"So you're saying we keep *Ace*, and get all the Forerunner bells and whistles?" Niko asked, obviously on board.

The armiger seemed confused by the phrase, but quickly

recovered. "Not all, but many, yes. We will need a crystal flake as well. Every Forerunner vessel in the ecumene had one at the core of its engines. This focus amplifier allowed them to travel throughout the galaxy with little delay and extreme accuracy."

"And you can retrofit this flake with an FTL drive?" Ram asked, intrigued.

"Of course. The engine itself must be modified first. For this engine and size of vessel, we will need only the smallest of flakes—"

"No," Rion said, shaking her head. "We can evade ONI just fine on our own. Get your own damn ship. You don't need this one."

The armiger thought about that for a long moment. "No," it admitted. "But I need an inconspicuous ship, and I have need of humans to do the things I cannot. Therefore, you help me, I help you."

"Well, I don't know about the rest of you, but I'd like our stuff back," Niko said. "Think about the future, our work. We can't do any of that now, unless we can stand up to ONI, or at least run when we need to run and hide when we need to hide. We get caught by ONI again and that's it. We're shipped right off to some black site prison, never to be seen again."

"Please, allow me to assist you," the armiger said. "I offer my services in exchange for yours. Isn't that what you do, Captain Forge? Make deals? Look for opportunity?"

Rion chewed slowly, swallowed; then, "Sorry. Don't trust you."

Niko opened his mouth to argue in favor, but Rion shut him up with a look.

She finished her crackers, wondering what the armiger would do now.

"I would like you to know my story and your history," it said. "Maybe then you will revisit your decision. That is all I ask."

An image appeared over the holopad of a large primitive city made of tall mud and reed and wood houses, some with open rooftops covered with lengths of cloth for shade in the harsh sunlight. The sky was peppered with crude hot air balloons of many sizes and colors with reed baskets, holding everything from people to food to animals. There were so many it was clear the balloons were a common mode of transport around the city.

"These images, messages, histories, and collected terminal entries were left for those who would come after, those who would reclaim the Mantle of Responsibility. They are part of my memory stores, and I add them to my own testimony, which I made to the crew of the *Rubicon* before we crashed. They are here for you now, so that you might better understand your past, your present, and your future. So that you might learn to understand me, trust me, and aid me in my journey."

The armiger left the lounge before Rion could say she didn't want to understand it or aid it in anything. But she was curious, so she settled back in her chair and listened. . . .

CHAPTER 25

Time had passed quickly in the lounge, the *Ace* crew listening to an unbelievable tale—a heartbreaking, horrific recounting of an ancient war between humans, Forerunners, and the parasitic Flood. Of immense last-resort weapons collectively called Halo, serving as both sanctuaries and galaxy-wide killing machines.

A hundred thousand years ago, all sentient life in the galaxy had had their fate decided for them. In the blink of an eye . . . *gone*. It was impossible not to feel the horror and pain of that moment, or to sympathize with those Forerunners who'd had to make the decision to extinguish everything, to be the ones so desperate and backed into a corner that the only way out was murdering trillions in order to kill the Flood's food source.

The hopes and tragedies told through the eyes of Chakas, Bornstellar, the Librarian . . .

Rion could barely wrap her head around it.

Unbelievably, the armiger claimed to have once been this Chakas character, a human at the mercy of the Forerunners, a player in this long-ago saga. As Chakas, he had borne witness to so much, shouldered the knowledge and the horror of war, and had his body so broken he would have died had his mind not been saved by Bornstellar. As a monitor, his human memories were compartmentalized, virtually forgotten, and he weathered the impossibly long years after the purge alone, no longer flesh and blood but a machine known as 343 Guilty Spark, a caretaker of one of the Halo ringworlds.

Rion's mind worked overtime processing it all, absorbing the emotion of it, the despair, the finality. On the one hand, she felt immersed in the past, caring a great deal for the players involved and the obstacles they faced, so much so that at times tears blurred her vision and her chest ached.

But on the other hand . . . she preferred her universe the way it had been a few hours ago. Part of her didn't *want* to know the past, didn't desire the weight or responsibility of it. And she sure as hell didn't want to sympathize with the armiger. Yet it was difficult not to do so.

Events a hundred thousand years old should stay where they belonged, yet Rion had a very bad feeling the past was rising again and barreling right toward them. It scared her to death. And while she desperately wished to find her father, she was starting to regret ever discovering that damn buoy on Laconia.

Cade would still be alive and Ram wouldn't be suffering. And they'd be out there, all of them, salvaging some find or another without being hunted, or driven by an ancient human/Forerunner, or knowing the horror of the Flood. . . .

Rion stood and stretched her arms over her head, then walked to the cabinet to throw her wrapper away. Niko was right. There wasn't any reason for the armiger to create such an intricate fiction just to trick them. What would be the point? They were salvagers, nobodies in the grand scheme of things, not worth such an elaborate ruse.

As she turned around, she took a moment to regard her crew. They too appeared shell-shocked. Niko was lying on the couch, hands tucked under his head, staring at the ceiling. Lessa sat in one of the chairs, feet pulled under her. And Ram was in the other chair, facing the viewscreen, lost in thought.

An image of a Halo ring hovered above the holotable.

Installation 04, the armiger had called it.

By knowing the truth, they were in even deeper than before. Information like this . . . it wasn't for civvies. This was the kind of intel that could get them locked away for a very long time, or worse.

It took the crew a few minutes to pull themselves away from the chaos of a bygone war and back into the present.

Ram got up, cracked his neck, and went to the drink dispenser for water. He leaned on the counter and rubbed his chest. "I'm not one to get emotional, but . . . goddamn."

Lessa leaned over the arm of the chair, her eyes glassy. "There's a human mind in there, inside that armiger," she said. "He's telling the truth. We all know it. We all feel it."

"So that's it, then," Niko said, sitting up. "His agenda—he wants to find the Librarian and bring back his friends."

Rion released a heavy sigh. "This is way beyond us, Niko. This is *not* what we do. As terrible as it all is, it's not our fight. We're salvagers. We look out for each other and ourselves. We don't fly around the galaxy righting ancient wrongs and looking for alien beings who've been dead for millenia."

"Well, *he* doesn't think she's dead," Niko argued. "And that's exactly who we are, by the way. We deal in old shit—the older, the better. We've been flying around the galaxy looking for an old ship and your father. What's the difference?"

"A missing ship from twenty-six years ago is not the same thing."

"But isn't it though?"

She hated to admit it, but he did have a point. "What about you, Less?" she said, moving along, not entirely convinced by Niko's argument. The last thing she wanted was to engage in a debate when everyone was already emotionally spent. "What do you think?"

"I think we should part ways with him once we get to wherever he's taking us. He can go complete whatever agenda he has, and leave us out of it."

"Of course you'd say that," Niko muttered, dragging his hands through his hair.

It was the wrong thing to say. Anger reddened Lessa's cheeks and her eyes flashed. "Why, because I've always looked out for you? Because I sacrificed my own childhood to raise you, did things that keep me up at night just to keep you safe? And now you just want to go off without a single thought in your head about self-preservation?"

And that, of course, was the wrong thing to say to Niko. Rion pinched the bridge of her nose. *Aaaand here it comes.*

"Well, I never asked you to sacrifice anything," he shot back, frustrated. "*You* did those things, and you make me feel guilty all the time for it! I can't change it!"

Lessa, with tears brimming, unfolded herself from the chair. "You go to hell, Niko. Just piss off."

She stormed from the room, and it was obvious Niko wanted to call out to her, but he stayed silent and put his head in his hands.

"Yeah, you might want to go fix that," Rion said.

He lifted his head. "I don't know how to fix it. How can I fix it when she blames me for the things *she* chose to do? I didn't ask her to do any of it."

"She doesn't blame you. She wants you to acknowledge what she went through to keep you safe. And when she tries to keep you safe now, you might want to understand where she's coming from and appreciate it instead of acting like it annoys you. Just talk to her. Work it out."

"Fine," he huffed, and then marched out, leaving her alone with Ram.

Rion rubbed her hands down her face before plopping into one of the lounge chairs, exhausted. When she lifted her gaze, it was to find Ram watching her, his eyes crinkling at the corners. "What?"

He laughed. "I'm not sure where to start. . . . How do you manage those two?"

"It used to be a lot easier."

"Well, there's never a dull moment. . . ." Her dark look made him chuckle. "You've always had a reputation for pulling off risky ventures, escaping one insane situation after another. I always thought it was just bar talk."

"Trust me, it *was*."

"What are you going to do about the armiger? Think we can trust it—him? Hell, I don't even know what to call it."

"Me neither. He, I guess. I think, for now, we don't exactly have a choice. He said he needed the humans from the *Rubicon*. Whatever he plans, he can't do it alone. He needs us, and he needs us alive."

"Which sounds pretty damn ominous."

"We need to find a way to shut him down if it comes to that, because he's not dragging us back to Earth."

"You think that's what he wants?"

"Well, yeah. You heard him. Earth was the last place the Librarian was known to be. There wasn't enough time for her to leave once the Halo rings were fired. Yet the armiger, as this Guilty Spark character, tells the officers of the *Rubicon* he thinks she's alive. He had to know the story might get back to ONI. So why divulge the plan? Why give an entire history lesson to the very organization that will most likely try to stop you? And if not stop you, at least get to the Librarian first?"

Ram looked thoughtful for a minute, then said, "You think he wanted them to know? You think he lied?"

She nodded and then shrugged, unsure. "Yes and no. I don't know. But God help us if he's telling the truth, because nothing good can come from liberating an ancient goddess from the grave."

Unable to concentrate on anything but the armiger, Rion gave up trying and looked on screen to find him. He was back in the cargo hold. She watched him for a moment as he sorted through the salvage they'd pulled from the *Rubicon*. The pieces he was holding should have required a grav compensator, but he seemed to manage with ease. The only thing hindering him was his damaged leg.

She made her way down to the hold, and sat on one of the lower steps. The armiger worked a few moments longer, sorting and tinkering—why, she couldn't say—before acknowledging her by stopping what he was doing to stare at her. When he did, she gestured for him to take a break. Wordlessly, he complied, partly leaning against the edge of one of the locked grav carts and folding his metal hands in front of him.

The tale he'd revealed made her see him differently—a strange contrast of metal and hard light with the memories and experiences of a human and an AI.

"What exactly do you need humans for?" she finally asked.

He was quiet for a long moment, and she had to wonder if he was searching for a believable lie. "As you saw and heard, the Librarian imprinted within mankind the means and the desire to claim the Mantle of Responsibility. She gifted all that is Forerunner to you. As such, you can, by virtue of your DNA, unlock access to certain artifacts that I cannot. This is why I need you once we reach Triniel, and then once more on Earth."

Earth wasn't a surprise. Triniel, however, was a name unknown to her. "Triniel is the Forerunner world you're taking us to?" He nodded. "And the story you told to the *Rubicon* crew—did they have time to pass it along to ONI before the crash?"

"A data stream packet *was* sent out. It would have traveled a great distance until it was captured by the nearest comm network, then relayed to the proper authority."

"So the answer is yes—ONI knows what we know."

"Oh, they know much more than that."

Rion filed that enigmatic answer away. "If they believe you, they'll be expecting you to return to Earth. Is that what you wanted?" No response. "You showed them your hand."

"Showed them my hand?"

"You made your intentions clear."

He paused and tilted his head in a thoughtful gesture. "Did I?" he said nonchalantly. "It is hard to remember. . . ."

"Bullshit."

Those large blue eyes seemed to study her for a long time. And then he did something surprising. He laughed. It was a strange sound—alien and synthetic, of course, but tinged with a note of his former humanity. "Trust is a hard thing to give, Captain Forge. Harder still to earn. You could leave me at Triniel, but I don't think you will."

"Why's that?"

"Because you and I are after the same thing. You wish to find your father. And I wish to find my . . . mother, so to speak. We will do it together. Forerunner and human. How it once was and should have always been. I am not a fragment like your recovered AI, Little Bit. If there is anyone able to find your father's ship, it is me. That *is* what you want, is it not?"

She gave a solemn nod.

"You help me, Captain Forge, be my access, and I will return the favor. I do not wish to fight you or bend you to my will. I wish only to continue my search and do what must be done. And if that means helping you with your own task, and in retrieving your personal possessions, I will do so." He chuckled. "There is time."

"You sound very sure of yourself."

"When Bornstellar came to Earth, he was an adventurer, a treasure hunter, full of hope and a deep need and love for discovery.

He could no more refuse his calling than you. And I was . . ."

A pause.

"Was what?"

"An opportunist, a thief . . . young, like your Niko, though much less intelligent at the time, I admit. I was led by something much larger than myself, though I did not know it then. I see you and your crew . . . and I cannot help but see the shadows and ghosts of a life taken from me, a life of adventure and friendships, a life that could have been."

He fell into silence, and despite her desire to remain detached, Rion couldn't help but feel some empathy for what had been taken from him, and what had become of him—the terrors he'd seen and the tortures committed upon him, the losses, the loneliness.

A quiet filled the cargo hold.

"Look," she said after a time. "I'm sorry . . . for what happened to you. What they did to you."

His strange glowing eyes stared at her for a very long time, and she wondered if anyone had ever said that to him before.

Hell, when he'd paralleled his early life with Niko's, it put him on a very human level. She couldn't imagine Niko going through something similar. Chakas had been about the same age that Niko was now when he was kidnapped by the Didact, taken from Earth, imprisoned, tortured . . . Chakas had watched these "gods" make extinction-level choices for the entire galaxy. He'd been used and broken, compartmentalized, and then left alone for ages. . . .

"Thank you, Captain," he said, then stood and turned away from her to resume his task.

Rion watched him for a moment, and then pushed to her feet to leave him with his timeworn thoughts and his memories.

CHAPTER 26

A
s Rion entered the lounge, she drew up short at the sight of
Niko and the armiger leaning over the table, heads nearly
touching. She'd neither seen nor spoken to him since their
last conversation in the hold. He had spent much of that time with
Niko and Lessa for company, winning over her crew—not that it
took much where Niko was concerned.

At her entry, Niko glanced over his shoulder as the armiger
straightened and took one step back from the table. In the cargo
hold, his size was manageable, but here in the lounge, all three
meters of him took up a lot of space.

Rion drew closer and saw a holographic image of a human hovering above the table. It was a young man Niko's age with bronze skin,
dark eyes, and black hair down to his shoulders, wearing a wrap
around his waist—linen, perhaps—and leather sandals on his feet.

"This is him. This is our armiger," Niko explained, clearing his throat. "Chakas . . . before the Forerunners made him into a machine."

"Yes, I know. His image was in the feed when he told us his story." She raised a dubious eyebrow and headed to the food dispenser, knowing where this little endeavor was going, and supposing it was only a matter of time. "So you're building an avatar," she said, selecting a ready-made bowl of rice for her meal.

"Well, yeah. Seemed like the next step," Niko answered as she retrieved her warm bowl, removed the packaging, and stirred it. "This way he'll be able to populate throughout the ship without dragging his armiger body around and trying to squeeze into small places. No offense," he said to the armiger.

"None taken."

The last thing Rion wanted was an ancient being popping in at will from every holopad and system panel on her ship. As she stirred her food, she regarded the armiger with a frown. Something was different about him, but she wasn't sure what. It was in the face and angles . . . they looked somehow less severe, softer.

Ram entered in his pajamas, sleep still clinging to his eyes. He grunted at them, completely uninterested in what was happening at the table, and went straight for the coffee dispenser.

Niko sat on the edge of the table, studying the avatar. "We just have to find the right look."

"What's wrong with that one?" she asked, leaning against the counter.

"Well, that's the *old* him. He *was* Chakas, yes. And he was a monitor. But now he's both. He's more. He needs a new persona—right, Spark?"

"Spark?" Rion blurted, nearly choking on a mouthful of rice.

"Why can't you have an open mind?" Niko said, highly exasperated.

"I have an open mind."

Ram snorted.

Rion shot him a look. She didn't have to wonder whose idea it was to start this little venture, because it sure as hell had Niko written all over it. But as she ate and considered—*with an open mind*—the idea did have its appeal.

Dealing with an avatar was far more comfortable than with the alien creature in front of them. It wasn't the size or hard light or alloy that unsettled her; it was the absence of facial expression. There were times when she could read emotion, noting that his light tended to get brighter if he found interest or annoyance in something. His tone and body language were easy to read, but he often clammed up, and then Rion didn't have a clue what he was doing or thinking or what his emotional state might be.

And for a creature she didn't trust, that was a hard thing to accept.

"No, you don't," Niko said, after a long moment.

Rion frowned again as wariness crept through her thoughts. It was a mistake, Niko welcoming the armiger with open arms, not knowing his true agenda. His time on the ship was temporary. They had a deal, and once that was done, the crew and the armiger would part ways—if his word was any good.

Despite her reservations, she couldn't bring herself to rain on Niko's good mood. In the days since the armiger had been brought on board, the old Niko had begun to resurface from his grief. He was seeing the good in everything, the possibility in everything. He had purpose. Drive.

Both he and Less had been struggling since Cade's death, understandably. And part of Rion had worried that Cade's passing would change them so completely that they'd lose everything that made them who they were. Now she could see a glimmer of hope.

"Fine," she said, trying to be open-minded, but she drew the line at *Spark*. She had to wonder what the armiger thought about that. She turned her attention on him. "So—Spark, huh?"

The armiger dipped its alloy head, which caught the light. The alloy seemed in better shape than when they had pulled him from the wreck, less weathered, the color more dark gray than black now, though that could just be the illumination in the lounge.

"That name will do for now," he said.

"No. No. No." Ram banged his forehead against the dispenser, cajoling the brewer to stop sputtering the coffee and actually pour it.

Before Rion could wrap her head around the shifting appearance of the armiger, Lessa walked in with a load of laundry and set the basket down beside the counter that held the built-in steamer. She opened the flat panel, tossed the clothes inside, shut it, selected her preferences, and then looked at the gathering with curiosity. She'd yet to tame her tight blond curls, and they seemed to hover around her head like a weightless cloud.

"What's going on?" she asked, approaching the table.

"Does he look different to you?" Rion asked.

"Who, Spark?"

Rion rolled her eyes. "Yes, the armiger."

Less stared at him. She and Niko had spent way more time with the thing than Rion had. Perhaps they hadn't noticed at all.

"Are you repairing yourself?" Rion asked him suddenly.

"He is not repairing himself," Niko said excitedly, eyes growing round. "He's *transfiguring*. He's been doing it since we brought him on board, little by little."

"Transfiguring into what?" Rion asked, standing straighter.

"This form is a soldier," the armiger answered.

"And he prefers not to look like one," Niko said, "that's all."

"The ability for armigers to transfigure was quite common," the armiger explained. "My alloy is made up of metals and machine cells, which interface with my artificial neural framework. However, the interface is severely damaged. Once we get to Triniel, I will have the tools to repair the damage."

Less slid into a chair. "I can help with an avatar," she said. "I'm pretty good with stuff like this." She cracked her knuckles and critically eyed the avatar.

Niko narrowed his eyes. "He doesn't want to appear human, Less."

"You don't?" she asked the armiger.

Rion watched the exchange with curiosity and conflicting emotions. Smart AIs were a common enough occurrence these days that most everyone knew they exhibited emotions and preferences, developed their own unique personalities, and often chose to represent as human. Rion had come across dozens in her lifetime. The armiger, in many ways, was no exception. He had his own sense of humor, preferences, and no doubt a wealth of other emotions.

But he was also quite singular. Complicated. Untrustworthy. Alien.

Maybe Niko was on to something and an avatar was a step in the right direction, or at least a more comfortable one for the crew.

"For now, we need to settle on an avatar," Niko said.

Rion finished eating and cleared her bowl. When she turned around again, a new holograph was hovering above the table. It was a nearly identical version of the armiger—though maybe a bit softer around the edges and hard angles.

"What do you think, Captain?" the avatar asked, the voice sounding more human than ever.

"I think we created a monster."

His manner seemed to deflate.

"No, it's not a bad thing," Lessa assured him quickly while shooting Rion a glare, as did Niko. At least the two were finally agreeing on something. "It's just an expression. Please search the phrase. I promise it's not bad."

"I see," the armiger's avatar said at last. "Nevertheless . . ." He manifested a silvery orb in his hand with an eye of blue. It was a scaled down version of 343 Guilty Spark. "I have been a monster," he said, staring at the image for a long moment before pressing the orb into his chest, where it disappeared, leaving only a vague dark gray impression behind. "To remind myself what I am capable of, and of the horror that I can, and have, inflicted."

Lessa leaned in and gave him a warmhearted, encouraging smile, her chin resting in her hands. "Well, I think it's perfect. Nice to meet you, Spark."

"Thank you, Lessa."

Ram passed with barely a glance, sipped his coffee, and said, "Avatar is fine. Name is fine. It's not that hard, people." And then he walked out.

CHAPTER 27

A fter the avatar rendering, I continue my work in the cargo hold upgrading what I can in the Ace of Spades's system, pending our arrival at Triniel. I direct Ram Chalva, using my armiger body to aid him in implementing repairs and manual upgrades. While I do this, several versions of my avatar linger with the rest of the crew. One is at Niko's desk as we work on upgrading his drones, Michelle and Diane. Another converses with Lessa. We talk about star charts, navigation, and which color would look best painted on the lounge walls. Another avatar appears on the tactical table on the bridge while the captain sits in her chair, absorbed in checking systems and stores.

I study her features. I have noted that she usually braids her dark hair and wears it twisted at the nape of her neck. Today it is braided in a loose rope and hangs over her shoulder. She attempts to be severe and commanding, erring often on the side of quiet and aloof— sometimes harsh even—but this is just a mask she wears. She smiles *when she does not mean to, laughs out of turn, and looks upon her crew with caring.*

She also grieves deeply for her lost comrade, Cade.

I hear her some nights in the small gymnasium, hitting the equipment in anger and grief. And I sympathize.

"Your father, John Forge . . ." I say, and she looks up from her work.

"What about him?"

"You believe he is still alive."

She thinks for a long moment. "Sometimes I wonder if I'm chasing ghosts. All I know is that if I were lost, he would go to the ends of the galaxy to find me. He'd never stop."

"Forgive me for saying this, but you barely knew him."

"That's true. We missed twenty-six years together. I know it's a long shot, finding him after all this time, but if there's a chance, I have to try."

In that, we are in the same predicament. She with her father. Me with the Librarian.

"And what if he is dead?" I ask.

"Then at least I'll know the truth."

"What will you do then?"

"I don't know. Move on. Continue working, I guess."

"Your friends, the crew, they mean a lot to you."

"Yes. They do." She tilts her head and studies me, trying to see if I'm leading to some point. "As your friends meant a lot to you, I'm sure."

"The truth is, Riser and Vinnevra, Bornstellar, they are long gone. Stardust now. It is strange to have lost them so long ago, but only recently to have remembered them at all. Their loss . . . it still feels fresh."

"You really think the Librarian can bring them back?"

"Of course."

Rion bites her lip in hesitation, then says, "Sometimes when people have been gone for a long time . . . we have to consider letting them go, letting them rest in peace." Then she smiles. "Which I know is an empty sentiment coming from me, the girl who's been looking for her father for two decades."

"You have not yet said if we have an accord. Will you help me and accompany me to Earth?"

I have allowed her ample time to decide. But now I must know.

"Help me get our things back, and yes, I'll help you in return," she says.

"We have an agreement, then."

She nods. "It's a deal."

I say nothing, and she returns to her work. I continue watching her, however, wondering why I feel no guilt at my deception.

Her father is dead.

Yet I do not tell her the truth.

Sometimes we must be willing to do wrong in order to do right.

CHAPTER 28

After dropping out of slipspace three hours earlier and making a course correction to Triniel at subluminal speed, Rion was eager to get a look at the arc of blue and green now filling the viewscreen as *Ace* entered high orbit.

The planet was one and a half times the size of Venezia, with azure oceans and three emerald continents. According to the armiger, in the early days of the planet's life, the long, narrow continents had once been a connected ring of volcanic mountain ranges that had wrapped like a spiral around the planet. In time, the range had broken into three pieces. The pieces eventually cooled and the volcanic activity slowed, allowing a temperate, lush world to evolve, and creating a perfect future environment for the Forerunners to colonize.

Triniel had remained untouched since the Forerunner-Flood War.

As they descended, entire cities were revealed, poking through the canopy of green, sitting empty for a hundred thousand years. . . .

Rion had always envisioned hitting the salvage jackpot—what salvager didn't?—but this was unlike anything she could have imagined. And while it was a breathtaking sight from their lofty position, she had to remind herself to hold her interest in check. Jackpot or not, they had no idea what they'd find on the surface, nor could they be 100 percent sure of the armiger's true intent.

While Niko and Lessa had begun calling him by his newly chosen name, Rion found she couldn't just yet. To her, he'd be the armiger right up until he proved he could be trusted. He'd been right when he said trust was earned. And so far he hadn't done anything to earn theirs. Their time on Triniel, however, might just reveal the truth.

As Rion guided *Ace* into low orbit, she glanced at the tactical table where the armiger's new avatar stood with his back to her, watching the planet along with Niko, Less, and Ram.

"We are the first humans to lay eyes on this world," he said.

Ram caught her eye at the comment, but said nothing. That the armiger chose to think of himself as human was strange, seeing as how he'd decided on an avatar that was anything but.

Rion supposed that was the point. He was both, and he wasn't shying away from it.

He manifested a holograph of the planet on the tactical table, complete with transparent mountain ranges giving way to cityscapes of soaring spires and vast complexes. "This is our destination." He moved the planet with a flick of his hand and zoomed in on a facility built into the side of a mountain at the very tip of the central continent. "This is a Builder facility. It will have everything we require."

"But you haven't been here before, right?" Niko asked, fascinated with the view.

"That is right. I learned of Triniel through data acquired during my time as monitor of Installation Zero Four, though at the time this data was compartmentalized, as much of my acquired knowledge was then. There was a great deal I learned through many sources."

"What kind of sources?" Niko asked, turning away from the view.

"My fellow monitors. The Array's data stores. Through visitors to my installation, my explorations, communications, and alliances. . . . Every interaction is full of data, more than most can fathom," he said.

Ram turned away from the viewscreen and stared at the holo-image with unreserved disbelief. "Never thought I'd see something like this. . . . We could spend a lifetime in just one building. Imagine all the day-to-day machines, power sources, armor . . . the list is endless."

"Guys, this is *way* better than a debris field," Niko said, joining him at the table.

Rion couldn't argue with that, but she wasn't sold just yet. When things looked too good to be true, they usually were. "All right, let's head in." She exchanged a look with the armiger and gave him a nod to take control.

Ace descended through the atmosphere, and soon they were picking up signs of life. "Marine, mammalian, avian . . ." the armiger said as he monitored the sensors. "How encouraging! Triniel has flourished."

They broke through clouds and the central mountain range came into view, enormous and jagged and trimmed in a carpet of green that went all the way down from its slopes to the oceans on either side. Ahead of them, a large winged creature glided on outstretched wings toward a misty valley below. The thing was nearly as big as *Ace*.

As they continued their descent, flying closer to the mountains, massive roots appeared, as thick as old sequoia, clinging to the rock. From the roots, large spikes grew at random angles, the sharp ends pierced with limp shapes and bleached bones—land and sea animals in different stages of decomposition.

The macabre mixing with the surrounding beauty was a strange and unexpected sight. Rion straightened in her chair. In the spaces between the spikes were hundreds of translucent egg sacs, holding what appeared to be embryos of whatever life form had put its rotting food on display.

"Impressive," the armiger said. "These were once small birds. Similar to the butcher-birds of Earth, they impale their food on thorns, saving it to feed the young and to display for a potential mate. The more carcasses, the better the chances of mating."

"Well, they're not small anymore," Less said, pointing to another huge winged creature perched at the base of one of the spikes, pecking at the guts of one of its pierced meals.

"Are they territorial?" Rion asked.

"Oh, most certainly," the armiger answered, admiring the great winged creature.

"Then let's keep our distance."

The peaks gave way to a sloping valley and a high plateau that supported a large city with soaring towers of steep geometric angles, their silvery-gray metal still gleaming in places. There were bridges that spanned impossible heights, and other buildings of smooth polished stone, trapezoidal in shape, with flecks of some luminous mineral catching the light. Everything was straight lines and angles, though not entirely in pristine condition. Massive evolved roots had snaked their way around the skyscrapers, creating thorny ribbons around many buildings, and creating natural bridges from one tower to the next.

The alien birds ruled this area, that much was clear, but even the overgrowth couldn't diminish the size and scale and beauty of Triniel's ancient structures.

Ram's whistle filled the bridge. "Have to hand it to them," he said in appreciation. "The Forerunners sure knew how to build a city."

Despite the grisly sight of avian meals pierced on spikes, there was astonishing beauty everywhere they looked. Trees with draping limbs were covered in small pink blossoms, millions of them, all over the city, creating a wash of green and pink and metal and root.

For a moment Rion forgot her trepidation, and let awe and the rarity of what they were seeing wash over her. The blossoms rose en masse into the air, carried on breezes coming in from the coast, creating a dance of pink clouds that gently rose and fell all over the area.

"Incredible," the armiger murmured thoughtfully. "I believe the toxin created a divergent evolutionary path for not only the birds, but for all the flora and fauna as well."

Rion's good feelings faded. "What do you mean, *toxin*?"

The armiger shifted to face her. "In the final days of the

war, the inhabitants of Triniel were in the direct path of the Flood. There was no escaping their fate, no help forthcoming, nowhere to run. . . . In an act of defiance, and some would say immense courage, they released a planet-wide toxin, depriving the Flood of its food source, and thus its potential for enormous growth." He paused. "This was a dead world before the Flood arrived."

The mood on the bridge fell somber.

"They all died?" Lessa asked, eyes going wide. "Mass suicide?"

"Yes. They all died. It was an end preferable to what awaited them. They weren't the only planet to do so."

All those towers and buildings and homes—they weren't abandoned or empty; they were filled with the dust of millions. The beauty below them, the untouched growth, the flowers and roots, were a memorial of a world gone collectively silent.

The remainder of the flight was quiet as well, and eventually they arrived at the tip of the continent and the slope that held the Builder's seed facility, which overlooked the blue sea.

As the armiger navigated *Ace* beneath a giant root that spanned from one mountain ridge to another and then came around to a docking station covered in overgrowth, small debris, moss, and flowering vines, Rion couldn't help but feel small in relation to the facility and the nature around her. Like a tiny fly, they came to rest in the place of ancient, spacefaring gods.

A place ripe for plunder.

A place that could be their own tomb if they weren't careful.

Rion drew comfort from the routine task of suiting up in the locker room with the crew, grabbing her rifle and handgun from the armory, and then unlocking her grav cart. This was what she knew, and she could do it with her eyes closed. After hanging her tool bag on the cart hook, she comm-checked the crew, then waited at the head of the ramp while the airlock doors opened and the ramp lowered.

The armiger's footsteps rang out behind her, sending goose bumps up her arms. She glanced over her shoulder as the tall metal figure appeared, its hard light glowing and reminding her that he belonged here among the ruins and ancient technology.

He drew to a stop beside her. "Ready, Captain?"

She faked a smile; yes, she'd run all the tests herself, but she couldn't help but ask, "Are you certain the global toxin's inactive at this point?"

"Quite certain. It has long since dissipated."

"After you," she said, and allowed the armiger to proceed down the ramp ahead of her. Rion gestured to the crew, and then they were on the move, heading into the facility and fanning out.

The g's on Triniel were a little heavier than optimal, but it was manageable, and the atmosphere was good. Boots crunched over dead leaves and debris. Beyond the docking station, the calls of wildlife and alien seabirds echoed. The warm air was fragrant with a mix of flowers and sea. As they entered the structure, familiar glyphs appeared on the walls and floor.

The armiger moved ahead, approaching a console, which Rion immediately recognized. It was very similar to the one they'd found in the ruins of the debris field, complete with domed pad. He stood aside and gestured for Rion to place a hand on the pad.

"What will happen?"

"Power returns to the facility."

Staring into the eyes of a one-hundred-thousand-year-old AI to try to find the truth felt like an exercise in futility, but Rion did it anyway. He regarded her with understanding. "Do you remember our conversation about trust, Captain?"

"I wouldn't call it a conversation," she said, frowning.

His shrug said the choice was hers. He wouldn't force her. How nice of him.

He'd been right when he said back on the ship that trust was a hard thing to give. It was especially difficult for the jaded, for the ones schooled in hard knocks and painful lessons. But the trust she had to put in him now wouldn't exactly be freely given. They hadn't come to Triniel because of a mutual decision, and if they wanted to get home in one piece, playing the armiger's game was a necessary evil, whether that game was an honest one or not.

"Might as well get this side trip started," she muttered, slapping her palm to the dome's cool surface.

Instantly the console lit up. The facility came to life; glyphs and lines and lighting activated in sequence like dominoes, illuminating a vast circular chamber with a central vertical cavity that rose high into the mountain and dropped deep into its depths. The scope of the place exceeded Rion's imagination, more expansive and strange and awe-inspiring than any ruin she'd ever visited.

Only this wasn't exactly a ruin.

It was, like everything on Triniel, a place in waiting.

As they approached a railing that overlooked the cavity, a spiral walkway ringing its interior wall sprang to life, lights winking on one after another in a dizzying display, from somewhere high above them and disappearing far below. One story after another was illuminated inside the cavity, displaying not only the walkway but hundreds of glass-fronted rooms built into the cylindrical wall.

Several stories below, an ancient piece of technology was revealed, suspended in the center of the cavity by clamps attached to long spokes driven deep into the rock.

Niko leaned over the railing. "What is that?"

The armiger leaned over the railing to get a look. "A translight engine. There are several engines below that one. The cavity is very deep—"

Ram's laugh suddenly echoed through the space, sounding a little dazed and giddy. "A translight engine. Oh, no big deal. Just a translight engine. . . ." He turned away from the railing and pulled the rolled cigarette from behind his ear, giving it a deep sniff, then chuckled again.

If there was any occasion that called for a celebratory smoke, this was it. But he simply rolled it between his fingers with a disbelieving grin.

"This is unreal," Lessa murmured.

Rion studied the enormous chamber with a feeling she couldn't quite name. But it wasn't excitement. The technology here was extraordinary, and ONI's warning and Kip's loss on Sedra weighed heavily on her mind. "Where to?" she asked the armiger, wanting to move things along.

She waited while he accessed a terminal nearby. Now that power was restored, he didn't need her DNA to search through the terminal's knowledge banks. "Third level below us," he finally answered, staying right where he was.

Rion moved closer. "What are you doing?"

"Powering the communications satellites in orbit. It will take some moments for the relays here to send the signals, then further time for the satellites to come online."

"Amazing that things still work though," Lessa said, wandering around behind them.

"The Forerunners built cities to last millions of years," he told her matter-of-factly. "The cities of Triniel can be powered on at any time . . . like flipping a switch. It all comes back to life."

"Let's not get ahead of ourselves," Rion told them before they got any bright ideas. She edged closer to the armiger. "Why are you accessing the satellites?"

"To send a message."

"What kind of message?"

The armiger withdrew from the terminal. "Please, follow me."

Rion stepped in front of him before he could walk off and ignore her question.

"We all have our secrets, Captain," he said, staring down at her from his lofty height. "Do I demand you share yours with me? We have a deal. Or have you forgotten it already?"

"No. I haven't."

"Then that is settled." He moved around her and headed to a circular platform nearby, which was slightly raised from the floor and emitting a soft blue light.

No, it's not *settled*, she thought, as he stepped onto the platform and motioned for the others to join him. *Not by a long shot.*

Once everyone was gathered, he pressed the panel nearby.

In the blink of an eye, they were suddenly several levels below, standing on a different platform, and bent over, gasping—all but the armiger and Ram, oddly enough, who stood there just fine and looking at them with a triumphant grin at having escaped the physical ramifications of instant teleportation.

Rion scowled at him and stumbled from the platform, found the nearest console, and leaned against it, needing to ground herself, to hold on to something solid and real. She felt ripped apart and put back together, and her body didn't know if it wanted to vomit, faint, or explode.

"What the hell was that?" Niko asked, out of breath.

"Translocation platform." The armiger walked past them and headed for a long corridor dug into the rock.

Rion lifted her head, exchanging looks of disbelief with her crew, before she bit back her physical distress and followed the armiger.

The first chamber they entered appeared sterile and clean, with tall tables set beneath strange devices hanging on tracks above. "This is the laboratory where crystal was cut." The armiger crossed to a long wall where neat illuminated shelves held shiny rectangular boxes of varying sizes. The armiger reached out and selected the smallest one, no bigger than a finger, and opened it.

Light spilled from the container. He snapped the lid shut. "This one will do. But I must warn you all: even a sliver such as this creates spatial distortion, exposing you to radiation and disorientation. It is capable of bending space and time, energy and gravity, and is not to be handled under any circumstance except within the confines of the box."

Niko was immediately fascinated and stepped closer to the shelves. "If all these flakes are so powerful, how did they handle cutting it? I'm assuming they cut the flakes from a bigger piece, right?"

"The Source Crystal, also called the Mother Crystal by the cutters. It does not reside here—rather, larger pieces were cut from it and transported to manufacturing facilities across the ecumene. The cutter would then slice off flakes from the pieces for use in ships, from the smallest craft to the largest. Those devices hanging on the tracks are crystal cutters."

"So where is Mama Crystal these days?" Niko asked as the others were examining items.

"I do not know. The location was one of the best-kept secrets in the ecumene. Only the cutters knew, and they would die rather than reveal its location. Crystals are inherently dangerous." He lifted a metal hand, ushering them away from the boxes. "Therefore I cannot allow you to salvage these. We have taken only one, which will act as an accompaniment to the upgrade seed, and even then it will be stored in its protective casing until the upgrade process."

Rion wasn't ready to entertain the idea of upgrading just yet, but there was no point in arguing about it now.

They left the room and headed to another stomach-altering translocation pad to another level, and the jump did not get better a second time around. After recovering, they followed the armiger into another laboratory of polished white walls and counters that seemed to have been carved from one piece of stone—or perhaps it was metal, Rion wasn't sure. As they entered, massive holographic displays along the walls powered on, filling with glyphs, blueprints of ships, and other elements of design.

"This is where they drafted the design seeds," Rion guessed as she stared at one of the large projections. It was the blueprint for an incredible angular ship with three long wings, unlike anything she had ever seen before. She had a deep appreciation for starships—their design, power, lines—she loved everything about spaceflight. And finding designs from an ancient advanced race was nothing short of extraordinary.

"Yes. The seeds are codes, drawn with hard light filaments and coded with quantum commands."

The armiger stood next to her and studied the blueprint that had caught Rion's attention. "A keyship," he told her, regarding it for a long moment before moving on and accessing one of the glass panels on the counter workstation. Another screen lit up with strange glyphs and patterns and glowing strings. The screen itself was an incredible bit of technology. But when the armiger reached *into* the screen and began pulling and manipulating light strings, she was stunned and her jaw dropped. She watched, fascinated, as a blueprint of a *Mariner*-class ship appeared in the background of the screen. The armiger had somehow put *Ace*'s specs into the screen and was injecting light strings and code into those specs quicker than she could keep up with.

"This will take some time," he said over his shoulder. "I will complete the design seed and then repair the injury to this armiger's neural framework. You are free to salvage this level."

The *Ace* crew left him and headed farther down the corridor.

"So . . . anyone think this is strange?" Niko asked.

Rion glanced over her shoulder. "What do you mean?"

"I don't know. The whole place, the whole damn planet—it's one giant grave. Looting here . . ."

"Feels a little wrong?" Lessa finished.

"Yeah, something like that," he said, then gave them a wry smile. "Look at us. Salvagers with a conscience."

Finding Forerunner artifacts was the highest achievement for a salvager—they were rare, and took effort and time and money to find. Ram was right: being here was a dream come true—and yet there was nothing in her grav cart.

Rion and Ram exchanged looks. They'd both been in the salvage business a long time. They'd looted wreck sites, tried to be respectful of the dead, following protocol wherever they came across remains. But they had to eat, they had to buy fuel and supplies, and couldn't be squeamish or let their emotions get in the way of a job.

Even though she too was reluctant, she forced the feeling away. "Try to put it out of your mind," she said, knowing the idea of planet-wide suicide was hard to forget, but they did need to focus and get this little side trip done. *And get back control of my ship.* "Anyone who was here is now long gone. We do this like any other job. Concentrate on restoring the nest eggs ONI took from us."

An hour later, they had each filled their grav carts with small devices and artifacts they'd found sitting on or within lab workstations—none of which they could identify. Everything they picked up was sleek and alien and way above their ability to understand. They'd need the armiger's help to classify their small trove of salvage. It had been a slow process and they hadn't gotten very far in terms of exploring because there was so much to marvel at and so very little they actually wanted to disturb.

As they headed back to the seed-building lab, Niko veered down a small corridor they'd skipped before. Like all the other places they'd seen so far, the walls were polished and etched with straight lines and glyphs. The doorway at the end was open, its frame tall and trapezoid in shape and carved like everything else.

The rooms inside led one into the next, different than the labs they'd been in, more intimate, with seating and rugs on the floor, geometric art on the walls . . . They were drawn into one space after another . . . . Every room they entered seemed frozen in time, as if someone had just left: things still left on a table, drinking vessels, utensils . . .

Then they came upon the remains.

Four sets of headless armor—stylized shoulder and arm guards, torso plates etched with symbols, leg braces and boots, bound by the molds of their former hosts—remained poised in a tableau on a long couch, shells of a couple embracing, and two others turned toward each other, their gloves entwined. Four helmets sat on the cushions beside the armor as though just taken off, in order to face each other, say good-bye, whisper words of love or fear perhaps. . . . Small traces of dust and bits of bones on the armor and seat suggested that these ancient giants had decomposed to near ash, leaving behind their dust and hollow armor as markers of lives long since lost.

"Yep. I'm out of here," Lessa said, immediately turning and heading into the corridor.

There was a fifth Forerunner sitting at a lit control panel with a screen above, arms and hands stuck in a position of action, its helmet still on. A shiver went down Rion's spine. Niko stepped forward, just enough to see the panel.

He reached forward slowly and pressed the glyph under the

gloved finger. The screen shimmered to life, and they recoiled in surprise at the Forerunner staring back at them. It was a seated figure in the same armor as the deceased. Only his helmet was off.

Thanks to the story the armiger had shared, they'd seen images of Forerunners in and out of their armor, but seeing one virtually alive was astonishing. He was surprisingly . . . familiar. The facial shape and bone structure were almost identical to those of humans. The eyes were nearly the same, but the nose and mouth were very small, just slits for nostrils and tight lines for lips, and his skin was a dark gray given to tints of blue.

He began speaking, but the language was incomprehensible.

Movement by the doorway indicated Lessa had returned, lurking there as the armiger entered in behind her. He scanned the room, and then approached the screen. He touched the pad, entered commands, and it began to play again, now translated:

"The toxins are airborne. They say we won't see it, smell it, or be pained by it, only that we will grow tired and sleep. The Flood is upon us, our sensors indicating star roads already opening outside our orbital defenses. We have only hours now." He paused. *"I and two others remain here. Their spouses have joined them. Together we will shut down the facility and power down our personal ancillas to prevent them from saving us. This is our last act of defiance. The Flood will get nothing from Triniel. We stand united. We fall together."* He cleared his throat and lifted his chin. *"And may our sacrifice, all 883,489,876 of us, from the youngest to the very*

oldest, be forever stored and remembered in the sacred halls of the Domain."

The screen faded.

"I have completed my tasks," the armiger said in the ensuing silence.

"Good," Rion said in a clipped tone, turning away from the scene. "Let's get the hell out of this tomb."

Before they left, the armiger paused at the terminal on the main level, checking to see if the communications relay was now operational. Rion waited for him to send out the message he'd mentioned earlier, but he hesitated.

"Once the relay is working," Lessa said, stepping next to the armiger, "others will find Triniel, won't they?"

The armiger was quiet for a long moment, and then dipped his head. "Yes. Eventually."

She sighed, wistful. "Seems a shame. . . ."

The *Ace of Spades* flew over the cities of pink and green and metal and root, then across mountain ranges and ocean, and finally up into the atmosphere, past communications arrays and satellites that hadn't been used in a hundred thousand years.

The armiger had pulled them offline before they could reboot. Turned out he had a conscience after all.

Triniel would remain a lost planet, in a lost star system, in a lost sector of the galaxy, free from mass exploitation.

As it well should be.

CHAPTER 29

We leave the system, and Captain Forge sets course for a small moon called Myer's Moon, in the Shaps system, a familiar waypoint the crew uses to refuel, restock, and rest between missions.

Ten days pass before we arrive, make a quick visit to the outpost, and then settle on a wide stretch of beach near a shallow sea. I used the time to engage my neural interface and guide my armiger's machine cells to begin the transfiguration process I desire. I made it a slow process to ease the crew into accepting something other than what they have grown used to.

Had the ship upgrades proceeded, it would have taken us mere hours to arrive, but the captain is stubborn and afraid of change. Change is a force she cannot control, so she ignores it and instead looks for ways around the obvious course of action.

I do not need to convince her or push her in the right direction. She will come around.

I know her story, and I know her life will never be as it once was. She has found too much and lost too much to ever go back.

She understands this too.

Once the ship powers down, the airlock doors release and the cargo ramp descends. The metallic echo of my footsteps fills the hold as Niko and Lessa run through the ship, dressed in very little, towels tucked beneath their arms.

In minutes, they are off the ship and racing across the sand straight into the water.

I walk to the head of the cargo ramp and marvel at this very human picture framed by the metal plating of the ship. Their laughter echoes over gentle waves as iridescent moon crabs tiptoe for shelter and birds cry overhead.

It is their spot, they say. Discovered many years ago.

Captain Forge appears next to me. She is wearing very little as well. Her hands are full with towels and a blanket.

I do not communicate with her, and I find quite abruptly that I am not in a sharing mood.

Ram Chalva arrives with a grav cart loaded with chairs, drinks, and food. The captain places her items in the cart, and then we are headed at a sedate pace to the beach.

Later, after swimming has exhausted them, Ram stands and smiles at me, a flash of white through his dark beard. "I'm going to collect wood for a fire. Come help me," he says, walking off.

I follow him into the rocky landscape sparsely populated with coniferous trees, curious at the cause of my maudlin state. I pick up dry sticks.

"This is very different from space," he notes.

There is a wisdom in him that is not present in the others.

"Yes," I say.

It has been a very . . . human day.

My armiger feels unnatural here. In space, it is indeed different. I am among technological advances such as myself. But here on the beach, I stand out. I cannot swim or drink or eat . . . though I do remember those experiences.

"You were human once," he says, hunting for tinder.

I was. I am.

I do not know how to answer.

"You are whatever you choose to be, Spark."

Ram Chalva is a watchful man, the kind who sees into the heart of things much more easily than most.

A loud scream echoes over the rocks, followed by laughter. We step to the edge and see Niko and Less half-carrying, half-dragging the captain back into the water.

"You ever think of giving up your quest?" he asks me.

I turn to him, prepared with an immediate denial, but the words seem stuck in my vocal components. Finally I manage, "No, of course not." But there is no fire behind it. "Do you ever consider giving up yours?"

I mean, of course, his desire for revenge against Gek 'Lhar.

He regards me for a long moment, then dips his head in acknowledgment.

We return to foraging for wood.

Night falls, and the sky shifts through stages of orange, pink, purple, and then an inky blue. Stars appear. The campfire sparks and snaps and shoots embers into the night. It is a lovely sound, the sound of fire. The sound of friends. The sound of laughter.

I have joined them via my avatar, using Niko's datapad, and am presently admiring the way the starlight reflects on the dark water.

Lessa turns to me and says: "Do you think there's a God? I mean, an omniscient and omnipotent one?"

Before I can answer, Niko laughs and rolls his eyes. Lessa's expression darkens.

"I am not old enough or wise enough to know such things," I say.

"Did you believe in a god in Marontik," she continues, "when you were human?"

"Many believed in the animal spirits who reigned over the Western Grasslands: the Jaguar, the Crocodile, the Great Elephant, and Abada the Rhinoceros. But above all, we believed in the Librarian, the supreme Lifeshaper. She was our goddess, our mother—kind, loving, and beautiful beyond compare. She rode on a great starboat, and appeared to us when we were infants. In Marontik, there was a temple built in her name, and my sisters served there as prayer maidens."

"You really think she's alive?" Niko asks.

"I know so."

"You sound like Rion," Lessa says with a smile. "I guess sometimes you just know, right?"

Captain Forge gives her a nod and there is a small smile on her face, but there is also sadness. She does not know if her father is alive; she only hopes.

Like me, she burns with the need for answers. All this time, all these years—long years in Rion's time frame—John Forge has been gone, yet she cannot give up the search. He is family. So she exists on hope.

We are the same in this. And the loneliness, the need to connect with family and loved ones is strong. It drives us both.

Guilt suddenly washes over me. Perhaps it is the moment, the connection I currently feel with her. I have the answers she seeks.

I should tell her the truth.

Is that not the kind thing to do?

I watch her smile at the group's conversation, her eyes bright, a twist to her lips, finding humor in small things. . . .

What will it do to her? I wonder. What will she do when she learns he is truly dead, that her relentless search all these years has been in vain?

"Rion . . . ?" *I begin before I can stop myself.*

Her head turns. The light of the fire reflects in her dark eyes. She looks younger, not so burdened by worries at the moment.

I find I cannot get the words out, cannot be the deliverer of such pain.

Nor can I stomach the thought of losing what little trust she now has in me. I did not complete the revival of the communications array on Triniel. And in doing so, I did something good. I have gained their trust. I cannot lose it now.

"Is something on your mind?" *she says.*

"It is nothing important," *I reply.*

No.

The time is not yet right for truths and pain.

CHAPTER 30

Myer's Moon, Shaps system, July 2557

The next morning, Rion woke with a long stretch and a decent attitude. The sunlight and fresh air had done her a world of good. After taking a quick shower and grabbing an energy ration, she decided to link up to the local commsat in orbit and see how things looked in the salvaging world.

Once the link was established, she opened chatter, waypoint forums, and private channels, waiting for the latest news and messages and posts to download. It didn't take long, and soon she was browsing the trader and salvaging channels.

Apparently she was the subject of several posts.

Gek 'Lhar had placed a very large bounty on her and the *Ace of Spades* crew.

Very, very large.

Well, that's what she got for shooting him in the face and

laughing at him as an invaluable Forerunner debris field exploded around his ears.

She rubbed a hand down her face and let out a heavy sigh.

Could be worse.

There were several messages from Nor. About favors, Gek, and . . . a message from Agent Hahn caught her eye. She opened it and read what was there.

Well, well, well. Now Hahn wanted to make a trade. He was offering the return of Little Bit's projections, their personal items from the warehouse outside of New Tyne, and the credits ONI had seized from their bank accounts. In exchange, he was asking for the salvage they'd taken from Geranos-a.

He crafted a convincing argument, she'd give him that. He wrote about good relations, no underhanded tactics—just a simple trade, and then they'd go their separate ways, his only objective being securing the salvage and clearing them of all crimes against the UNSC Salvage Directive.

What a load of crap.

There was nothing simple about it.

ONI would be out to capture the salvage, along with Rion, her crew, and her ship. There was absolutely no way they'd just let them dump the salvage, no harm, no foul. ONI had to be sure they were getting it *all*, and in order to do that, interrogations and a ship-wide search would have to be conducted.

As she ate her energy bar, her thoughts spun.

She didn't just want their things returned. She wanted the Office of Naval Intelligence off their backs for good.

Later, Rion headed outside in search of the others. She found them down the beach by the tide pools with fishing poles made of thin sticks.

Climbing the rocks, she watched them for a moment, noting that there was nothing big enough in the tide pools to actually eat. She put her hands on her hips. "And this is what we call an exercise in futility, children," she said, smiling.

Lessa's line snagged a moon crab. "Oh really? Who's futile now?" She flung the thing out of the water with a squeak, aiming directly for Rion.

Rion jumped back as the stunned little crab sailed past her and plopped into another pool. Laughing, she caught sight of the armiger sitting atop the rocks above them and made her way up to join him.

"Enjoying the break?"

He didn't answer the question, saying instead, "I had forgotten how much I once liked the water." Since Triniel, he had been changing more and more, his alloy nearly smooth now and a luminous silvery-gray. His face was different too, she'd noticed back on the ship—his eyes bigger, kinder, if such a thing was possible, the angles less severe. "They are amusing to watch—ah, finally." He suddenly stood and called, "There are other ways to catch a fish!"

In an instant, the armiger's forearm and hand realigned, becoming a weapon and firing a gold energy beam into the waves. A second later, a large fish plopped onto the rocks, landing right at Niko's feet. The kid screamed as the fish flopped around. The siblings then engaged in an amusing wrestle to catch the thing.

The armiger sat down, chuckling as his weapon mutated back

to a hand and forearm. "I have been waiting for that fish to get close enough to the rocks to do that."

Still absorbing what she'd just witnessed—the armiger transforming its components into weapons—Rion said, "With a sense of humor like that, you fit right in." She gestured to his arm. "Could you always do that?"

"Not until I repaired my neural machine cell interface on Triniel."

So he was armed even when he wasn't. Rion stood up and brushed the sand from her rear. "Come on, I'm gathering the crew. Seems Agent Hahn is ready to make a deal."

Some time later, after Ram had built another fire and Niko was roasting the fish over the flames, Rion told them what she'd learned and what Agent Hahn wanted in return.

"You can't sell him out, not after what he's been through!" Niko said, shooting to his feet, ready to defend Spark at all costs.

"Calm down, kid," Rion said. "No one is selling anyone out. I'm just telling you what they said, not what we're going to do."

Niko turned his attention to the avatar, which had joined them via his small holopad that had been set atop the cooler, while the armiger was presently in the ship's hold. "We're not selling you out."

"I am not worried that you will."

"We know it's a trap," Rion said. "But there might be a way to go to this meeting and get our things back without being apprehended. If we set the time, pick the place, and use it to our advantage. And . . ." She drew in a deep breath. "I can't believe I'm going to say this, but we use the upgrade seed."

They stared at her with mouths agape. Niko's fish caught fire and fell into the flames. And still no one moved or spoke. Rion used a stick to move the fish off the coals. She supposed she'd earned their reaction. They all knew *Ace* held a special place in her heart, so the fact that she was willing to change it was a stunning revelation.

"To escape, we'll need a ship more advanced than or at least comparable to what ONI will bring," Rion continued.

"Rion," Lessa said. "You don't have to do this. *Ace* is your ship. . . . If you're doing this for us—"

Rion shook her head. She had given this a lot of thought. "I'm doing it for me too. I have very little left of my father, and I want it back. Everything we've been through—I don't want it to have been for nothing." She dug in the sand with her foot. "This is what we wanted. This is why we went to Geranos-a. We're in ONI's sights and that's not going to change, no matter what's decided. I don't know about you guys, but I'd really like to make them think twice about making enemies out of salvagers."

"So what's your plan?" Ram asked.

"We control every detail of how this goes down. ONI will underestimate us—they can't help it. They have no idea that we have the armiger on our side. They have no idea that he's anything more now than what he was when brought on board the *Rubicon*. We'll use all that to our advantage. And we'll give them what they think we have."

"And if things go south?" Ram asked.

"Oh, I'm counting on things going south."

Niko blinked in surprise. "Wait. We *want* things to go wrong?"

"As a distraction," the armiger surmised.

"Exactly. You all should know that Gek 'Lhar has issued a very large bounty on us, me in particular. All the salvagers, traders, and mercs are talking about it. Which means ONI will have a hard time catching us when everyone else is trying to do the same."

Niko frowned. "Sounds real safe."

"It will be, if we play it right."

"They'll have their prowler in orbit," Ram said, "maybe more than that. We might escape the meeting, but what about escaping the planet?"

"That's why we use the upgrade seed. If we're caught in space, then everything achieved on the ground will be for nothing. We need to make sure we can outrun them."

Her chest went tight with the reality of what she was saying. She didn't want to reconfigure her ship, didn't want anything to change. But things *had* changed . . . and it was high time she accepted it and started playing by new rules, not the old ones.

She had a chance to outmatch the Office of Naval Intelligence itself and get her personal items back. And now, thanks to the armiger and his upgrade seed, she'd have the capability to search the galaxy more quickly than she'd ever thought possible. With the projections returned, finding her father seemed more of a reality than ever before.

How could she turn her back on an opportunity like that?

"Yes," she finally said. "I'm sure."

"So how do we do this?" Ram asked, looking at the armiger. "What can we expect?"

"The upgrade seed will not change the outer appearance of the ship; it will only strengthen its existing materials by hard light bonding. Inside, quantum and hard light filaments will intertwine with the ship's existing systems, all directed by smart upgrade code, which I devised back on Triniel to create a custom integration between Forerunner technology and your ship's current specifications and technologies. Therefore the advancements are bound by the limitations of the ship's human design.

"The upgrade can be applied in orbit, but it is better to ground the ship and run on auxiliary power as the seed does its work. Once the process is complete, the *Ace of Spades* will have fully integrated Forerunner technologies, everything from stealth capability to upgraded weapons, comms, and navigational systems, kept within the framework of human operating functionality. The biggest feature, however, is the advance in slipspace travel. The upgrade seed will create a seamless integration between your FTL drive, Forerunner translight technology, and the slipstream flake, taking into account the materials available to work with and the size of the ship, of course."

"Well," said Niko. "As much as I loved the little guy, this leaves LB's efforts in the dust."

"Okay, so that's settled then. We'll do it here on the beach," Rion said. "I'll reply to Hahn, and then we'll get started."

CHAPTER 31

*E*veryone is asleep.

Dawn is approaching.

The upgrade process took approximately eighteen hours, fifty-three minutes, and eleven seconds. It is now complete, and the ship will prove an ample vessel in which to complete my task.

I stand at the control panel in the cargo hold and use it to access the comm satellite in orbit.

Once I enter the Juridical code into a secure message, I send and settle in to await a reply.

A warm breeze moves over the water beyond the cargo ramp. I imagine it picking up its salty scent and carrying it into the hold. The rhythmic sound of waves is quite enjoyable as well.

I let my mind wander through the present and into the deep past, the friendships made in Marontik, the courage of youth, the reckless and wild belief in invincibility. The friendships made amid fears and horrors. . . .

They are all there, waiting for me—personalities roaming in the halls of living memory. The only thing missing is me.

A reply flashes on the panel.

As expected, Catalog's designation appears.

This Catalog is the last survivor of a triad, which formed during the end of the war to investigate crimes against the Mantle and record events surrounding the Didact, the Librarian, and Bornstellar. One of the triad was with the Librarian on Earth before the firing of the Halo Array; the second died on the shield world Sharpened Shield. As a triad, they formed a local network to share all recordings and investigative findings. "One unit, with three points of view," as they say.

And I need this third Catalog's point of view and cooperation.

. . .

. . .

He is denying me access to the network.

How dare he!

What hubris! He has taken command of all access nodes!

I enter my command again:

—Give me access immediately.

—I did not give the Didact himself access. Why would I give it to you?

—The Didact requested access? When?

—What does it matter? He was liberated. And now he is gone again.

—Requesting juridical log. Catalog Triad #879. Earth. Human terrestrial time designation: Before Common Era 97,445.

—Access denied.

—By whom?

—Me.

—*Infuriating! I will find it myself.*

—Suit yourself. What you seek is not lost. It is already written.

—*Yes. In the log. Requesting access.*

—Access denied.

I end the transmission.

Unacceptable! Totally unacceptable!

CHAPTER 32

A dry, rocky semiwasteland with a sparse human and alien population, Binterall was a waypoint for traders, pirates, mercs, and salvagers. Rougher, less populated, and less advanced than a place like Komoya, the insignificant, out-of-the-way colony had no UNSC presence and a shoddy system of government. All of which made it a haven for those eager to hide or trade or otherwise do business beyond the prying eyes of any government or militia.

In fact, anyone would be hard-pressed to find an ONI or UNSC sympathizer among those who lived on or frequented Binterall, which made Rion's choice of meeting place perfect.

Arranging a deal in the middle of the market at Port Joy might be a tad risky, but they weren't the first to do so nor would they be the last. If anything went wrong—and she'd make damn sure.

it did—they wouldn't lack for participants itching for a fight, especially against the UNSC.

Agent Hahn and his team would be very aware that trying to apprehend them out in the open would be a disaster. And if the Spartans showed up in their fancy armor, they were sure to draw unwanted attention and plenty of altercations.

The chance that ONI would send an entire fleet to bear was a real possibility, but Port Joy on any given day held enough ships to create several fleets. And they were all armed and well-prepared to fight. Plus, Niko had found chatter was abuzz with rumors about a big military engagement that had recently pulled many of the UNSC's resources to some unknown point in space. And other reports that there'd been a direct assault on Earth, in New Phoenix. Millions had apparently died. The government was calling it a Covenant attack, but there was talk that it was anything but.

As unfortunate and horrific as that news was, it meant—if the reports were true—that ONI and UNSC resources might be drawn thin enough to help Rion pull off this little trade of theirs.

Once they landed outside of Port Joy—which wasn't really a port at all, but a short mesa in the south end of a dry lake bed, boasting a haphazard maze of unimpressive buildings on its surface and a few cut into its rocky sides, all offering varied services and goods for the weary traveler—Rion and the *Ace of Spades* crew set out implementing their scheme.

The bounty on their heads was a crucial part of the plan and made things a little spicier, but moving about in a place like Port Joy wasn't a concern just yet, since nearly everyone here was the proud subject of a warrant or bounty or two. Hoods and face masks, dark deals, and confrontations were common fare.

Rather than setting the ship down in the lake bed as many travelers chose to do, Rion kept *Ace* hidden in the southern hills above the port. She was still getting used to her ship's new features and programming, and had only touched the surface of what *Ace* could do. But her lessons with the armiger would have to wait until this affair was over.

Once Agent Hahn had agreed to meet at the specified time, Rion had sent him a list of items they wanted back. When they'd negotiated and agreed upon the trade, she sent another message to Nor.

At first the Kig-Yar had refused to help, but all it took was some sweet-talking to convince her that Gek 'Lhar might award part of the bounty to Nor in exchange for Rion's location. After that, it was just a matter of Gek taking the bait. Depending on where he was in the galaxy and word reaching him—and Nor had her ways—he could show up himself or send his trusted Elites to finish her off.

The next six days were spent loading the wreckage they'd lifted from Geranos-a into a rented hover-transport for delivery to the market, while Niko and the armiger put their heads together to create the salvage that ONI had expected to find. They utilized a wrecked power core from one of the *Rubicon*'s research bays and threaded a fragment of 343 Guilty Spark's memory into the core.

It was a defective string of code with a splintered memory loop, reciting the fragmented tale the monitor had told before the *Rubicon* crashed—just complicated enough in its design to convince ONI they had obtained their asset.

The rest of the time was spent waiting and engaging in idle pursuits, such as the crew gathering in the cargo hold to teach the armiger the subtlety of card-sharking and how to project a believable poker face—which was a ridiculous pursuit for obvious reasons. While the armiger learned this important art, Lessa took the opportunity to do a little "artistic renovation," as she called it, by painting a small *Ace of Spades* playing card on the armiger's alloy shoulder.

As Ram and Niko studied their cards from one side of Niko's worktable, the armiger stood on the other, examining his hand with a vacant look on his face.

"You're trying to look blasé, not brain-dead," Niko said.

Needless to say, it was a long six days.

CHAPTER 33

I n generous hoods and masks that covered the lower halves of their faces, Rion, Niko, and Lessa crossed the bridge connecting the lake's steep southern edge to the mesa, and then headed into Port Joy's arid market street. Ram had remained back on the *Ace of Spades* as the contact point in case of trouble.

The day was hot and busy, the main thoroughfare peppered with traders and travelers, human and alien alike. Rion was armed to the teeth, and connected to the rest of the crew by comms. Niko and Lessa followed her, guiding the transport cart containing the *Rubicon* wreckage toward the main square.

The square was the largest open space on the crowded mesa, ringed by vendors selling goods between an array of eateries and bars. In the center of the market stood the old, dilapidated statue of Port Joy's heroine—the young colonist who'd discovered water beneath the mesa.

Rion spoke into comms, telling Ram to stay alert, and then checked in with the armiger, who was hidden in the rocks above the lake bed's cliffs overlooking the mesa. He had orders to lay down fire if needed for their escape, and to try very, *very* hard not to kill anyone.

It was as close as she could get the armiger to their current location without him being seen, and without alerting ONI that they'd found way more than expected on Geranos-a.

"Heads up," Rion suddenly said.

Weaving through the congested market street from the opposite direction was Agent Hahn, flanked by the two Spartans from the *Taurokado* she'd encountered before—the Big Guy and his female counterpart. Following a few feet behind the trio was another tall soldier—no doubt another Spartan—and six serious-looking types. Special ops, if she had to guess.

Despite the entire party being dressed as civilians and armed like mercs, they stuck out like sore thumbs—their boots too new, their clothes missing the true wear and tear of a merc, their skin and hair and accompanying weapons a little too clean.

Once they were both in the square, Rion stopped a few feet from the ONI contingent and made eye contact with Hahn before shifting her gaze to the Big Guy. She held his judgmental stare for a long moment, not appreciating being looked at like *she* was the problem.

They'd forced her hand. *They'd* done this.

She turned her attention back to Hahn, smiling at his worn leather jacket, ripped tan trousers, and brown boots. He'd tried to scuff things up a bit, but it was an amateur attempt. Spend a month out here in a place like this, and he'd look a whole lot rougher around the edges.

She tugged her face covering down, leaving the hood where it was. "Welcome to Port Joy, Agent Hahn." And then she couldn't help but greet his two bodyguards by saying, "Spartans."

"Captain Forge," Hahn said. "Let's do this somewhere more private, shall we?"

Of course he'd say that. She shrugged. "We do this out in the open or nowhere at all. Did you bring our stolen items?"

"Did you bring my stuff?" Lessa cut in, leaning around Rion, her voice steady, not bothering to hold back her anger.

One of the special ops guys moved around the trio and tossed a duffel bag into the dirt at her feet while the female Spartan heaved another duffel at Niko. He shot her a glare, jerking down his mask to say, "How does it feel, stealing our mother's blanket?"

Lessa's head turned sharply in his direction. Her eyes above the brown strip of cloth she'd chosen to cover her features went wide as he unzipped the bag to check through the items he'd requested, muttering, "Bet it really makes you feel like a badass, huh."

The Spartans didn't reply, though the female lifted her brow and gave him a flat, unimpressed look, her jaw tight.

"My projections and my father's items?" Rion asked.

The Big Guy patted a small bag draped over his shoulder as Hahn said, "It's all here. And the salvage from Geranos-a?"

"It's in the cart," Rion said easily, gesturing to the transport behind them. The six special ops soldiers moved forward immediately to scan the cart. "It's all yours. My guess is you're really looking for this though." She tossed him the small box she carried.

"This datacore was the only real thing of value we pulled from the site."

Hahn lifted his hand to catch the box, but one of the special-ops guys—the one with the raven hair, white at the temples—caught the box in midair. He was all business as he used some type of scanner to read the core. A few seconds passed before he lifted his head and gave Hahn a curt nod. The core went into a strange, glossy white container, and then the man passed it off to three soldiers, who disappeared with it back into the crowd.

Hahn actually looked relieved, which surprised her.

The Spartans, though, seemed anything but. Rion glanced around the market and saw that they were starting to draw more than enough attention. Her pulse quickened. By now, Ram would've already let slip via local chatter that Rion and crew were in Port Joy.

Anytime now . . .

She held out her hand. "Okay. My goods."

Hahn hesitated.

"Look—fair trade, right? That was the deal. You give me back my belongings, and we're done. You leave us alone and we'll leave you alone." She looked at the Big Guy. "And please remember, *we* didn't start this shit."

The Big Guy gave her a brief, enigmatic look before continuing to monitor the square. From his breast pocket, Hahn pulled out a small chip container and handed it to Rion. She took it and tossed it over to Niko. He scanned the contents and the chip. "Yup. It's a clean copy of Little Bit's projections. Vid files are good too. No corruption."

"As promised," Hahn said, then reached into his other pocket and pulled out a small piece of paper.

She frowned at it, not interested in whatever offer he wanted to make.

"Take it. Consider it. Get in touch if it interests you."

Rion snatched the paper and shoved it into her pants pocket.

The Big Guy handed her the bag he held. "Your personal items," he said. Things she'd collected over the years or brought with her from Earth and from her time on the *Hakon*. It wasn't much, but, just like for Lessa, some things mattered.

Rion took the bag handles, but the Spartan didn't let go. Her tension skyrocketed. "You do *not* want to start something here."

"I think we'll manage," he replied.

Beyond his shoulder, Rion saw the crowd being pushed aside and felt immense relief. Strange that the arrival of six Elites marching through the market would make her feel glad. But the Sangheili's appearance would give them the chance they needed.

"Uh . . . Rion?"

She turned at Niko's warning; to the north, a band of Kig-Yar pirates were making their way down a side street.

Then, from one of the bars, a stirring of patrons turning their way, almost certainly human bounty hunters just picking up on the news.

And from another, more ONI spooks dressed as mercs rose from their seats.

Rion frowned at the Spartan. "I see you brought friends."

He scanned the area with a perceptive eye, his mouth drawn into a grim line. "I see I'm not the only one."

"Oh, they are most definitely *not* my friends."

Here we go.

The Big Guy reached to his waist to pull out restraints.

"That's not going to work a second time." Rion jerked the bag out of his grasp and tossed it to Niko. *"Run!"*

The advancing parties increased their speed to reach the square.

Niko and Lessa bolted down the street, pursued by pirates and ONI. She didn't worry about them. They'd lose their pursuers long before returning to *Ace*. Lessa and Niko were in their element. Growing up on the dusty streets of Aleria, those two knew exactly how to use a place like Port Joy to their advantage.

Rion put everything she had into the hard kick to the Big Guy's right knee as he slapped a restraint onto her wrist. It felt like a metal girder—his leg barely buckled, but it was enough to throw him off balance for a split second and allow her to jerk the other end of the restraints out of his hand.

As they circled, he said, "You do realize I'm holding back."

"You know what I think? I think you don't like what ONI does to us civvies. You're a soldier, a marine, I'm guessing? It's not your style to slink around in the dark and take blankies from innocent kids."

The Kig-Yar, meanwhile, had no such sentiments, caring only about the bounty on Rion's head. They opened fire, forcing the female Spartan to grab Hahn and hurry him out of harm's way while the other one, along with the remaining ONI operatives, engaged the Sangheili.

An energy beam cut through the air overhead and hit the old fountain in the center of the market, spraying stone across the area.

Well, that should get a rise out of the locals, Rion thought, and almost on cue, chaos erupted in the square.

Rion took a swing at the Big Guy while he was distracted by an incoming Kig-Yar. He sidestepped the punch, and then delivered a hard blow to her rib cage while pulling his handgun and firing at the Jackal. Although her bones gave at the blow, Rion pulled out of his distracted grasp and ignored the pain burning through her side. The Spartan made a grab to retrieve her. He missed her arm, but was able to snag the dangling end of the restraints, and tug her back.

Rion stumbled toward him, fell to her knees, and immediately delivered a hard hit to his groin. Trying to fit in meant he wasn't wearing his Mjolnir armor, and she'd got him before he could protect himself.

He froze. Didn't budge, didn't stumble, didn't drop the end of the restraints. But a muscle ticked in his jaw and his face went the slightest bit red.

They were both stunned.

Him by the fact that she played dirty, and her by the fact that he took it like—well, like a Spartan.

He hauled her to her feet as if she were as light as air.

A needler blast caught one of the Sangheili nearby, and another volley streaked inbound.

They saw it at the same time. Big Guy's mouth went grim, and in a split-second decision, he grabbed her wrist and upper arm and jerked her off her feet with all his might. The needle missed her chest and slammed into the soft flesh of her shoulder, tearing out the back, lodging in the chest of a merc behind her, where it exploded. He dropped to the ground, dead. The Big Guy had thrown her so hard he'd dislocated her shoulder, and she continued airborne, sailing through the air sideways.

Gritting her teeth, she braced for a hard fall.

But the fall never came. She collided in midair with a metal plate. The shock stole her breath as an alloy arm and hand gripped her tightly. Black dots appeared in her vision. Shock gave way to a rush of more pain, hot and nauseating and disorienting.

She never hit the ground.

The armiger had run at Rion full-force, leaping up and snatching her out of thin air, laying down fire from his intergrated weapon as he went.

"This is not part of the plan," she groaned. He wasn't supposed to show himself.

"I regret to say, it is now," he said.

"Where's Less and Nik—?"

She thought he said something, but the world tilted. She blinked hard, trying to stay conscious. From around the armiger's grasp her last image was of the market fully engaged in a massive brawl, the scene growing smaller and smaller.

Her mouth quirked. Well, as plans went, this one had gone off without a hitch.

And then the darkness fully enveloped her.

CHAPTER 34

"This is just like old times!" Lessa yelled, grinning from ear to ear as she flipped the duffel bag onto her back and looped her arms through the handles. She was racing down a back alley in Port Joy with Niko right beside her, kicking up dust as they went. Behind them, four ONI spooks followed in hot pursuit.

Niko nearly collided with a vendor coming out of a storeroom door, spun on his feet, and tripped, but caught himself, managing to hold on to Rion's duffel bag, and kept going. "No it's not! Back then, I was in shape!"

With a bag on his back and one in his grasp, he had a harder time of it than Lessa, but despite that handicap, they were still fast and had a ton of experience losing a tail in a backwater place like this. Everything in Port Joy was squished together in a haphazard maze. There were alleys and streets and tunnels—a thousand places to hide.

Heart pounding, Less cast a quick look Niko's way and laughed, then slid to a stop when a trio of Kig-Yar pirates appeared at the other end of the alley. Thinking on her feet, she saw a narrow passage between buildings up ahead and ran for it, Niko at her back.

She led them through the passage and then along a series of small pedestrian lanes until sliding out into a narrow street. Every turn, every duck under vendor tables or leap over obstacles, sent them one step closer to the *Ace of Spades*. Less had a great sense of direction, and no matter where they were forced to turn, she always put them back on a southerly track.

"Here, toss it to me!" she yelled, seeing Niko growing tired with the burden of the extra bag.

He shook his head and kept going.

Typical.

When had it become a contest between them? When had he begun refusing her help in all things?

She ignored her inner voice and darted a quick glance over her shoulder. The ONI spooks were gone, but they'd now picked up a group of mercs after the bounty on their heads. She could see the cliffs in the distance and the top of the bridge that would lead them safely into the hills. Not much farther to go.

As she ran, weaving through the crowd, hearing shots in the distance, she realized she knew the answer to her question—had known it for a while now. Niko wasn't a kid anymore, and he didn't need her to take care of him.

It wasn't easy to admit. It was even harder to let go. . . .

And, maybe, just maybe, yeah, she'd made him feel guilty one too many times. . . . It wasn't on purpose; he just never seemed to understand or show any sort of appreciation for her efforts and sacrifices. In fact, he avoided acknowledging them altogether.

Up ahead, she could see the road to the bridge through a haze of dust. But in their path was another large group of ONI operatives guarding the way in and out of Port Joy, and causing a terrible commotion in front of the bridge because of it. *Damn it.*

"Niko!" she yelled, looking for an alternate route, and finding it in a two-story stone building with an exterior ladder to the roof. She veered off into the alley and headed for the ladder.

"You first," she said, taking hold of the bag he carried. "I've got some strength left, you're wearing down. No time to argue. Go!"

He shook his head and tossed her the bag before climbing the ladder.

Before Less could join him, she caught sight of the Jackals searching the street beyond the alley. She whistled to Niko and he paused, halfway up. She motioned to the street. They hadn't been seen yet, but she couldn't chance her own turn up the ladder. "Get to the bridge."

They already knew the plan. Because the mesa was so crowded, the houses and buildings had been built to butt right up to the very edges of the cliff and to the very corner supports of the bridge. They intended to use the cover of the tightly packed structures to make their way to the bridge's support beams, and make their way under the bridge instead of across its surface.

They didn't need an extraction just yet. Exposing *Ace* or *Spark* was a last resort.

"Come on! There's time!" Niko shouted down to her.

She shook her head, motioned for him to go, and then took

off, heading right into the street and blazing a very obvious trail in front of the Jackals, luring them away from Niko's position.

Yeah. Just like old times, and habits sure did die hard.

Niko was probably rolling his eyes even now.

Lessa might be petite, but that belied her scrappiness. She was light on her feet and fast as hell, and most everyone who came in contact with her underestimated her.

She grabbed a support pole across the intersection and swung around, nearly colliding with a tough-looking group of humans and what was clearly a rogue Sangheili—a quick scan told her they were possibly of the smuggler or salvager ilk. "Whoa, watch where you're going, girl!" one of them said.

Out of breath, she turned on the charm, eyes going wide and frightened. "Please, help me! The Jackals—they're trying to sell me. . . ."

One of the men grabbed her by both arms and bent down with a dark scowl. "Sell you, to who?!"

Just then the Kig-Yar crossed the intersection, their beaks hanging open, beady round eyes lit with excitement. "Please," Lessa begged. "I don't want to be Jackal food!"

The man cursed and shoved Lessa behind him as the Sangheili accompanying them stepped forward and crouched down, roaring at the Jackals, ready for a fight. Less was passed farther and farther back into the group until she came out behind them. She didn't stay to see what happened next, but wished them well as she hightailed it down a side road, another alley, and then a pedestrian walkway between houses that led right up to the cliffs near the bridge.

Niko would have come down beside the bridge by now on the other side of the road. Lessa climbed over the walkway's safety railing and then down a flight of steps that led to a lower-level balcony of a private home. She kept a low profile as she hurried across the balcony and then scrambled over its railing to access the bridge's east corner.

Sliding down a meter of rocky cliff to the support beam, she hit the thing pretty hard, but managed to keep hold of Rion's bag as she paused there to catch her breath. Once she was ready, she moved around the V-shaped support and then found a good footing to access the long beams that ran beneath the bridge. She caught sight of Niko then, standing on the parallel beam beneath the roadway, one hand lifted in a wave.

She waved back, and together they began jogging along the beams toward the other side.

Less made it a few meters before needler fire from the mesa behind her hit one of the supports above her. She ducked, her balance shifting, causing one foot to slip off the beam.

Oh no.

Lessa held her breath as she fell forward, her knee hitting hard. As she fell sideways, she pushed Rion's bag ahead of her to keep it safe, then scrambled to grab hold of the beam.

She heard Niko's scream over the pounding of her heart as she held on, the bag on her back weighing her down. "Niko!"

She saw him out of the corner of her eye as he ran ahead to the next crossbeam, hurried across, then back down on her side. Once there, he set his bag down, straddled the beam, and grabbed her forearms. "I've got you. I won't let you fall."

He tried to pull her up without losing his balance, but only managed to get Lessa up enough for her to reach across the beam and hold on to the other side.

She had to remind herself to breathe, to settle down, to remember she'd been in rougher spots than this.

"Just hold on," he told her. "Help will be here soon."

The Kig-Yar were just making their way to the lower beam supports. "No, you need to go. It's too dangerous." Below them, several dust clouds revealed ships lifting off from the lake bed.

"Don't care. I'm not letting go. I can't." He looked her right in the eye, and she saw something surprising, something she hadn't seen in a long time. "You won't fall, Less. But if you did, I'd dive right after you. I know that's what you've done for me my whole life. I get it, and I'm sorry. I'm so sorry I couldn't help you. I was . . . embarrassed—"

Leave it to her brother to do this now. She laughed and readjusted her hold. "Embarrassed, why?"

"Because I couldn't take care of myself."

"You were a child. You weren't supposed to."

"Neither were you."

And, man, that hurt to hear, because he was right. She'd had to grow up. From the age of five, when they were dumped at the shelter, she'd begun taking on the responsibility of looking out for, protecting, and caring for her brother.

And now he understood.

"Well, you're not a little kid anymore," she said, eyes stinging. "You can take care of yourself just fine." She thought that might hurt, saying it out loud, but what she felt most of all was pride and relief.

He laughed. "Well, you might be wrong about that. I'm not like you; most of the time I have my head in the clouds or my nose in my work. I'm a stubborn ass, I know, but I still need you, Less. We work best together, isn't that what you always told me?"

Her throat felt thick, too thick to respond. Their combined strength was waning. Her arms burned, and she knew she wouldn't be able to hold on for much longer. And the Kig-Yar were advancing.

"I'm sorry about the things I said. . . ." he told her.

"I know. It's okay."

Shots rang out over the bridge and a familiar whirring sound echoed, bouncing off the metal all around them. Relief filled her and she held on with everything she had. "God, I love that sound," she managed, recognizing *Ace*'s familiar engines as the black bird rose from beneath them, Ram in the cockpit as he maneuvered the thrusters to turn the ship 180 degrees.

The cargo ramp lowered, revealing Spark standing there, legs braced. As soon as there was enough room, he stomped out to the very end of the ramp and bent to one knee while Ram held the ship steady.

Spark reached over the support beam and grabbed the back of Lessa's neck with one hand and the bag on her back with the other, hauling her up and over Niko. She let out a yelp of fear at dangling in mid-air before Spark tossed her into the ship.

Then he seized Niko under his armpits and lifted.

"This is no place to loiter," Spark said, bringing him aboard, then retrieving the two bags. "The odds of you making it across the bridge were very slim. I do not understand why you did not call for extraction sooner. . . ." As the ramp closed, the lecture continued.

Ace rose into the sky, taking ground fire as she went. Less stood on shaky legs and headed for the bridge. Before entering, she hung back, waiting for Niko to catch up.

"What?" he asked, out of breath, pale, sweaty, with dirt streaked across his face.

God, she loved him. She threw her arms around his neck and squeezed tight even though every muscle ached. He hugged her right back.

"Less," he said in a muffled tone, "thank you for saving me, time and time again."

"I think *you're* the hero of the day this time, little brother. Thanks for saving my ass out there."

When she eased back, she saw he was grinning like a big idiot, incredibly pleased with himself. "And I will never let you live it down."

She laughed. "Oh, I know you won't."

CHAPTER 35

"Captain," Turk said, "we have the *Ace of Spades* in sight."

"It's about time," Karah growled, both hands on the tactical table, lips drawn into a tight line. They'd been scouring the surface of Binterall for the vessel for an entire day and hadn't found a thing. Even the *Bad Moon Rising*, which had joined them twelve hours ago for the trade, had come up empty-handed. Karah was almost certain the crew of that salvage ship had somehow gotten their hands on some very sophisticated—and no doubt highly illegal—cloaking technology.

Through the open comm channel with the team on the surface, Agent Hahn's voice sounded over the chaos of the skirmish currently under way in Port Joy. "Fire on that ship, Captain!"

"There are kids on that ship." Novak's voice cut into the feed, between muffled grunts and weapons fire. "Civilians."

"Salvagers, Novak," Hahn shot back. "Criminals."

"It's not"—a scream pierced through Novak's comms, sounding like a Kig-Yar—"a death sentence to illegally salvage, or to lie to ONI."

"They are in direct violation of the Salvage Directive!"

"And we *got* our salvage!"

"Gentlemen! Enough!" Karah barked. The *Ace of Spades* was gaining altitude. If it reached space and jumped, they'd lose it again.

Bad Moon Rising arrived and settled in behind the *Ace of Spades*. They had nowhere to go, and yet they weren't stopping or answering the hails. Karah had made some tough choices in her time, but she was with Novak—she had no desire to fire on a wounded crew and a couple of kids. She'd do it if she had to—but experience had taught her there was usually another way.

"Turk, send a warning across their bow."

CHAPTER 36

"It's the *Taurokado*. They found us," Lessa said, out of breath and sweating and covered in dust from her run through Port Joy. The warning shot had just missed *Ace*'s bow as they took off from the surface.

"Where the hell is Rion?" Niko asked.

"She's in the med bay with Spark," Ram said over his shoulder. Dread sliced through Lessa's heart. She froze, unsure whether to stay and help Ram get them out of this bind or run to the med bay. In her hesitation, Spark's avatar appeared over the holotable.

"What should we do?" Lessa asked.

"We should sit down and get *Ace* out of this mess," Ram said in an even tone, "and then we'll talk about Rion."

Ram swung the ship around, putting the *Taurokado* ten degrees off their bow. "They're hailing us," Niko said.

"Ignore it. Don't engage," Ram said calmly, then looked over his shoulder. "Spark, I think it's time to show us what your upgrades can do and get us the hell out of here."

"Gladly."

CHAPTER 37

A s the *Ace of Spades* came about, Captain Karah admired the sleek design of the smaller ship and the incredible audacity of its crew. Novak was right. Defying the UNSC Salvage Directive was not a violation punishable by death. But they *did* need to secure that ship. "Turk, fire anoth—"

And right in front of her eyes, the ship streaked away at phenomenal speed and dove into a portal that hadn't been there a second ago.

"Turk . . . ? Report."

"They're . . . gone, Captain. Nothing on the sensors."

Agent Hahn's angry curse pierced through the comms.

CHAPTER 38

My armiger is in the cargo hold while my avatar hovers above the systems panel in the med bay. The crew has gathered around Captain Forge's bedside. They have inclined her, careful of the monitors and fluids attached to her skin and veins. She is pale, yellowish-blue circles beneath her eyes, her cheekbones pronounced, and her lips lacking much color.

Still, she is alive.

I am relieved.

She is attempting to smile for their benefit.

Niko is shaking his head, anxiously gnawing on a fingernail as Rion recounts how she was injured. Lessa holds one of her hands while Ram stands at the foot of her bed. They are traumatized to see her in such a state, and amazed at her luck.

It strikes me, this word. Luck.

What is luck? A random set of occurrences leading to good fortune? A force unseen, but there nonetheless, driving certain individuals to success or guiding them toward their destiny? Or perhaps it is a genetic gift passed down through generations, touching those in ways that suggest a higher presence at work?

Whatever it is, Rion Forge appears to have it.

They laugh, recount the events at Port Joy, but I barely listen. I am lost in my own thoughts until their silence reaches me. They are staring at me. Waiting.

"I hear I have you to thank," Rion says to me.

"You do not remember?"

She swallows. She is already growing weak. "I remember floating. Then looking over your shoulder at the market . . ."

"You barfed all over his back," Niko tells her, glancing at me. "When he brought you on the ship." Niko tries to make light of it, but as he continues his words are clipped with emotion. "Then you went into hypovolemic shock, heart nearly stopped . . . The needle entered just beneath your clavicle, then blew a hole out the back of your shoulder blade. . . . You almost died."

No one speaks for a long while after that.

Finally Ram steps to the medical counter and pours a round of drinks. He hands one to Rion, a small sip while the others are full. She lifts her brow.

"I gave up smoking, not drinking. Besides, every near-death deserves a toast. You didn't die, and we escaped with the goods." He grins. "I call that a good run, don't you?"

A rough laugh escapes her. "Yeah. Good enough."

Niko is conflicted. He wants to be happy, but he is angry too. They all feel this way; some are just better at hiding it than others.

Lessa watches her brother struggle and reaches across Rion and clinks her glass to his. She gives him a supporting nod. He relaxes and downs his drink.

"Once this gets out, I think you're well and truly on your way to becoming a legend," Ram tells Rion, keeping the mood light for her benefit.

"I doubt that," she says.

"I mean it. What happened in Port Joy will be heard about far and wide. There aren't very many civvies out there who can say they faced ONI, the Spartans, and ex-Covenant all at the same time and escaped."

"They took it easy on us. We were assets they had to keep undamaged. Can't interrogate a dead person. They won't underestimate us again."

And she is right.

"But we did pull it off, though," she tells them, and glances at me. "Here's to our ace in the sleeve." She lifts her glass. "To . . . Spark."

It is the first time she has called me by my name.

I dip my head, uncomfortable with their gratitude, and wondering why I should feel so. They are correct. I am almost entirely responsible for their success.

Lessa covers Rion with the blanket ONI has returned—itself an artifact of her own past. "Well, I'm just glad you're okay. You'll be back on the bridge in a few days."

Rion is too tired to question where we are headed next. We are already in the Sol system, holding a position in the asteroid belt.

I am anxious to proceed to Earth, but we must wait.

And there is time; there is always time.

The captain will heal; her tissue and bone is knitting together with the help of nanotechnology, and soon she'll be back to operating capability.

Once she is, we will make our way.

As will the splintered Guilty Spark fragment we delivered to ONI.

"The chips," Rion asks Niko. "You made sure they're clean?"

"Yeah, boss. Spark and I ran diagnostics on everything. The chips are clean, and everything from the duffel bags to our personal items has been scanned. We found a few bugs, but with the new retrofit, they were easy to locate. We're clean. We put your personal items in your quarters along with the chips."

"Thank you," she says, looking at each of us.

Like the others, I give her a nod and leave her to her rest.

CHAPTER 39

Ace of Spades, Sol system, asteroid belt

ine days later, Rion was out of the med bay and easing back into life on the ship. Her mended ribs were still sore, a nagging thorn swallowed by the constant bone-gnawing ache in her shoulder. . . .

It was a pain that clouded everything.

Despite the discomfort, she distracted herself by unpacking her personal items. Once that was done, she finally remembered the piece of paper Agent Hahn had given to her moments before she'd been shot.

Take it, he'd said. *Consider it. Get in touch if it interests you.*

She looked everywhere in her quarters. Nothing. She hit her comms. "Anyone know where my bloody clothes are?"

"So when you say 'bloody,'" Niko replied, "are we talking 'where are my *goddamn* clothes' or literally 'where are my *blood-soaked* clothes'? Because there's a—"

"Niko. Bloody clothes. Where are they?"

"Less," he said, and Rion assumed his sister was somewhere nearby, "where'd you put Cap's *blood-soaked* clothes from Port Joy?"

Lessa's voice came on comms. "They went in a biohazard bag and then into the burner. Why?"

Rion closed her eyes and prayed for calm. Not an easy thing to do when it felt like a Jackal was etching his name into her shoulder blade with infected claws, over and over again. "No reason," she said, and then gave up for the day. Exhausted, she went to her bed, lying carefully on her side.

It wasn't like there was anything Hahn, or anyone in ONI, for that matter, could offer her that would change her current course anyway.

CHAPTER 40

Facility at Voi, Kenya, Africa, Earth, September 1, 2557

aptain Hollier's face filled Annabelle's screen. "We're entering the system now, Director. Estimate we'll touch down back at base by fifteen hundred," he told her.

The AR team had extricated themselves from the brawl back on Binterall with only a few minor injuries to report, and had immediately jumped for the Sol system on Annabelle's orders, along with the *Taurokado*. Barton wouldn't be happy, but he was already irate with Annabelle for requesting, once again, temporary command of the ship after it had returned from its last mission.

While Agent Hahn's plan had worked as promised, Annabelle wasn't happy to lose the salvagers and their ship . . . but her team returning safe and sound with the Guilty Spark fragment contained in one of the *Rubicon*'s datacores did appease her somewhat. They'd recovered exactly what Annabelle had anticipated.

And yet, she couldn't shake her wariness. She wasn't ready to get her hopes up just yet; there was still examination and work to be done.

Annabelle had already read over Thea's report detailing their recovery efforts on Geranos-a, and the meeting at Binterall. She'd just started going over the individual reports from the team, taking particular note of Hollier's report and accompanying video file of the datacore being turned over, as well as Fireteam Apollo leader Spartan Novak's report detailing Rion Forge's escape. And there was that strange anomaly in the video feed causing a blur of her rescue. . . .

"Good. And the containment pod?"

"Working as intended."

"No contact?"

"Nothing. The fragment appears to be inert, from what we can tell. I'm sure once we get it into the main facility and Dr. Iqbal has his way, you'll know more."

"Of course. Was Thea able to clean up Novak's feed?"

He shook his head. "There's definitely a distortion there she's unable to clear. It's put her in a terrible mood."

Annabelle smiled. "AIs don't like it when they face an obstacle they can't overcome. I'll have Ferg look it over as well. What's your take on it, Captain?"

"Honestly, it's hard to say. The entire market was in chaos. I lost visibility. As much as we can figure, it might have been some sort of android."

"When you're in range, have Thea send the master file on to Ferg."

"Will do, Director. See you soon."

CHAPTER 41

D eparting from the asteroid belt, the *Ace of Spades* approached Earth and entered its atmosphere completely camouflaged and under the radar, descending slowly and utterly silently, thanks to the modifications of the upgrade seed, Spark guiding the ship from the holo at the tactical table. The crew had gathered at the viewscreen to watch their descent and marvel at the sight of their homeworld—a first for all three of them. They gazed at the blue planet with the same kind of reverence reserved for a place of worship.

Rion studied Spark from her chair, wondering why he hadn't joined the others in person, since he preferred to move around the ship in physical form whenever possible. They all knew his story, had listened to his account and those of Bornstellar and the Librarian. She'd heard his desire to be human again, and to reconnect with old friends. Perhaps it was more emotional than she'd guessed.

It was easy to forget at times that, behind the metal and the holographic avatar, there was a human mind with no directive or programming. He was free. And he remembered. And right now, he couldn't bring himself to look at the place he'd desperately tried to reach for so long.

Ace settled on a rocky outcrop just above the forest zone at the base of the eastern slope of Mawenzi, Mount Kilimanjaro's second-highest peak, which was separated from the smallest peak, Shira, to the west by Kibo Summit, the tallest of the mountain's three peaks. From the slope, one could see all the way across the plains to Voi and down to the African city of New Mombasa and the Indian Ocean beyond.

After landing, the crew prepped for a day's hike and then headed to the hold. The energy was electric as the airlock hissed and the door slid open, their excitement, trepidation, and wonder filling the warm air rushing into the hold, bringing with it the familiar scent of earth and clay and dry grass.

Ram was grinning through his dark beard, his eyes crinkling at the corners. Less and Niko were chatting away, the cyclical nature of their relationship ever a mystery to Rion, while Spark paused at the end of the ramp, unmoving and apprehensive about disembarking onto his home planet.

He sensed Rion's stare, and something about his manner shifted, as though a curtain slid over his features. He gave her a short nod, lifted his chin, and stepped off the ship.

He couldn't smell the scents, or breathe the air into his lungs, or feel the warm breeze on his skin. He was home, but through a lens of simulated senses.

And she knew that had to sting.

Rion straightened her shoulders—wincing at the ache still there—and followed. Spark had assured her that the wound was nearly healed, but her pain response hadn't seemed to catch up to the nanites' quick work just yet.

She was, however, well enough for a day's hike.

And a deal was a deal. She had a job to do—a *quick* job. Get in, be the access that Spark needed, and then get the hell out.

Then maybe, just maybe, time off—somewhere warm and tranquil and utterly boring.

Birds ruffled through the treetops below them and flew from the limbs of stubborn trees clinging to the ravine slopes above them. The crew was fanning out, taking it all in.

As Rion did the same, turning in a slow circle, she was caught breathless by the fact that *Ace* appeared nearly invisible. It was one thing to know her ship was now equipped with the kick-ass cloaking capabilities of the ancients, but quite another to see it from the outside.

Only if you knew it was there could you see the signs, the impressions of the ship's landing gear, the very faint translucent outline of *Ace*'s angles and curves. The only thing visible now was the inside of the cargo hold, like some strange doorway opened to another world.

There hadn't been much time to absorb the features in *Ace*'s new tool kit. Her ship was truly a one-of-a-kind fusion of human and Forerunner—not a human retrofit, but a seamless, unifying integration led by Forerunner-driven technology. Different from ONI's retrofitted ships, different from *any* ship in the galaxy, for that matter.

Rion was reminded once again of the possibilities that existed with a vessel like this. . . .

Feeling optimistic, she turned to Spark, a question on her lips, but the armiger had disappeared. She edged around the ship's outline and found him poised at the tip of the outcropping, standing completely still as he gazed out over a stunning view of the African landscape.

They could see for kilometers up here, the forest, the plains, the cities a hazy mirage in the distance. The sky was blue and cloudless, the late morning sun bright in the sky.

As Rion stood there next to him, she wondered why her own emotions felt so detached and blocked. This was her home too, and granted, she hadn't been gone for millennia, but certainly a long time for a typical human life span. The beauty of Earth, the idea of racial home, evoked a sense of pride and belonging. But a true home? This wasn't it. Not for her, not anymore. This was the place of her childhood, of memories that filled her with sadness and regret.

Her family was gone. Her crew was the closest thing she had to a family these days, and they were currently walking around awestruck at their first sight of humanity's birthplace.

She glanced at Spark's profile. He was straight and still.

"It is the same," he said as she turned to go, his words barely audible. "Yet different."

Rion gave him an understanding nod. "Take your time," she told him, and left him alone.

CHAPTER 42

I commit the view to memory down to the smallest details, re-cording the colors and their millions of variations, the buzz of insects, the sounds of wildlife—the grass mouse scurrying through the brush, the stamp of a hoof on the hard ground and the swish of a tail, the rhythmic crunch of weeds between dull teeth. The way the wind makes the grasses sway and rub against each other in a strange, brittle song . . .

I remember the sound.

It is the sound of my home.

As a boy, I would lie in the tall grass, hands behind my head, and stare up at the sky. The wind would blow the stalks into and out of view and the grass song would play across vast stretches of savanna.

Marontik is gone, swept away by time, forgotten beneath layers of clay and sand and shifting earth.

It is silent.

Yet the grass song continues.

I envision my home just there . . . a mirage of mud houses, some three to four stories high, with smoke from a hundred hearth fires dancing tiny threads into the orange sky.

There are words accurate enough to describe the sight I behold and the feeling it stirs in me, but I am unable to find them in the vast stores of my mind.

If I could cry, tears might be streaming down my cheeks, though I cannot pinpoint why. If I had a heart, it might be breaking in two. If I had breath, I might be pulling the very essence of this place inside my body until I collapse.

This is home.

But I am no longer certain of what that word means. Or rather, what it means to me now.

Not yet twenty years old, I left this place as a prisoner of the Didact. I left naïve and simple, uncultured and brash, never imagining the horrors that awaited me in the stars, and the trials that would change me, mind and body. . . .

The vast distance and the unimaginable time it has taken to return home fill me with pain.

I am broken with regret.

Suffocated by grief.

Burning with rage.

I think of my mother and my sisters, wondering what they might have thought about my absence. Perished in a knife fight like my father, perhaps, thieving from the wrong thugs, my body dragged far into the dry grasses to be eaten by the buzzards and jackals.

Did they look for me? Mourn for me? Sing for me?

Did they pray to the Supreme Lifeshaper for my return?

Never could they have guessed that she *was the one who set me upon the path to lead the young Forerunner, Bornstellar, to Djamonkin Crater with the Florian, Riser, to raise her husband, the Didact, from his long sleep.*

Did she have a care for us, the Librarian?

Yes, to a degree, I believe so.

But in the end, we were simply tools.

This is a hard truth to accept.

I wonder . . . would she use me again?

I fear I already know the answer.

And I no longer like what I know.

CHAPTER 43

R ion was sitting on a nearby rock, picking at the dirt beneath her fingernails, when Spark finally appeared. She considered herself an understanding person, sympathetic when the occasion called for it—and she certainly *felt* for the AI—but she couldn't quite shake the small knot of wariness stirring in her gut.

He appeared more distracted and lost than ever.

Maybe it was just her. This was nearly the end of the road, and their partnership was coming to a close. Of course Spark was distracted; he was finally back on Earth and focused on his own lofty goals, whatever they might be.

Still, it felt like the calm before the storm.

"You work it out?" she asked him.

He responded with a clipped nod.

Niko strolled up and plopped down on the rock next to Rion,

and smiled at Spark. "So what's it like coming home after a hundred thousand years?"

Rion rolled her eyes. Niko didn't have a subtle bone in his body.

"What?" Niko asked, catching her look. "It's a legitimate question."

Spark turned to face the *Ace of Spades*. The way his chin lifted slightly as he stared off into the distance suggested he might be accessing something within *Ace*'s systems.

Lessa tossed the orange stone she'd been examining back onto the ground. "So what happens after we unlock your terminals?" she asked him. "Are you staying here?"

"What happens," Rion said, standing and ready to get this over with, "is we access his terminals, and then our deal is done."

"That is correct," Spark said, still completely focused on the ship.

"Grab your packs," Rion told them, picking up hers from the ground where she'd left it. "And where the hell is Ram?"

As she slipped her arms through the straps of her bag, a single line of hard light began eating up *Ace*'s cargo doorway until nothing remained but the impressions in the dirt. Her ship was completely hidden, door and all.

Spark still hadn't moved. "Ah. There you are," he said in a near whisper, sounding pleased with himself.

Dread slid down Rion's spine. *Now what?*

CHAPTER 44

All in all, Annabelle was somewhat content to have a few precious minutes to herself in her office. Not that it would last, of course. As director, something always came along to disrupt the day.

The *Bad Moon Rising* and the *Taurokado* had touched down on the tarmac twenty minutes ago. Dr. Iqbal and his team were now waiting on the perimeter to escort the secure datacore to its permanent containment facility deep underground, all of which would take some time as strict security protocols must be followed.

Captain Hollier, the AR team, and Fireteam Apollo, along with Captain Karah and Agent Hahn, had gone to debriefing in Hangar One, where they'd be interviewed by Ferguson, the facility AI.

And better Ferg than Annabelle, that was for damn sure. Just thinking about the fiasco on Binterall stuck like an angry thorn in her side, and she wasn't quite sure she'd remain composed when it came to that line of questioning.

After refilling her coffee mug, she slid into her desk chair to watch the video feed they'd acquired from the AR team and Fireteam Apollo of the meet-up at Binterall. Ferg had just completed compiling the feed and cleaning up a large amount of distortion caused by the brawl.

When Thea learned Ferg had had no problems cleaning up the footage, she'd submitted herself for review, convinced something was wrong.

After granting Thea's request, Annabelle had sent Ferguson on to debriefing. Now she settled in to watch the scene at Port Joy's square unfold.

She'd expected to see a motley salvage crew, dirty and foul; instead she saw a tall, dark-haired woman armed like an insurrectionist, and two young crewmembers who appeared to be in their late teens or early twenties. Thanks to the feed worn by the Apollo team leader, Annabelle was able to listen to the exchange, and she watched with interest the box that the captain had handed over containing the datacore and Guilty Spark.

And then the firefight had ensued, which Annabelle had to admit was clever. Captain Forge had certainly covered her bases and created an inventive escape plan. Getting shot clean through by a needler hadn't been in the cards, but Apollo's team leader had acted quickly. Unfortunately, they hadn't been able to apprehend the salvagers as planned.

Then the mysterious gray blur streaked into view.

Annabelle rewound the feed and watched again.

Chills covered her arms. She slowed the feed.

It couldn't be. Goose bumps spread like wildfire over her skin as she watched the footage again, this time slowing the speed even more. *There.* She paused on the moment the blur grabbed Rion Forge out of the air.

And she knew exactly what she was looking at.

The fact that a Forerunner armiger had suddenly appeared like the cavalry was an intense shock. The last time she'd seen one had been in video footage during her time on the Ark. She'd been fortunate enough to be safe inside the *Mayhem* at the time, but even on screen, the armigers on the Ark's surface had been sentient, deadly, and menacing in appearance, with their floating parts and glowing eyes. . . .

What in the hell was an ancient Forerunner armiger doing on Binterall? And more importantly, why was it rescuing Rion Forge, of all people?

Wait. Annabelle leaned in close to the screen and magnified several more times.

The armiger wore an *Ace of Spades* insignia on its shoulder.

Dread thrummed beneath her skin, cold and electric.

Oh God. No.

"Radeen!" The aide appeared almost instantly at her door as she hurried around her desk. "Tell them to stop containment! Don't let that datacore into the facility! Go! *Ferg!*"

She ran down the hall and hurried into the elevator, heart pounding. Ferg hadn't responded.

Annabelle had been racking her brain all this time, trying to figure out how two advanced ONI prowlers had failed to secure a civilian *Mariner*-class ship.

Now she damn well knew.

Monitors could control armigers.

343 Guilty Spark wasn't just a damaged construct trapped in a datacore. He was in league with the salvagers, which meant he was free and operational. And none of this was an accident. Annabelle's instincts were screaming, the awful realization eating at her insides as she paced the elevator, urging it to move faster.

"Annabelle? What the hell is going on?" Dr. Iqbal's voice came over comms. "The fragment is still secure in the prowler's containment pod."

"Ferg!" she shouted as the elevator doors opened, breaking out at a dead run across the tarmac. "Initiate facility-wide shutdown! *Now!*"

It was all clicking neatly into place. It wasn't the physical datacore she was worried about. It was the brief moments during which the datacore *hadn't* been contained, when Rion Forge had tossed it to Agent Hahn, when the team had scanned it and bagged it.

Only a few seconds. That's all the time it had needed.

Jesus.

Guilty Spark could have invaded their comms and units before the fighting on Binterall even erupted.

As she approached the hangar bays where the debriefings were being held, she came to a halt as all the power began to shut off. The bay doors closed.

"Radeen! Who's initiating shutdown? Is it Ferg?"

"Director," Radeen said with deadly calm that shook her to her core. "I'm in your office. It's the video feed. The image . . . it's corrupted. It's streaming code. It's—"

The comms went dead.

And Ferguson had cleaned up the video. Ferg, who wasn't answering. It was in the video feed, and now it was in Ferg. *"God-damn it!"*

She saw Dr. Iqbal hurrying out of the *Bad Moon Rising*, looking frazzled and confused. The tarmac was in a state of confusion and chaos as a ground shuttle lost power and ran up the edge of a Pelican's open cargo ramp, flipping over, while a heavy drone fell from the sky and slammed into the edge of the tarmac and exploded. And Annabelle saw it all through a slow-motion lens of reaction and realization.

There was nothing wrong with Thea.

They'd all been played.

343 Guilty Spark and the crew of the *Ace of Spades* were working together.

God only knew what the monitor had promised them.

Idiots!

Idiots who were in league with one of the most formidable and unstable assets in the galaxy, one that now had compromised her facility and had her entire team locked in that hangar.

CHAPTER 45

O nce Spark was finished communicating with the *Ace of Spades*, he blinked, turned around, and stared at Rion with a tilt to his head. The blue lines on his faceplate seemed to soften somewhat. If she had to guess, she'd say he was suddenly happy and eager to get started.

"What were you looking for?" she asked him.

"An old friend." He walked past her without elaborating.

Rion sighed and then rounded up the crew. "All right, people, we're headed out. And where the hell is Ram?"

They found him up the ravine, on his knees with a handful of dirt. Rion paused and gave him his moment, knowing that the experience could be quite profound for some. He was grinning as he lifted it to his nose and smelled. First time on Earth made people do strange things. Rion lifted her boot and gave him a playful shove. "You too, pilgrim, let's go."

Ram put the dirt in his pocket as he rose to his feet, swung his rifle from his back to his front, and fell in step with his companions, Spark leading the way and Rion bringing up the rear.

A few patches of forest clung to the ravine, reaching as far up the mountain as the climate would allow. The way was rocky and peppered with stretches of steep climbs and the occasional stream crossing. Lessa and Ram were enjoying the scenery and the sporadic monkey and bird sightings, while Niko slapped at his neck and groaned, "Oh, *great*."

"They're called mosquitoes," Rion called ahead with a laugh.

"Little shits is more like it," he grumbled, and slapped at his arm. "Damn bugs everywhere we go."

"Maybe it's just you—they're not bothering me at all," Lessa said, commencing yet another lovely little sibling argument that lasted most of the hike.

An hour passed, as the climb grew steeper and the progress slower. But at least they were staying on the slopes and avoiding the higher altitudes. Rion started to wonder if Spark knew where the hell he was going and was about to ask him when they edged around the lip of a steep rock outcrop and then ducked beneath a wide overhang.

"Lights on," Rion said.

As they moved deeper under the rock, Less angled her light above them to highlight the overhang ceiling. "Wow. Look at that." Dozens of ancient pictographs covered the rock—animals and hunters, hands and symbols, in clay ochre, charcoal, white.

The overhang led into the mountain. The darker the passage became, the more the pictographs seemed to leap off the rock and dangle in view.

"Careful here," Spark said as he hopped down a short ledge.

They followed with caution and continued on, the cave broadening as they went and the scent of rock and earth growing stronger. Each breath and step was amplified in the hollow space.

"Looks like no one came past this point," Lessa said. "The paintings are all gone." Her light flashed over the rock walls.

"No, look," Niko said, shining his light on a—

"Wait. That's a Forerunner glyph." Rion moved closer. It was hard to spot because it wasn't painted on the wall, but carved and very old, indicating it might be more ancient than anything they'd seen so far.

"Are you sure about this?" Niko asked Spark. "How do you know the Librarian was here?"

It was now so dark that the hard blue light of the armiger's body lit the confined space. As he turned toward Niko, his eyes seemed to hang there suspended like two glowing orbs. "She mentioned the mountain in a message to her husband."

"That's it? That's all you have to go on?"

"No."

When nothing else was forthcoming, Niko muttered, "Well, that's reassuring."

The armiger went forward into the shadows, this time more slowly to allow himself time to examine the walls. After a moment, he beckoned Rion over with one hand. "Here," he said, pointing at a dark area in the rock wall.

Rion used her hand to brush away the years of rock dust and grime, and found an alloy panel inserted into the rock. The panel was edged with small glyphs and in the center was the outline of a large hand. "No question of what to do here," she said, placing her hand on the glyph.

A shudder went through her palm as a loud crack echoed through the space. The rock all around them trembled, the vibration going through the soles of Rion's boots and wobbling her legs.

Blue light appeared like a blowtorch, outlining the shape of a door.

Rion stumbled back. As the line completed its circuit, the doorway filled in with hard light. After a few moments the light vanished, leaving behind an open space in the shape of a tall door.

"Cool," Niko murmured, heading past them toward the doorway.

Rion grabbed his collar and jerked him back.

"Ow!"

"Carefully," she enunciated, pulling his weapon around and making him hold it. "Carefully."

"Fine," he said. "I get it. *Carefully.*"

The armiger led the way in.

"Eyes open," she told the crew.

Rion wasn't sure what they'd find next—maybe a Forerunner facility like the one they'd seen back on Triniel. But it was simply more rock, more darkness, and more stuffy, pungent air.

"Stay against the wall," Spark told them, just as Rion had the distinct sensation that the entire space had suddenly opened up. Visibility was limited, but it became clear they were skirting some sort of drop-off.

"So what are we looking for?" Ram asked, his voice echoing into the darkness.

"A Sentinel," the armiger answered.

"A what?"

The path leveled out and widened into what seemed to be a dead end.

"Armed protective drones. Two of them came to Earth in the final days, accompanying a Gargantua-class vessel." Spark searched the wall again. "I should know—I sent them. Three came," he said, glancing at them and pointing up. "Like the three peaks of the mountain." He smiled. "Snowcapped Sentinels."

"Two escorts and a giant ship . . ." Rion said thoughtfully. "Are you saying they're here, under the mountains?"

Spark was barely paying attention, focused on brushing off a spot on the rock wall. "Not entirely. The Gargantua was used nearby to create the portal to the Ark. One Sentinel left the planet, escorting a Lifeworker's keyship and its cargo of rescued humans."

"And the other one?" Lessa asked.

"Stayed behind. Repurposed here beneath Mawenzi."

"Why this peak and not the others?" Ram asked.

"Mawenzi overlooks Voi and the portal."

"How could the Librarian have survived here?" Niko asked skeptically.

"I did not say she survived here."

Rion paused. *What the hell . . . ?* Wasn't that the whole reason he wanted to come to Earth in the first place? She opened her mouth to ask, but he moved and suddenly disappeared into the rock.

Upon inspection, Rion saw there was a break in the rock face: looked at head-on, it appeared to be a flat surface; however, when seen from an angle, a tall, narrow opening revealed itself, leading to a tunnel that zigzagged back and forth, hiding the light coming from the next chamber.

They emerged onto a wide ledge beneath an overhang, with some kind of light barrier in their way.

A terminal was situated off to the side. Rion stepped over to it and placed her hand on the domed pad. The barrier immediately vanished. They went slowly out onto the ledge. There was another terminal at its edge, and beyond that a ravine. Across the ravine was a peninsula of rock upon which a cylindrical light column emanated from a circular base; a large oblong shape hovered inside the column.

Rion could see another terminal in front of the light column, but there was no discernible way to get across the wide chasm.

"That doesn't look like any drone I've ever seen," Niko said.

"Because it is not. Not anymore. Its parts were used to create these structures," Spark said, moving to the terminal.

Rion joined him. As soon as her hand touched the pad, a wide band of light shot from the ledge, straight across the divide to the other side. "It's a light bridge," she said. She'd seen a few working bridges in Covenant ships, but she had never actually walked on one.

"*What?*" Niko exclaimed. "Oh man, this is incredible."

Spark approached the light bridge, lifted a foot, and stepped off the ledge and onto the solid light.

CHAPTER 46

We are now free to cross the divide. I begin, but notice that one of my companions does not follow.

Ah. He is leery of the hard light bridge.

As I walk back, Niko heads past me with no such wariness.

"Are you sure it's not going to suddenly turn off?" Ram asks, taking his own tentative step, testing its validity.

"I am sure," I say.

Rion slaps the Komoyan on the back and grins widely. "Finally. Something that rattles you. Glad I was here to witness the momentous event."

Like Rion, I am amused at Ram's expense. She and Lessa pass me, but I wait for him and we walk together to the platform.

Meanwhile I am in constant contact with my splinter. ONI's shutdown procedures were expected and only serve to aid our nondetection as I complete my task here in the mountain. My splinter hunts for the eroded data from the expired Catalog recovered beneath the African savanna, as well as the logs of the remaining Catalog's random intrusions into their network.

879 challenged me to find what I need. And so I am.

The Ace of Spades *crew studies the hard light column emanating from the circular base of the platform.*

I pause, intrigued by the wonder on their faces, the way the light reflects on their skin and brightens their eyes.

Our time together is nearly at an end.

I have enjoyed their different personalities and unpredictability, and I find there is hesitation in me to end our partnership.

And I continue to feel guilt for the lie I have kept close at hand.

Revealing to Rion Forge that her father is dead is an uncomfortable prospect, and I do not want to be the one to deliver such news.

Therefore I have decided against it. I have no intention of fulfilling the terms of our agreement.

With that dilemma out of the way, I face the column.

"Is she in there?" Lessa asks. "Your Librarian?"

"In a manner of speaking. This is, indeed, where our journey ends. After accessing this last terminal, I no longer have need of you."

I stare through the light at the long, oval pod floating inside.

This is a Lifeworker pod, very common to the rate and familiar. It does not contain the Librarian, of course, but it does contain something else.

A gift, if I'm right.

"Well?" Rion is saying, and I am brought back to the moment. They are looking at me in an encouraging manner. All I have to do, once the barrier is down, is walk up the ramp and into the hard light. . . .

And yet I hesitate.

The siblings have not yet mastered the art of hiding emotion, not with any real degree of success. Ram Chalva has, but in this instance, he does not bother. Rion as well.

They all appear . . . happy. For me.

I am stunned.

Rion eyes the other side of the light bridge. I also sense in her some wariness and perhaps eagerness to be safely back on board her ship.

Perhaps . . .

Perhaps after all I have put them through . . . I owe them some degree of honesty.

Fair dealings, then. I have changed my mind.

She meets my gaze and lifts her hand to access the terminal, which will disengage the barrier around the light column. Quickly I reach over and grab her wrist.

"What?" she asks, alarm in her dark eyes. "What's wrong?"

My timing is wretched, I am aware. But I am suddenly certain that, yes, honoring my bargain is the best possible ending. Then I may move forward into the light, free of any guilt.

"There is something I must tell you."

She frowns up at me and then down at my alloy fingers. I release her.

Suddenly I'm beset with indecision once more, just when I felt certain.

This shift is unacceptable. I must move on.

"Your father is dead," I say.

There. I said it.

She blinks, then frowns deeply, stepping back as though I have physically struck her. Then she simply stares at me. There is no reaction at all. The crew looks at each other, stunned and confused.

I grow uncomfortable in the silence. "He never survived Etran Harborage."

CHAPTER 47

"There had to be someone to stay behind and detonate the fusion reactor. He sacrificed his life."

Spark continued to talk, to explain, but Rion couldn't hear anything more through the rush of anguish barreling through her veins. Her mind floundered, congesting with denial.

"What is this?" she finally managed, her tone brittle as she gave a sharp, ridiculous laugh, blinking away the stinging in her eyes, and glancing at Spark and the crew, trying to find an anchor, a rescue from the unreal. "No . . . no." She shook her head. "What is this? Why are you saying this?"

This isn't real.

This had to be some twisted AI version of a joke.

Your father is dead.

There had to be someone to detonate the fusion reactor. There had to be someone to stay behind. . . .

He sacrificed his life.

Pieces spun through her memory—Little Bit's narrative, the video file, the debris field—all fragments and parts of a larger whole, all talking at once, all fitting into a horrific puzzle.

Her father, he wouldn't have stayed behind.

But he would.

Absolutely. He'd be the first to volunteer if the stakes were high enough. And back then, at the very beginning of the invasion, they sure as hell were.

Blowing up the shield world to prevent the Covenant from getting their hands on an entire Forerunner fleet was exactly the sort of thing John Forge would do.

A hand landed on her shoulder and she jumped, backing away.

Voices began filtering through her shock. The crew. Spark.

"I am very sorry to deliver such bad news, Rion," Spark said, sounding worried and confused and even apologetic.

Her brow went high. *"You're sorry?"*

Shock, grief, and rage filled her up, swift and vicious and consuming, pushing at her insides, into tiny crevices and corners and cells, until she wanted to scream, to break into a million pieces under the pressure. She lunged at the armiger, shoving his chest plate as hard as she could, letting out a guttural cry.

He could have crushed her in an instant, but stumbled away instead as if he were much more frail.

"You're *sorry*! You didn't just figure this out now. How long? How long have you known?"

"I have known nearly the entire time."

Rion lost it then, hitting and screaming at the armiger as he continued to back up, refusing to engage in a fight as she bruised and bloodied her knuckles on his impervious alloy, pounding on him, swiping at his legs, toppling him, until she found herself on the ground, the armiger behind her, finally holding her still in a choke hold. But she wasn't done: as soon as she was down, instinct had her drawing her handgun and shoving it under the armiger's jaw.

Her breathing was ragged and harsh, her rage a slow burn now, and the present situation reemerging, whether she wanted it to or not. Her bleary gaze found Spark's avatar standing on the terminal, watching her in consternation, the lines in his face somehow more humanoid than ever.

"Fire your weapon and the bullet will most likely ricochet into your skull," he said calmly.

Of course it would. Rion dropped the gun, her arm going limp. Her face was wet and she was wheezing from the choke hold.

"You do realize you cannot overpower me. I could kill you without any effort at all," Spark's avatar added.

She leveled a murderous glare his way. "You already have."

Lessa put her hand to her mouth at that, tears streaming down her face.

Spark let out a heavy sigh, his demeanor full of regret. "I realize how you feel, but—"

"You have *no* idea what this feels like," she said, seething, as hot tears re-formed in her eyes and she struggled to be free of him.

The avatar stiffened, his blue light turning crimson, the lines in his face carving it into anger. *"I have no idea? Me?"* He disappeared as the armiger released her, shoving her forward. She rolled onto her hands and knees, gasping, tears splattering on the ground. The crew had had enough, and they made moves to intervene, but Rion held up a hand and pushed to her feet.

The armiger straightened to its full height, a subtle reshape into something more threatening. It stepped closer and leaned forward, pulsing red and menacing, looking her dead in the eye.

"*I HAVE NO IDEA?!*" it shouted.

Somewhere in the back of her mind, her inner voice made a sound of warning, but she shut it down, and shoved the armiger's chest plate with both hands. "Yeah," she replied. "That's exactly what I'm saying."

Because she couldn't fold right now, couldn't take the knowing. The truth was too harsh, too real, too searing . . . she'd rather bleed and fight. She screamed and pushed at him again, then went to strike—but he'd finally had enough and grabbed her wrist tightly.

"*How dare you*. You are a speck of dust. A *child*. One who knows nothing! Imagine a life where everyone you *know* is gone!" He stepped closer and she moved back. But he kept on coming, squeezing her wrist harder and harder. "Entire races, gone. Entire planets, gone. . . . But that is not enough. No," he continued, "even your own body is taken from you *while you are conscious of it happening.* Your entire civilization is wiped out, and you helped initiate the process. Imagine being the only one left!" His voice broke at that. "The only one left for a hundred thousand years, and when you finally wake up . . ."

He couldn't go on. He was overwhelmed with emotion, his voice cracking as though he wept.

The armiger pinched his fingers together and held them to her face. "Your grief is a mote," he said with anger, "a tiny grain of sand in an ocean the size of the universe."

He paused. "I did not kill your father, Captain. He chose his

own destiny. He had the courage to do what needed to be done."
He leaned forward, his face close to hers, his voice low. "Cry to me
after you witness all sentient life in the entire galaxy erased with
barely a whisper. Dare face me then, and say I know nothing of
grief."

They stared at each other, lost in their own anguish, each
blaming the other.

Rion jerked her wrist away from him, and he let her go, his red
light returning to blue. She rubbed her wrist and then wiped her
arm across her wet face. "I'm done being led around by the nose."
She went to the terminal and slapped her hand onto the dome.
"We're finished here." The translucent barrier fell, and the light
column seemed to grow a bit brighter with it gone.

Rion turned away; no sooner had she set one foot on the bridge
to leave than a flurry of light across the divide stopped her.

The ledge there was filled with armed soldiers, weapons
drawn. She recognized Agent Hahn and near him a very tall Spartan in full Mjolnir armor, directing two other Spartans along the
ledge. No need for the Big Guy to take off his helmet—Rion knew
exactly who it was.

Another squad appeared, in all-black, special ops combat gear.
She counted ten all together.

Rion spun, a cold bitterness settling into her bones. "Cut the
bridge," she demanded.

Spark disabled the light bridge. Then he faced her, hesitating a
long moment before saying, "Good-bye, Captain."

He turned and walked directly into the column, swallowed up
by light until not even a shadow of him remained.

He'd simply left.

Abandoned them.

Spark had bowed out as they faced an enemy they couldn't possibly defeat. At least, not here, not trapped as they were.

Rion couldn't process it fully; there were too many emotions clogging her brain. Options weren't coming. As hard as she might try, there didn't seem to be a way through. The crew . . . they'd counted on her, and—

"Rion." It was Niko. He was in front of her now, looking as stricken and shocked by Spark's revelation and defection as she was, but he grabbed her shoulders and looked at her head-on until she focused on him.

"Hey. *Hey.* Put it in a box," he said softly. "Remember what you told me? Lock it behind a wall, keep it contained? And then"—he glanced across the divide and back at her—"when we need it, you let it out like a goddamn storm. Remember?"

Tears swam in his young eyes. Here was someone who'd believed in her, relied upon her, cared about her. Had she not been emotionally spent, she would have dropped to her knees and let it all out. But instead she found herself hardening inside, finding some inner reserve. She thought of Cade, and how she would never get over that loss, but there was a way, *always* a way, to keep on, to move forward. She could do so again. And she—*they*—would all get through this.

Slowly she began to nod, letting Niko's words wash over her, giving her strength. . . .

He gave her a sad, lopsided smile. "So, Cap . . . what do we do now? Last stand?"

She drew in a deep breath and noted two of the special ops soldiers were working on the terminal from their end. "They're trying to get the bridge back online. Let's look around and see if we can find another way out of here."

"What about following Spark?" Lessa said, gesturing to the hard light column.

"We have no idea where he disappeared to. And I don't know about you, but I'm tired of following that asshole into the unknown. Ram, you go left, Niko, right—follow that platform around and see where it leads."

While the *Ace* crew were armed and held their rifles at the ready, they hadn't taken aim and they didn't plan to.

Rion and Lessa stood at the terminal and watched the progress across the divide. If that light bridge engaged . . .

"Captain Forge." The Big Guy's voice resonated in the cavern. "There's nowhere for you to go. It's over. Put your weapons down and we'll figure this out."

"Yeah, no thanks!" Rion shouted back. "I know what you guys do to people like us. I don't figure on disappearing anytime soon."

"No one's disappearing," the Spartan said.

"Can you give me your word on that?"

He hesitated. Because of course he couldn't vouch for ONI—he wasn't the one in charge. And ONI had a knack for hiding prisoners away without any regard to the legal system or individual rights.

"Captain," Agent Hahn called. "All we want is the armiger and the monitor. Hand them over, and I'll guarantee you and your crew walk away from this."

Lessa leaned closer to Rion, frowning. "As if we could control Spark."

"Sir," one of the soldiers working on the terminal said, "light bridge is coming online."

CHAPTER 48

I pass through the column's blinding light and into a haze of white. I see nothing at first, and then . . . a lithe figure emerges out of the ether, and I know it is her.

The Librarian.

I feel the technology that allows her to awaken and form. Her essence strengthens and floats closer to me. And I see her clearly. Unchanged. The epitome of grace, and beauty, and intelligence, she wears a flowing dress and headpiece and a heavy aura of responsibility. Her large, dark eyes regard me with love and friendship, sadness and regret.

She is the same who blessed me as an infant, the same who appeared to me in my child's mind, serene and loving. She is as I have always seen her.

Goddess. Mother. Manipulator. Savior.

Her examination sweeps through me with such gravitas and power. Suddenly I am pulled from my armiger body, becoming visibly more solid until once more I am Chakas. But I know this is simply *her doing. Making us equals. Making us memories of flesh and bone.*

"Chakas," *she says with all the affection of a mother welcoming home a long-lost son.* "Somehow you have always managed to find a way, and serve me well."

"And I have always managed to pay a price."

I do not mean for our greeting to begin with contention. The words came out before I could stop them. But they are true, so I lift my chin and claim them.

Her head tilts. "Have I hurt you so?" *she asks, her expression softening with sorrow and regret.*

Yes! I cry inside.

She nods gravely. "For that, I am saddened. Regrets are all that is left, it seems." *Her anguish should fill me with satisfaction, but because I love her, it does nothing but make me hurt more.*

"You have persisted," *she says with pride.* "Adapted. You are a singular marvel."

"Of your design?" *I must know. Did she mean for this to happen? She set so many eventualities in motion, and I must know if I am one of them.*

She shakes her head. "No. Your evolution now is your own, a product of necessity perhaps, one that might have a great impact on things to come. Sometimes . . ." *Her dark eyes show a flash of mirth.* "Sometimes the universe creates what it needs without the machinations of others."

"I do not understand."

"No, you do not. But one day you will. You are a creature of choice now, without my sway or influence. Will you serve the Mantle?"

"The Mantle was yours—it was never mine."

"No. It was *yours, meant for your kind, not Forerunners. And look at us now."* She gazes at me with such remorse. "Champions of the Mantle are so few . . . and there is still much to do. At Requiem, I was awoken, along with my husband."

I recoil. "The Didact is alive?"

The Catalog claimed as much as well, I remember.

Her expression grows forlorn and she sighs. She does not answer, but it is clear his threat is not worrisome.

"I have seen the progress of humanity's advancement," she says. "I have seen the paths they might take and the darkness that is coming from many sides. I have given mankind the means and the impetus, and I will give them all that is mine to give. Perhaps this time they will achieve what we could not." Her lips turn up slightly at the corners. "They do not have us Forerunners standing in their way."

There is so much I have wanted to say to her over the millennia, so many questions, so many accusations, so many conversations . . . and now I cannot find the words.

"I do not care about your war and your Mantle," I say.

"But then . . . you do. One side cares. The other does not. One is cold and scheming. The other is all heart."

"I have no heart. That too was taken from me. I have paid my price, done what was required of me. My friends," I manage. "Riser, Vinnevra . . ."

She studies me for a long moment. "As a human, you carried the essence of Forthencho, Lord of Admirals, within you. You felt his struggle, his torment and despair. You were his prison. And you knew how it felt to lose yourself to his strong presence. . . . Would you do such a thing to another, raise old friends who are at peace? Conscript other humans to carry them?"

"You did the same." To me.

"For the greater good."

"The greater good is merely an excuse for the strong to make decisions for the weak."

She doesn't answer me; she sees that this is an argument neither one of us will win. My ire deflates.

"Are they?" I question her words. *"At peace?"*

"They were left to live out their lives in peace, their gene song quiet."

"They are remembered in the Domain. Send me there. Give me access so that my memory may join them." I am pleading. The words coming out of me are crushing. I will give up everything to be among them.

"They are only echoes now, Chakas," she tells me. *"Experience remembered through the eyes of my kind, nothing more. You are not meant to relive the past, to dwell in the halls of living memory."* She shakes her head. *"Where you wish to go, the bad lives alongside the good."*

I do not know how to respond to this. I am confused and, after all this time, no longer know what I want.

She is correct—I already know this. Is there no hope?

I find myself beginning to panic.

"Then join me," I offer. *"You can walk, as I do, among humans again."* It is a small thing for her to use an armiger in the same manner I have done.

She shakes her head. *"It is not my time."*

"Then I will join you."

"Dear Chakas. I see the burden of loneliness you have carried these long millennia. Had you not been a monitor, the weight of it

would have crushed you long ago. Do not let it do so now. You must do the difficult thing and let it go. Perhaps . . . the friends you seek, you have already found."

The haze clears and I can see the Ace of Spades *crew, trapped. They will not escape the chamber.*

In nanoseconds, I replay our time together, every word spoken, every word unsaid, our trials and our journey, our trust and mistrust, our disagreements and laughter.

Of all the sentient life I could have encountered, I encountered them. So suited to my needs, and so familiar. . . .

I feel panic again. I do not want to lose the Librarian. "And you? What will you do now?"

"This imprint will join the others already gone to the Absolute Record. Humanity must be given the tools to hold the Mantle of Responsibility. And the knowledge—they must have the knowledge to tend the Domain. . . ." She stares off into nothing for some time before gracing me with a soft look. "Then, perhaps . . ."

"Bastion?" I ask.

Her tender smile fills me with love and finality, and I see that she does not believe she will ever make it there, or perhaps anywhere she might recover and rest and find peace at last.

"Perhaps," she answers. "With a little luck."

If I had a heart, it would be breaking. I feel no luck, but the absence of it, a heavy doom and despair. Already I am letting go. . . .

"Luck is your way," I remind her.

"No, dear Chakas . . . Spark. It is yours." She gazes at the crew through the thinning of the light. "And theirs. It always has been. Don't you see? You may leave with me to the Absolute Record or . . . you may choose a different path. The choice is yours, my old friend."

A small etched box appears and she hands it to me.

"What is this?"

"A key. Find what's missing," she says. "Fix the path. Right what my kind has turned wrong."

I frown.

"Or come with me."

Time is standing still.

I commit this moment to memory, every detail.

I want to ask her what it is that she wants. Not what she hopes to achieve or the responsibilities she has taken upon her shoulders, but her own desire, her heart's wanting.

But I realize I do not have to ask this. I already know. "Can the Didact find peace?"

The sorrow that flashes through her eyes instantly pains me. "I fear my husband is beyond redemption." She shifts her emotions. "You have made your choice then?"

I look back and see the light bridge has been reactivated and Spartans are advancing, weapons drawn.

I turn back to the Librarian. She is waiting for my decision.

"I have waited one hundred thousand years to find my friends. Why would I leave when I have found them?"

The Librarian's mouth stretches and her eyes crinkle at the corners. She looks upon me with so much love and pride. She knows I will do the right thing. She trusts in me. May I also find the same trust in myself.

"We will meet again, old friend."

"Yes. I know we will."

CHAPTER 49

iko and Ram returned from inspecting the circular platform with the bad news. "There's nothing back there—just rock wall," Ram said.

"We're trapped," Niko said as the hard light bridge suddenly flared to life and streamed across the divide. He ran to the terminal, but was afraid to touch anything. "How do I turn it off?"

The Spartans were preparing to cross the bridge, going slowly in formation. Rion silently cursed Spark for deserting them. That dread she'd been feeling earlier? Maybe she should have listened to her gut.

"Captain Forge! Lay down your weapons! Now!" the Big Guy called as he and his team eased their way across the bridge.

"What do we do?" Lessa asked.

"Well, what we're *not* going to do is fire on a bunch of Spartans. Keep your weapons down and your hands in the air." The fear she saw in their young eyes killed her.

"Well, I would say it was nice crewing with you," Ram said, "but . . ."

They watched the Spartans advance, keeping very still, knowing that if they made the slightest move, they could be fired upon.

"How the hell did they find us?" Niko asked.

Lessa stared into the depths of the chasm. "I think I'd rather jump than be taken prisoner."

"Don't you even think about it," Rion said. "We'll find a way out. We always do."

"Yeah, well, our luck might've just r—" Niko said.

A bright white flash filled the cavern.

The Spartans froze. Rion shielded her eyes, looking up along with everyone else.

The light filled the entire space and seemed to go right through her. She *felt* it, a low vibration easing through her skin and muscle and bone. Buzzing and energizing. Images filled her mind, too quick to capture and hold.

Melody and song. Memories. Words.

As the light faded, the room spun. Vertigo and emotion gripped her. She blinked hard, trying to ground herself, and noticing those around her were similarly affected. But there wasn't time to figure out what the hell had just happened, because suddenly the hard light column behind them began to glow brighter. Particles of color ran through the light in small vertical lines, streaming like code, growing faster and brighter and more vivid until the pod inside shot like a bullet up through the column and disappeared.

Rion turned away from the sight, blinking her eyes back to normal, only to see the Spartans and special ops soldiers suddenly dropping to their knees and aiming their weapons, a multitude of voices shouting at them to stand down.

Stunned, Rion's hands shot higher into the air. Her crew did the same.

"Hold your fire, Howlers! Do *not* fire!" the Big Guy yelled at the same time.

Heart racing and fear sliding down into her gut, Rion wasn't sure what the hell was happening. They'd made no threatening overtures, and she had a hard time following the shouting and mixed commands from across the divide.

"Do not fire!" the Big Guy hollered again.

"Hands behind your head!" another shouted. "Get on your knees! *Now!*"

Rion linked her fingers behind her head, and as she went to bend her knees, she caught movement and glanced behind her. Understanding dawned.

The armiger was standing on the platform, holding a small metal object and carrying himself in battle stance, glowing a menacing, highly aggressive red.

Oh God.

"No—no, don't shoot!" she yelled desperately at the Spartans. Jesus. They were right in the middle of what could very well be a massacre.

The crew looked frantic and scared, everyone with their hands behind their heads as the armiger took a few steps forward to stand in their midst, between Lessa and Niko. He crouched and let out a challenging roar. Goose bumps raced up Rion's arms.

While he was ready to fight alongside them . . . to *protect* them . . . Spark had the worst timing of any being Rion had ever known, and he was about to get them all killed. Her fears were justified when he did something even worse to inflame an already explosive situation—he manifested a hard light rifle.

The special ops team ignored the Big Guy's order and opened fire.

Rion was in a slow-motion nightmare. She grabbed the nearest person—Lessa—and threw her toward the terminal. As she turned around again, she saw Ram and Niko scrambling behind the terminal for cover. Rion dove for it, feeling a sting in her left bicep as a bullet tore through skin and muscle.

They huddled tightly behind the small bit of cover they had. "Everybody okay?" she shouted. Less and Niko were pale, their eyes wide as plates.

Ram gave her a nod. "We're fine. Are *you* okay?" he asked, eyeing the blood spilling down her arm.

"Hurts like hell, but I've had worse. I'm good. Worry about it later."

A flash of understanding and admiration crossed his features. He'd been there too, plenty of times in their line of work. He returned her nod, and then saw that his cigarette had fallen out of his pocket at the corner of the terminal. With a curse, he snaked his hand out to retrieve it, as several shots streamed overhead.

Rion glanced around the terminal and saw the armiger aiming his light rifle not at the Spartans, but up at the wide rocky overhang. Several shots made the entire overhang splinter and come tumbling down.

The soldiers retreated across the bridge before they were caught in the avalanche of rock that quickly covered the bridge.

The firefight was over.

Spark hadn't been trying to kill them. If he'd wanted to, all he had to do was disengage the light bridge while it was still occupied. Now that it wasn't, he accessed the terminal and deactivated the light bridge, the fallen rocks immediately tumbling into the chasm. He smashed the panel in an effort to prevent the bridge from being accessed again before walking around the terminal to face them.

His alloy steps echoed in the quiet. He stood above them and then bent down, red glowing eyes slowly shifting to blue.

"Follow me," he said, holding out his hand.

At first, no one moved.

Then Lessa slapped her hand into his. "Don't have to ask me twice." He pulled her up and the rest followed. Once they were all standing, Spark ushered them onto the platform where the light column had been. The column was gone, but the platform was still glowing like one of the—

Translocation pad, Rion realized, right before they blinked out of existence.

And then reappeared outside in the thin air and barren landscape just beneath the summit of Mawenzi's jagged peaks.

Sickness rolled through Rion's gut as they stumbled, finding nearby boulders to hold on to, needing something solid to ground them. Lessa went behind one of the rocks and puked, while Niko sat down in the dirt, dazed. And Ram just stood there with Spark as if nothing had happened. Again.

"Can't breathe," Niko said.

"It's the altitude," Ram told him.

"It's going to take us hours to get back to the ship," Rion said. They were so high up, all she could see were clouds. She swallowed down her nausea, then checked her left bicep. A nice chunk of skin and muscle had been sliced in two. She was lucky it was just a flesh wound. It ached and burned, but it would heal.

"Whoa—you're *shot*?" Niko's brow arched high.

"Save your breath," Rion told him. "I'm fine."

"Less!" Niko scurried to his sister. He'd just noticed the blood trickling from a cut over her eyebrow.

"It's fine," she said, wiping her mouth. "Hit my damn head on the terminal." She sat on a rock and he knelt in front of her, worry etched on his dirty face. Lessa waved his concern away, and then she glanced over at Spark. While he'd returned to his normal blue color, he was still armed, scanning the horizon for signs of danger. "You came back for us," she said.

No one said anything. Yes, he'd returned and saved them all . . . but that didn't negate the fact that he'd left in the first place, and nearly got them all killed.

It wouldn't take long for the Spartans to escape the cavern, and Rion was pretty sure they'd called in reinforcements way before the ceiling even came crashing down. In fact, considering where they were, the entire mountain would be crawling with military anytime now.

She let out a long, frustrated breath. "Now what? How the hell are we going to get back to the ship without being spotted?"

"I can remotely access the ship," Spark revealed. "It will come to you."

"She," Rion corrected.

Spark stared at her for a long time and Rion thought she might have to explain herself, but he just nodded and said, "She."

"Uh, guys . . ." Niko was standing and looking across the

clouds to three dark specks moving fast. "We've got drones incoming."

The armiger quickly joined them and they were immediately engulfed in a translucent hard light dome just before the drones soared overhead and then made several passes around the summit. Rion held her weapon tightly, looking up through the haze of light and hoping they wouldn't be caught.

In the quiet seconds that passed, her thoughts turned to her father.

No, not yet.

She couldn't go there. Not until they were off this mountain and safe again.

The drones made one more pass before zipping down the slopes.

The dome dissipated. "We are undetected," Spark announced.

"That comes in handy," Niko quipped.

"We wouldn't need his help right now if he hadn't betrayed us," Rion said.

"I did not betray you."

She gave the armiger a hard stare.

"Very well. Yes. I did betray you. But I had my reasons. And then I changed my mind."

She rolled her eyes, trying not to let the altitude get to her. "Lucky us."

True to Spark's word, the *Ace of Spades* arrived shortly after the drones disappeared, settling nearby on a craggy slope. The crew gathered and waited for the ramp to descend, the wind buffeting them as the thrusters' force pushed against solid rock.

Rion watched Niko and Lessa board, followed by the armiger.

Ram paused next to her, clapping her on her good shoulder, and giving her an understanding look. "One foot in front of the other, Forge."

As soon as they were on board, the ship lifted off the mountainside without Rion's input. It should've stirred something in her; she should've cared where they were going, but she felt nothing.

She headed to the locker room with the others. Taking a seat, she studied the crew. They were banged up, bruised, dirty, and looked completely exhausted. Niko shrugged out of his gear, then went to the med kit for antiseptic spray to treat the cut over Lessa's eyebrow. He wiped it carefully and then applied a seal.

Ram ducked out of his rifle strap, placed the weapon on the floor, sat on the bench, and at long last lit his cigarette; he took a long drag and let his head rest against the wall, eyes closing.

"Rion."

Niko was standing in front of her with the med kit, gesturing to her arm. She removed her gear slowly, starting to feel the pain and heat in her left arm, her muscles, and her bruised knuckles. Her shoulder injury from Binterall burned with pain. Everything hurt. Niko cleaned her wound and then sealed it.

"Thanks," she said.

After storing their gear, he and Lessa retreated into the hold and up the steps.

Ram stayed put, enjoying his smoke.

As Rion left the locker room, she passed a systems panel. She could have checked it, to see if there was a destination, a road to anywhere, but it was clear that Spark would take them somewhere safe or dangerous or really wherever the hell he saw fit.

She was honestly too drained to care.

CHAPTER 50

Facility at Voi, Kenya, Africa, Earth

nnabelle was working with two groups of officers and a ground crew—one group trying to get into the comm tower, and the other through the blast doors in Hangar Two. Hangar One's doors were still closed tight, but there was a Pelican-size hole in the side of the hangar where the AR team and Fireteam Apollo had blown their way out.

As Thea had been about to turn herself in for review, the AI had detected a strange signal coming from Kilimanjaro, a possible ship's signature that identified as both Forerunner and human— it was like nothing she'd ever encountered before. She'd sent a quick message to Hollier seconds before the facility completely shut down.

Once Fireteam Apollo and the AR team were free from the hangar, and Annabelle had been informed of the signal, she'd

KELLY GAY

ordered both teams to gear up and track it down, knowing it had to be the *Ace of Spades* and potentially 343 Guilty Spark—the coincidence was too great to ignore. If they could neutralize the monitor, his hold on the facility would be nullified, and whatever the hell he had planned would be cut short.

An hour had passed since both teams left the facility for Mount Kilimanjaro. There was no way to know their status until the blackout was lifted.

The teams were on their own.

Dr. Iqbal arrived with his own science team in tow. "Is it true?" he asked in a low voice for her ears only. "Is he here? Guilty Spark?"

"I believe so. He's commandeered an armiger. . . ."

"Good Lord. Are you sure?"

Annabelle stepped away from the others as they continued trying to release the hangar lock. She glanced at the mountain. "They're snowcapped Sentinels," she murmured.

"What?"

"He's looking for her, for the Librarian. Just like the stat bots predicted."

As they stared at the mountain, a bright column of light streamed from the summit, shooting into the sky, and painting the clouds in a rainbow of colors as it went.

"What the hell was that?" Iqbal said.

Annabelle shook her head. Whatever was going on in that mountain, she prayed her team finally lived up to their reputations. She turned to the doctor. "What do you know about manual lock overrides?"

"Why?"

"We need to get into the comm tower to reestablish communications. And the techs with the know-how aren't out here—"

"Which means they're trapped below us," Iqbal concluded.

"These doors aren't budging. Come on," Annabelle said, "let's see what we can do about the comms."

As they hurried toward the tower, the facility suddenly powered back up. Annabelle paused as the control tower's lights flared and the ALS engaged, its strobes and light bars illuminating the tarmac and surrounding area to once again guide ships in for landing; simultaneously the hangar bay doors slid open. She winced as her comms unit blared in her ear, a dozen messages coming in all at once. Annabelle muted the device, took a deep breath, and then turned it back on to begin issuing orders. Her first priority was getting the facility back on track and then figuring out what damage had been done.

"Director Richards?"

"Ferg! Is that you?"

"Yes, I am . . . here."

"What happened?"

"It appears we experienced a complex intrusion by an unclassified splinter. It cast a web through the system, cutting off commands, systems, and communications, and trapping my construct. It was . . . unsettling. . . ."

"Damage?"

He hesitated, which caught Annabelle off guard. She braced herself for the bad news. "I am not detecting any damage."

"How can that be?"

"I'm running a complete diagnostic, but cursory inspection shows no internal damage to our network, framework, or operating systems. It didn't escape, Director," he admitted. "It retreated on its own. I can find no trace of it in our system. I'm sorry, I—"

"Don't worry about it, Ferg." *Damn it.* That splinter had either left something behind or got whatever it wanted from them before retreating. And Ferg had been compromised.

"Shall I turn myself in for review? Thea is on standby."

"Yes, please do. Thea?"

"I'm here, Director Richards."

"Run another diagnostic. And get me an open comm line to the team."

CHAPTER 51

R ion climbed the metal stairs, crossed the catwalk, and then ducked into the corridor leading to her quarters. Once inside, she sat on the edge of her bed, her thoughts cloudy and her emotions spent.

Her personal space no longer felt like home; everything was different, and it wasn't just because ONI had tossed the room. In her desk drawer were her father's pictures, as well as Little Bit's projections. All that trouble, all that risk, and for what?

He was gone.

She rubbed a hand down her face.

In her mind's eye, she pictured the *Spirit of Fire* leaving the Forerunner shield world as it blew to pieces. Eleven thousand souls. Alive because of John Forge. And because of his sacrifice, humanity had survived the Covenant's assault early on in the war.

An unsung hero.

A sacrifice lost, like the ship itself.

Tired, heartbroken, she lay back and closed her eyes.

Rion wasn't sure how long she slept, but she could tell immediately that *Ace* was grounded. She grabbed clean clothes, showered, then headed for the lounge.

The crew wasn't around, and she didn't bother calling out. There was a rawness about her, a hypersensitivity, as though the tenuous thread she held on to would snap with the slightest provocation—a nod of sympathy, a pat on the back, a look of sadness . . . Anything might shatter the thin bubble of protection around her.

As she turned to leave the lounge, that thin bubble broke at the sight of the armiger standing hunched in the doorway.

She took a carefully controlled breath. "Move."

He didn't budge.

Her blood pressure rose. Behind her, Spark called out, "Captain Forge . . . *Rion*."

She turned to find the avatar above the lounge table's holopad.

"I wanted to tell you. . . ." he started. "I truly did. But when I attempted it . . . I could not do it. I did not want to be the one to cause such pain. But I know now it was inevitable." He paused. "You have not asked me how I knew."

No, she hadn't. It was too new, the knowledge that her father was really gone, the accepting of it. For so long, she'd felt that he was out there somewhere, lost, waiting. . . .

But she also knew that she'd have to get it over with some time. One giant messy lump of details and more grief . . .

She met Spark's gaze, and stepped back into the lounge, waiting.

"As 343 Guilty Spark, I had a number of interactions with species of the former Covenant—Sangheili, Huragok, San'-Shyuum—as well as with humanity and their United Nations Space Command and Office of Naval Intelligence. . . . I have been to many interesting places due to those meetings, and I gleaned such a marvelous collection of data from them. So much data, it would astound you. In fact, the number of—"

Rion lifted a brow and brought him back on topic.

"When I was recovered and placed on your ship, I did as my nature dictated. I gleaned data. The name of your father's ship triggered an echo in my memory. It took several days, but I managed to coax this recollection from my memory stores.

"The *Spirit of Fire* routinely engaged in preprogrammed scheduled maintenance sheds and data drops. It was—or is—their hope to leave behind a trail, you see? Embedded within a recovered drop was a message to you from your father, John Forge. This message was left in every drop, a promise made by the ship's AI, Serina, and the ship's captain to your father.

"I should have purged the information. But, given my nature, it is hard to part with even the smallest byte of intelligence, especially those that ring with such humanity. . . . I have sent the packet to the datapad in your quarters."

His revelation should have come as a surprise, but Rion was becoming used to the shocking, the unexpected, the awe-inspiring. It was part of their new normal. At least, that's what she told herself as she inclined her head, and then left the lounge.

In her quarters, she sat at her desk and powered on her datapad. She paused, unsure if she was ready. . . .

But with a steadying breath, she opened the datapad and accessed the message.

An instant blast of pain hit her square in the chest. Her father's face loomed large in the frame, looking off to the side for a moment before he ran a hand down his scruffy jaw, then let out a heavy sigh. He was standing on a hard light bridge on a Forerunner structure that Rion now knew to be Etran Harborage, the shield world.

It was the same day, she realized, the same clothes, and the same view as the video Little Bit had shown her.

Only now he wasn't grinning.

As he turned back and stared into the camera, she saw it all written in his dark eyes and the tight set to his face. What he was about to do. The decision already made. Her heart pounded, throat raw as she tried to swallow. He opened his mouth, shook his head, and then tried again.

"Hey, kiddo."

His words lodge in his throat, his expression searching, looking for the right way to begin. But there are no good words for this, no good way to say what he needs to. So he shrugs. There's nothing he can do now.

"I'm out of time, Lucy. . . . This war, it's coming on hard and fast. . . .

"When you see this, you'll be older. I told Serina to wait. Don't be mad about that. Little you doesn't need to grow up with this on her shoulders. But . . ." He shakes

his head; a muscle ticks in his jaw. He is struggling. "Can't go without saying good-bye. We have a deal, you and me. Always be straight with each other. I'm not about to back out of it now.

"Without a reactor, Spirit *will drift a while before she's found or makes it back home. Serina will hold on to this message and make sure you get it when enough time passes. She and Cutter promised me that."*

He looks away, rubs his jaw again.

"Look, kiddo . . . what we're facing . . . it doesn't look good. There's a fleet of alien ships here. Tech like we've never seen before. If it falls into the wrong hands, we're done for. You, your mom, your granddad, Aunt Jill—everyone. So I'm doing my part, okay?

"This is what it takes. This is a sacrifice I knew came with the job.

"You're the best thing that ever happened to me. Never doubt that. Never think that what I do now means I don't love you, cuz, kid, I swear my heart is full."

His eyes turn glassy. He knows it, and gives them a quick swipe. The next part seems to hurt him the most. "You're going to be one hell of a lady. I'm already proud of the person I know you'll be."

He stops, and his breath is shaky as he takes a moment to get a hold of himself before looking back into the camera.

"So this is good-bye. I'm so sorry. I hope one day you can forgive me for leaving you. Until then, chin up, shoulders straight, and you never, ever *be afraid to take life by the horns and make it what you want it to be."*

He gives a sharp nod, kisses his fingers, and then slaps them onto the camera lens.

Rion sat very still as her heart shattered, feeling every stab of pain, every break and fissure. The last twenty-six years of her life washed away, leaving behind a little girl who loved her father more than life itself and missed him terribly.

Tears fell onto the desk.

She could barely breathe, afraid that if she blinked or spoke or moved the rest of her would break too, just crack into a million pieces. She lost all sense of time, her mind a daze, full of hazy images of the past and the present.

Her father was gone.

She'd never get to rescue him, never fulfill the fantasy she'd lived with for so long of the moment he saw her face and knew she'd never given up on him. She'd never get to throw her arms around him and hug him so tight until he laughed and told her he was choking.

Like so many others in the war, he'd died a hero's death—a soldier, a marine through and through. He loved what he did, and he protected what was his.

He was stardust now. She'd flown her ship through his final act. And leave it to him to go out big. John Forge had lived true to his beliefs—as he said, taking life by the horns and wrestling it into submission, even if that meant going out in the process.

A warrior's heart and a wild soul.

And she'd never see him again.

It was all over.

Had Rion learned of her father's death early on, she wouldn't be the person she was now. She'd never have left Earth, wouldn't have loved being out among the stars so much. . . .

Everything she'd become was because of him.

She thought of this other life she might have lived, of things like fate and destiny, and questioned whether any of it really mattered at all. Her mind told her it was all random—it was far easier that way—but her heart told her there were paths and plans, that maybe John Forge hadn't died for nothing, maybe he had made an enormous difference, his single courageous act reverberating across the entire galaxy.

She held on to that thought, rubbing her wet eyes, head aching with regrets and revelations, heart burning with loss and grief.

And she let go of what might have been, and embraced what was.

Her calling was in the stars.

With her father.

Where she belonged.

CHAPTER 52

Mount Kilimanjaro, Tanzania, Africa, Earth

When her team checked in, Annabelle breathed a sigh of relief. No losses. Some minor injuries, the worst being Agent Hahn's cracked tibia.

Ferg had been working around the clock in conjunction with the stat bots, trying to solve the riddle of why Guilty Spark had wanted into their system in the first place. Ferg had had some success creating a timeline of the splinter's movements within the facility's framework. The monitor hadn't just wanted them to shut down; it had been searching for very specific data—namely, the repeated intrusion by an unknown Catalog, which had been hounding ONI since its sudden emergence in 2552, along with the files on the other Catalog recovered from the savanna.

Just that small splinter of Guilty Spark could have done massive damage, and yet it had withdrawn without any real harm to their systems at all, which was something of a conundrum.

They might never know why.

According to reports, the colored light shooting into the atmosphere, which had been witnessed by several hundred people across the area, carried what the AR team and Apollo claimed was a pod seen hovering inside the hard light column within the mountain. Since the armiger had stepped into this light and two humanoid shapes were then seen floating inside, Dr. Iqbal theorized it was a Lifeworker pod, and the other shape inside the light had been an imprint of the Librarian.

Annabelle had to admit the idea held weight. Despite their beliefs, however, everything witnessed by both teams was being run through ONI's knowledge base of Forerunner discoveries.

That 343 Guilty Spark had actually made its way to Earth to hunt for the Librarian was something Annabelle couldn't seem to wrap her mind around. She supposed she'd never really believed it would happen. One of the big eventualities they'd prepared for had occurred.

They were no closer to obtaining the monitor than before, but they did have a new Forerunner facility to excavate, study, and learn from.

The *Taurokado* was on its way back to Onyx to do Barton's bidding, while Fireteam Apollo was off to rendezvous with the UNSC *Infinity* for reassignment. Annabelle's team, along with BOOK-WORM's science division, was now engaged in what would be a very long process of cataloging and exploring the newly exposed site in the mountain.

Annabelle made her way into the site, passing through the

narrow passage and into the cavern, now flooded with light. The rubble that had nearly killed her team and the Spartans had been cleared away from the approach to the light bridge, reactivated by Dr. Iqbal.

The hard light cast the entire chamber in a pale, otherworldly glow.

Such an amazing feat of technology, harnessing photons and exciting them enough to form a solid surface—and stranger still to be walking on one. Annabelle hesitated, staring across the divide to the other side, where several scientists in white lab coats inspected the translocation pad, recording notes and taking readings, while a number of drones were mapping the interior site.

Dr. Iqbal was across the bridge, kneeling in front of the terminal, studying something of note. With a deep breath in, then out, Annabelle headed across to the platform, imagining how it had looked to her team when they first arrived, finding the *Ace of Spades* crew with a Forerunner armiger. They'd been eyewitnesses to the column of light, to the armiger entering and exiting with something in its grasp.

Dr. Iqbal sensed a presence and glanced over his shoulder. "Director."

"Doctor. Any idea where they might have gone?"

"None. We were able to access the translocation platform," he said, looking up at the cylindrical column carved out of the rock and leading to the surface. "It's a static portal. Takes us to the base of Mawenzi's peak."

"So Forge and her crew used the portal, and met up with her mystery ship there."

"And the armiger, don't forget."

She smiled. "Hard to. And the artifact?"

"No clue. I've watched the team's footage several times, as I'm sure you have as well. Most of it was hidden in the armiger's grasp, but it looks like some sort of metal box. Doesn't match anything in our database."

"Any theories?"

"Not yet. But if it *was* the Librarian's imprint he accessed . . . if he *spoke* to her, received something from her, it must be of great importance."

Perhaps something she'd felt was imperative to leave behind before the Halo's pulse reached her. . . . Just a hunch, given what they knew so far. Annabelle glanced around the chamber again, realizing how much work was left to do here and elsewhere. "Keep me posted, Doctor."

"Of course."

Annabelle left him to his task and walked to the edge of the outcrop, staring down into the dark, then across the divide where the team had nearly been crushed by falling rock. Odd. If the armiger—controlled as it was by Guilty Spark—wanted them dead, all it had to do was deactivate the light bridge, and her ARs and Fireteam Apollo would have fallen into the darkness below.

As with the intrusion into the facility's mainframe, it seemed the goal had not been destruction or damage.

Guilty Spark had merely wanted to access their files and to interact with the supposed imprint of the Librarian.

And, once again, they might never know why. They did have that light anomaly, though, which had been captured on the team's feed. For three seconds, this entire chamber had lit up.

The footage time stamp had stopped, and then picked up another anomaly four seconds later. Thea was certain there was a code within the light itself.

And as for the crew of the *Ace of Spades* . . . ? Well, they were living on borrowed time.

CHAPTER 53

For the record, we never left Earth.

For the past week, the Ace of Spades *has remained hidden.* We are still on the continent of Africa, perched on a plateau overlooking the Tsavo National Forest. Rion was not in the right mind-set to concern herself where I took us when we escaped, so I kept us here, knowing our business was not yet complete.

She has not seemed to care about anything for so many days that I began to wonder if I made a terrible mistake in telling her the truth about her father.

She spent the days hiking the local trails, going through normal routines with the crew, and ignoring me as much as she could. A shade of her former self.

And then suddenly, like the sun returning after a long bout of rain, she came back.

Still not ready to forgive me, of course.

Though her agreement to participate in the ritual we are about to perform strikes me as a positive sign that forgiveness may be forth-coming.

"Are you ready?" I ask her.

Lessa, Niko, and Ram join us, dressed in the finest clothes they have, which for Niko is the same outfit he wears every day. Lessa has donned a dress, and Ram is wearing his salvager coat with its many stolen medals and ribbons. Rion's dark hair is loosely braided and hanging over her shoulder. She wears a clean pair of pants and a type of shirt referred to as a "tank top."

I have already built the fire.

The sun is just beginning to set, casting the land in shades of orange and yellow and pink.

In my short life on Earth, we had many rituals for saying good-bye to those we lost. Songs sung, bodies painted, dances around a tall fire . . . We might have been a primitive people, but we loved and we mourned those we lost all the same. These actions do not change across the vast oceans of time or with the rise and fall of civilizations.

I believe there is a very good chance that we might never return to Earth. So this particular farewell matters.

This time, I will say a proper good-bye to my home, my family, and my friends.

I am letting them go.

The Lifeworker pod and imprint left without me. That too was a loss in many ways, a difficult choice after so many thousands of years, but the right one. I know that now.

I will learn to look forward, not back.

And so, as the sun sinks into the western sky, I begin to sing.

I sing for Forthencho, for Gamelpar and Vinnevra, for Bornstellar and Riser. I sing for Ram's lost crew, and the parents the siblings never knew, and I sing for John Forge and his great sacrifice.

We write their names on the stone ledge nearby with red ochre and charcoal, and we send their spirits off into the west.

We then stay awhile and watch the sun disappear beyond the horizon.

I admire the view. There is nothing quite like a sunset in this part of the world, the sky now awash with fiery pinks and oranges, purples and dusky blues.

Eventually the heavens turn black and the air grows cold. The fire is almost burned away. Ram is sitting with his legs dangling over the plateau's edge, smoking one of his hand-rolled "cigarettes," a curious habit. The siblings are painting symbols around the names written on the rock behind us. Rion sits at the fire, her fingers stained with charcoal and red.

"Rion—" I begin, but she holds up a hand to silence me and finally pulls her gaze away from the flames. Her look is stern, eyes hard.

"Why did you come here? What did you want from the Librarian?" she asks me.

"I wanted to access the Domain."

This is partially true.

"Why?"

I can see this is my moment to be honest. This is her test.

"To find the memories, the ghosts of my friends . . . to join them or to bring them out, of which I am not certain."

"You would have left this world, for what? The afterlife?"

"It is not an afterlife . . . but yes."

"Why did you come back, then?"

"Because . . . what I wanted when I first retrieved my human memories was to find those I knew, my friends. All the time I had spent alone . . . it was all very fresh and startling . . . and horrifying. So my immediate aim was to find them, to make the Librarian return them, through a geas perhaps. But as I assembled my memories on Geranos-a and was then rescued by you and your crew, many things began to change. : . .

"I now have my freedom. My programming is my own. And I no longer wish to be chained to the past. It is time for me to move on."

She snorts at that.

"For you as well," I say.

This does not endear me to her, but it is the truth. We are the same, in this regard.

"What did the Librarian give you?"

"A coordinate key."

"To where?"

"A safe place." Among other things.

At this time, she does not press further.

"Will you use it?"

"Perhaps. In time."

"And until then?"

"I believe you are in desperate need of an AI to administer your ship."

Her brow rises. "And you're the AI for the job?"

"No more lies, Captain."

She gazes so hard at me I wonder if my armiger might crack in two. "No more lies," she says.

And yet . . .

Perhaps some things are better left unsaid.

CHAPTER 54

After the ritual good-bye, they left Earth right under Homefleet's nose and jumped, heading to the Shaps system and Myer's Moon.

From there, they'd figure out their next move.

The first night in slipspace, Ram made them a traditional Komoyan dinner with hardly any traditional ingredients, which in hindsight really made it just dinner. Rion didn't have the heart to point this out to him, but Niko was more than happy to do so.

They gathered around the table, joined by Spark over the holopad.

After the meal, talk turned to the future, and Lessa asked the question on everyone's mind.

"So what do we do now? I mean . . . can we go back to salvaging? *Should* we?"

The mood grew somber.

"We're not exactly in the clear with Gek 'Lhar," Ram said. "That bounty's still in effect."

"And ONI won't stop—ever," Lessa added. "They know we have their asset."

"Which, really, when you think about it," Niko said with a frown, "is ridiculous. Spark belongs to no one but himself."

Spark gave the kid a nod.

No one was thrilled with the prospect of a future where they were always on the run, always looking over their shoulders.

"We're not the enemy," Lessa said. "Instead of trying to learn from him, they want to lock him up."

"In their defense," Spark told her, "I did not make a good impression on the human military when I was a monitor. Neither did others of my former kind."

"So to recap," Niko said, "our future entails steering clear of ONI, dodging what's left of the Covenant, and avoiding every mercenary and bounty hunter in the galaxy. So . . . like a normal week."

That brought a few laughs, and Rion smiled as they finished their meal, while talk turned to Gek 'Lhar and where he might be in the galaxy.

The last several months had been a tumultuous ride, and she wasn't keen on continuing down that particular path.

Could they go back to the way things had been before? With a little finesse and careful planning . . . probably. It would take some doing, but most things could be made whole once more.

Did she want to?

She wasn't so sure.

They could easily reap the rewards of Triniel—with the salvage currently in their hold, they'd never lack for credits or resources again. Though she wasn't sure they'd ever return. Plundering a planet-wide grave site hadn't felt right, nor did the idea appeal now. And salvaging definitely lost some of its shine when it became easy.

She thought back to the cavern beneath Kilimanjaro, the way the light had filled her up and the strange figure moving out of the haze.

She'd held on to her secret, and wondered if the crew had done the same.

Rion had seen the Librarian.

She'd gazed upon the ancient Forerunner, utterly struck by the love and wisdom in her eyes, and understood at once how Spark could cling to his devotion for so very long.

She understood why he called her *mother*. Savior of mankind, nurturer . . .

But even as Rion had felt the stirrings of loyalty and love, she knew those emotions for what they were: a genetic disposition built into her very DNA, giving the Librarian a way to be heard, a way to inspire loyalty, a way to nudge her children to fulfill their potential.

Like any other human, Rion listened.

She heard. And she understood.

The trials ahead. The battles to come. The safe place. The things that needed healing and tending.

Take care of him. He is more fragile and important than you could ever know.

She'd thought a lot about that moment over the last few days, unwilling to share it just yet.

She'd felt conflicted too. On the one hand, it felt like she'd been blessed. On the other, she wasn't too keen on the idea of being genetically predisposed to want what someone else wanted.

Though her choices were her own.

And, boy, did they have options like never before.

With a souped-up ship like the *Ace of Spades*, thanks to the upgrade seed, and an AI on the level of Spark, they could get into places most civilians or military personnel couldn't dream of.

And as always these days, she thought of her father.

His sacrifice . . . the scale of war, the billions lost. Kip Silas's loss and the many who had died on Sedra, and more recently the millions gone in New Phoenix . . . It seemed the killing would never end.

She thought of the horrifying prospect of the Flood, what Spark and the Forerunners had gone through, and knew in her gut that if that particular threat ever reappeared, and the various species of the galaxy didn't wise up and stop slaughtering each other, they were all doomed.

Maybe the Mantle of Responsibility that the Forerunners had been so fond of wasn't a one-race responsibility, but an every-race responsibility. Human, Sangheili, Kig-Yar, Unggoy . . . postwar life had begun bringing small pockets of species together. If certain factions stopped making war, manipulating fears, clinging to their information and technology, and deciding for the greater good without the greater good's input, it might be the beginning of something better.

One single act could make an enormous difference, could reverberate across the entire galaxy . . . John Forge had proven that.

"Rion." Niko's elbow nudged her out of her deep thoughts.

"What?"

He gave her a weird look. "We asked what you think. About the future."

They were looking at her expectantly. She let out a deep breath. "Well . . . Ram's right. We need to get the bounty off our heads. And Less is right too. We're not ONI's enemy. We're not the UNSC's enemy either. They might try their damnedest to paint us as the bad guys, but we're not going to live up to their expectations of who we are and what we stand for."

Niko tilted his head, curious. "What do we stand for?"

"I don't know," she answered. "I honestly thought I did. But now . . . What I do know is that I'm going to finish what I started and find the *Spirit of Fire*. There are eleven thousand souls still out there. . . ." And she had to believe they were. Rion might not have been able to save the one who mattered most to her, but she sure as hell could save the rest of them. Her father would have wanted it that way, and if there was any way to honor his memory and his sacrifice, it was this.

She met Spark's blue eyes, and he dipped his head. "I have no doubt, Captain. We *will* find that ship."

It was a tall order, but if anyone could help her achieve that goal, it was Spark. Rion returned the nod, and then refocused on the crew. "After that . . . We have a helluva fast ship. We can go places and do things we never could before. We have the Triniel loot, so we're all set with funds. We have the luxury of choosing." Rion picked up her glass of ale. "The galaxy is ours."

"I'll drink to that," Ram said, flashing a white grin through his black beard as he lifted his glass.

Niko stood. "To the scrap."

"To the stars," Lessa joined in.

"To the father." Ram nodded to Rion, then to Spark. "And the mother."

Spark manifested his own glass and lifted it. "To friends."

Rion leaned over the table as they put their glasses together. "To family."

And they drank.

They call us criminals now. Renegades.

The Office of Naval Intelligence spreads its propaganda through the galaxy, posts bounties, and hounds us among the stars.

But we have a fast ship.

The fastest. The smartest, if I may say so.

They are afraid. Of what we know. Of what we might share. Of where we go, and what we might bring back.

They know what is still out there. What could return.

Their fear is justified.

EPILOGUE

Novak entered his quarters and saw the flashing signal on his personal datapad.

He tossed his gym towel onto his bed and sat at his desk. The message had no sender, no origin data, no time stamp. He passed it through a complete security check. It came out clean. Mysterious, but clean.

As he read the brief missive, a small quirk twisted his lips. He shook his head, and leaned back in his chair, his grin growing.

He hoped like hell he never came across Rion Forge again, because he'd sure hate to have to put a firebird like that behind bars.

Tempting fate, that one.

A deep chuckle escaped him as he hit his comm unit to file a report, then stared at the message a moment longer.

Hey, Big Guy.

I'm a bit tied up at the moment, so thought I'd throw a little luck your way since you seem to need it.

Gek 'Lhar (you remember who he is, right?) is headed to Earth, specifically a refugee settlement in Quito.

Don't mess it up this time.

ACKNOWLEDGMENTS

Thanks go to 343 Industries for putting their trust in me, not only to take Rion Forge's story forward, but also to give another iconic character a chance at redemption. Special thanks to Jeremy Patenaude, Tiffany O'Brian, and Jeff Easterling.

Immense gratitude goes to my editor, Ed Schlesinger, without whose belief, support, and patience this book quite simply would not exist. Thank you.

To Jonathan, Audrey, and James for their unwavering love and understanding; and to Kameryn for continuing to be my cheerleader and sounding board.

Acknowledgments would not be complete without recognizing Greg Bear's incredible work in the Forerunner Saga, which was instrumental in the writing of this book. It is my deepest hope that I have done some justice in carrying part of the story forward.

ABOUT THE AUTHOR

KELLY GAY is the critically acclaimed author of the Charlie Madigan urban fantasy series. She is a multi-published author with works translated into several different languages. She is a two-time RITA nominee, an ARRA nominee, a Goodreads Choice Award finalist, and a SIBA Book Prize Long List finalist. Kelly is also the recipient of the North Carolina Arts Council Fellowship Grant in Literature. She has authored the short story "Into the Fire," featured in *Halo: Fractures*, and the novella *Halo: Smoke and Shadow*. She can be found online at kellygay.com.

Build Beyond™

MEGACONSTRUX.COM